Stories of a Digital Spalpeen

D. M. O'Dowd

Published by The Digital Spalpeen, 2024.

This is a work of fiction. Similarities to real people, places, or events are entirely coincidental.

STORIES OF A DIGITAL SPALPEEN

First edition. February 23, 2024.

Copyright © 2024 D. M. O'Dowd.

ISBN: 979-8227032454

Written by D. M. O'Dowd.

Table of Contents

Introduction 1
Election Fever...4
I Want to Break Free 18
Finding Headser..30
Plucking Crows 41
That Beats Banagher 55
Marmalade I...65
Marmalade II 76
Peig Sasta 90
Sigmund's Men... 106
The Tripp to Tipp... 119
Some Tulips 133
The Two Paddies 147
The Three Marys 157
The Life of Lobster 170
Australia.. 187
Two for Joy 199
The Digital Spalpeen... 211
Meeting the Duvel 227
The Invincibles 239
Amor Vita 251
The Parting Glass... 265

This book was written by a Human, from West of the Shannon. This book is a dedication to all those Humans, Wild Men and Wonderful Women that came before, led the way, giving gifts of grit and humour.

Introduction

If you were born in Angola, you might collect Yombe sculptures and watch Nollywood movies. You might have spent your youth playing basketball under the marigold trees. You probably weren't born in Angola. If you were born in Mississippi you might believe Jesus was a Republican, eat gumbo for breakfast and spend your Friday nights in car parks drinking moonshine. Chances are you were not born in Mississippi. If you were born West of the Shannon, in a small Market town, where everyone either knew you or knew your people. You would likely have spent your youth on the sidelines of a GAA pitch, desperate for the shift, drinking Linden Village. If one day you woke and said to yourself fuck this for a cake and arse party, someone's got to take the Horse to France. The rest may well have gone like this.

*****

The Digital Spalpeen
Standing at the station
It's another rainy day
it breaks my heart to leave here
it breaks my heart to stay

Back to bad old Boston
sure, it's just a skip away
but the ones who always tell me that
are the ones who always stay

D. M. O'DOWD

Take me away, far away from here
I got ambitions you see,
Bright lights, blonds and endless TV
I got the world at my feet
Blue eyes and an accent so sweet
I never thought that one day
Like the moment, those blue eyes would fade away

Cousin Andy was a boxer
Boxed from Brooklyn to the Bronx
But he settled with a family
When he lost the golden gloves

I got a brother down in Sydney town
Met a girl there from Japan
Now he's living there in limbo
Searching for the promised land

Take me away, far away from here
I got ambitions you see,
Bright lights, blonds and endless TV
I got the world at my feet
Blue eyes and an accent so sweet
I never thought that one day
Like the moment, those blue eyes would fade away

Money was my Mecca
I thought I had it made
All the neon signs were flashing

STORIES OF A DIGITAL SPALPEEN

Every busker sang my name
But when the world becomes your Oyster
The Pearls look all the same
So you look for friendly faces
The place where people know your name

Take me away, far away from here
I got ambitions you see,
Bright lights, blonds and endless TV
I got the world at my feet
Blue eyes and an accent so sweet
I never thought that one day
Like the moment, those blue eyes would fade away

Election Fever

Back when Pluto was a planet, things were different, cars came with cigarette lighters, Men rejected umbrellas (in favour of plastic bag on the head) and teachers were not your friends. There was no answering back, you did what you were told and if you didn't you got it. You couldn't swear or nothing, no fucking way, if you did you got it. They had their differences, one might use the lat on the hand the other a bang across the head or shake the guts out of you. For Nelly it was the lat, she made it her own. I would hear about Nelly and the lat from the day I was born, along with "Wait till Nelly gets her hands on you". I heard it the time I caught sight of the door ajar and was gone on to the road or when I took the lolly stick and scraped off the chewing gum from the street and ate it or when I held the cat out the top window or when I took the fathers fags and twissled the tobacco out of them one by one.

"Jesus Mary and Joseph, what am I going to do with you, you're as mad as a fecking March hare .... wait till Nelly gets her hands on you".

It was a nice warm summers day when I decided to take me tractor to the top of the rock and let her roll. She had no indicators but other than that she was as good as any other machine on the road and me as good a driver as any . Oh the trundle of the wheels on the hot tar, the warmth of the sun on my willing knees. I was making pace until usurped by a shadow of a man with bangs of silage radiating off him. Davey was half ashamed explaining to the mother the tailback on O'Connell Street all due to my escapade. She nearly fell over with fright, which soon turned to annoyance.

"I'm worn to the bone trying to keep an eye on you," she said, "I can only hope Nelly can do what I can't," and looked to the sky.

"Aragh I suppose he didn't mean any harm," Davey argued on my behalf, his eyes following her around the kitchen as she ping-ponged from the cooker to press to the fridge.

"I don't know," she said in half agreement. "I have ham or corned beef Davey, which will you have ?"

"Any of the two."

"Tamata ?"

He took the sandwich in his grip and crossed his legs, his bony knee sticking out from the trousers, the sinews of his neck stretching and relaxing as he mulched the soft bread. The tea was finished in a slurp and he exclaimed he would be off.

"You'll have another one Davey" the mother jumped to attention.

"I won't now, thank you very much," he answered and stood.

"Did you get thin ?" the mother wondered, but Davey only laughed and handed back the plate.

"Now Sir," she said, turning her attention to me, "what am I going to do with you?" "Will you have cream crackers with cheese and a cup of Maxwell House?"

"I will," says I and she was off again looking for the Calvita.

"You'd feel sorry for him too," she mused pouring the sweet milk into the coffee.

"Who Mammy ?" I asked.

"Davey" she remarked as she swirled the remaining liquid in the saucepan gazing out the window.

"Drank two farms of land," she said, "poor aul bugger".

The fateful day arrived. The face was near chaffed off me from Palmolive and warm water. I was dressed in my dungarees and my favourite black jumper with the red lines that looked like snakes. A pair of white socks folded onto my feet to make the sandals look presentable (you couldn't keep me in shoes the mother said). Waiting at the school door I caught my first sight of Nelly, brown and squat.

"Morning Ladies," she says crisply.

"Morning Mrs Ewing" the mothers answer in chorus.

We waited half stricken in fear as Nelly leafed through the big bunch of keys while the breeze tossed her rust curls from left to right, finally coming on a big one the size of her hand, shuffled it into the lock and with a loud crank the door creaked open. I think it fair to say at that point I had my first moment of weakness. Looking at the mother a tear had gathered in her eye and she didn't know what to do with herself, I could have said "Sure come on Mammy we'll be off on home, and you can pull a stick from the hedge and I'll jump around like He-Man till you tell me go easy and we'll have two big bowls of chicken soup like we often do and you can blow on mine if it's too hot, and butter me up to big slices of Pat the Baker for dipping and while the soup is simmering I'll be out in the street with Bosco collecting election stickers or running after *Bang Shilo* shouting "Bang" back and forth till you tell me go easy on poor old Shilo that he hasn't been right in the head since he was in the British Navy or if Shilo isn't around maybe old Joe Brady would come out of Mannion's pub with a belly full of Porter and myself and Bosco can take turns to land a punch on his paunch until he is winded and you tell us go easy that old Joe was the King once but that was a long time ago, what do you think Mammy ? ". She wiped the tear, making out it was the wind that caught her unexpectedly and likewise, I followed the procession into the cold school.

Nelly we soon learned had her set routine, the morning commencing with her instructing Liam Brennan to the well for a jug of spring water (I was jumping up and down to go), the Kettle was boiled the pot scalded and the tea made. A drop of milk and two heaped spoons of sugar, a blow of the hairy lip, sitting back Nelly never failed to comment "That's nice now". She threw the legs up on the low stool, and took out her Irish times, opening it like a Japanese dressing curtain, no one had a clue what she was up to in there but could hear grumbles of discontentment, the surface of the paper shimmering with indignity, a tut and ta, hum and haw until the tea was drunk to the dregs the paper tower crumpled to rubble.

"Haughey is only a crook," she said standing me the crooked eye.

"Yes Mrs Ewing," the whole class answered.

"And Fitzgerald is nothing but a dreamer".

"A dreamer Mrs Ewing," we agreed.

"And this whole election a feckin farce," to which no one knew what to reply.

She clapped her hands briskly, "now class, I am going for a puff of fresh air" she announced tapping her finger on the box of blue silk cut in the pocket of her cardigan "No noise while I'm gone" she said, her suspicious eyes crawling over the innocent heads as she hopped off for her puff.

"How was it ?" the mother asked "Did I like Mrs Ewing ?" and a ball of other questions. I was jiggered tired from *buntas canite*, numbers and letters and all kinds of new stuff that I could only reply

"fine" with a shrug of the shoulders and fell into the car.

We gave Mrs Gallagher a lift to town, she had been waiting patiently at the school wall for the offer, managing a look of great surprise when it eventually came. The car sunk as she got in, she was that stout a woman with big pink glasses and teeth that stuck out as far as the four cross roads. They started straight into the chat, the election, the state of the country, how the farmers were crippled and not a good man left in the country. Somewhere in between, I was told to stop kicking the seat. I let the window down and counted the cows scratching their necks on the barbs of the wire fences. We passed the miser who trod along slowly, his hair thick and matted hanging like vines, the thinning crown coppered from the summer sun. His coat, a frieze colour, was fastened at the waist by a length of bailing twine, his shoes split open on all sides, his toes I imagined black as spuds as I strained to get a proper look. I listened to the mother and Mrs Gallagher discuss the great details of his existence, how he had stacks of money stored in a shoe box under the bed but was too tight to spend it and Hell nor high water would he let not soul or sinner into the house.

"Ah it's a disease" Mrs Gallagher opined.

"It is" the mother agreed. "He won't be too worried about the vote" the mother said.

"Nor the milk quota" said Mrs Gallagher and the mother laughed saying it was the best one she ever heard.

Arriving in town I hoped I knew what was coming as Mrs Gallagher flicked open the clasp on her purse, extracted a note and pulled it close to her nose to evaluate through the murky lenses, satisfied she turned and handed me a folded pound. The mother protested, attempting to intercept the transaction but there was no stopping Mrs Gallagher. I smiled and said nothing, the deal was done, I would be over to Lizzy Taylors in the blink of an eye.

Davey was in town, purchasing a pair of Dunlop's in the shop so he checked in with the mother to see if the gasúr[1] had gotten himself into any more scrapes.

"He'd keep you on your toes," she opined, I was sitting at the table at the time, "come on, ate up," she said taking the fork from my hand and mashing in the spuds with the carrot and the meat and shovelling a forkful into my gob. The auld fella over the far side of the kitchen was in beside the range.

"What you make of this election Davey?" he asked.

"Aw now," said Davey, throwing the head back as if to say why bother.

"Come on now Davey," said the father in half jest "Wolf tone would turn in his grave with talk like that".

"Sure they're all the same to me" Davey finally commented, "Finna Fail or Finna Gale, Haughey or Fitzgerald" he says.

---

1. https://en.wiktionary.org/wiki/gas%C3%BAr

The father sat back in the chair, "I don't know Davey" he said in reflection "eight hundred years of struggle and we have come to this ?" followed by a sigh.

"Don't be going on with talk the like of that" the mother scolded.

"Isn't it our history ?" he protested.

"You'll be taken up" she snapped, shutting everyone up.

"Haughey's only a crook and Fitzgerald a dreamer" I announced.

There was a look of bewilderment on the face of Davey followed by another great laugh all around.

"Where did you get that at all ?" asked the father.

"Mrs Ewing," I said matter of fact.

"Isn't she a sympathiser ?", Dave asked the mother.

"Well now," the father settled himself.

"You can tell her this from me," he says "that Mr Fitzgerald is a good honest man at the vanguard of the just society and in politics for all the right reasons", he paused.

"Did you get all that ?", "I did" I confirmed.

Like the father, I was a Fine Gale man and in an effort to affirm allegiance, I restricted myself to collecting FG stickers only, covering all in sundry with them. The face of Gareth Fitzgerald, stretched between the green and orange bands became a member of the family. He was on the handlebars of my bicycle, every window and door in the house, his folded features displacing the head of the Liver bird on my school bag, as well as covering the right and left breast of my school jumper from that day on. It was only after Mrs Ewing had arrived back in from her *puff of fresh air* that she noticed.

"Take them off," she said crossly, "we'll have no political propaganda in this classroom".

I looked at her bewildered as to what she was referring to.

"Take them off" she barked louder, pointing with a finger like a bayonet. The song of loyalty sang in my heart.

"I won't Mrs Ewing" I said defiantly, thinking of the father's words.

She stood stock straight and wondered for a moment had she had heard right before returning to me with a blank stare. In a low determined voice she uttered through gritted teeth to, "remove that dreamer from your school jumper, left tit and right". I could see the tiny beads of sweat glistening on her upper lip. I couldn't turn my back on the father now retorting proudly that,

"Gareth Fitzgerald was a just a man of a dacent society".

"Dacent," she says "dacent is it ?" and for a moment I thought I was off the hook as she chuckled to herself until without warning she made a run at me and had me by the lug. It was easy to know she played handball for the county with the grip she had on me, taking me to the top of the room as fast as my scandals could carry me.

"Now, ya little guttersnipe," she says with a wheeze, composing herself. She opened her cupboard and slid out a long thin lat which once served as an ornate veneer to a table.

"What's that ?" I asked with alarm.

"You'll soon find out," she says flexing the lat like the Count of Monte Cristo.

"Out with your hand," she says to which I obeyed, "open it up" she barked, poking me in the chest with the sharp end.

I looked left at one of my classmates, Ann Marie Colemans curls were standing on her head, Thomas Corchran frozen in fear, his mouth around the bottle of orange. They had all heard of the lat. I rolled open the hand and it came down with a crack, followed by four more, each punctuated with me recoiling the hand into my belly before slowly sacrificing it again.

"Sit down now" she instructed after the fifth pointing the way to my seat with her weapon of torture. I turned to make off, "hold on" she said, changing her mind and holding the lat against my belly as a barrier and as quick as one two she whipped the stickers from my chest before letting me go. I sat holding my poor hand but it proved more difficult to hold the tears but I managed, I wasn't going to let either the auld lad or indeed Garreth Fitzgerald down.

The mother knew it on me, there wasn't the expected litany of questions that might normally drive her half daft with the how, where, what and why of life. Strangely it looked like she was missing my interest.

"Did something happen?" she enquired cautiously.

"No Mammy" I said, nervous that she might get it out of me,

"What will ya have for your tea ? A Donegal catch with a tin of beans ?"

I still had a craw in me stomach but not wanting to raise suspicions said

"Sound."

The beans bubbled, the mother still probed, and the auld lad entered the kitchen.

"How is the big man ?" he asked.

"Good" I answered.

"Oh" he stopped, "cat got your tongue ?"

The mother was back on the case, "Did something happen at school ?"

"No Mammy," "tell me now, did Mrs Ewing give you a slap ?"

"No Mammy."

"What did she slap you for ?"

"For saying Garreth Fitzgerald was a good man," unfolding my hand.

The father beamed but the mother was not so impressed, taking the injured paw and tenderly running her thumb over it to assess the damage. "She won't get away with that" she says in a stern voice and instructed me to "sit up now and have your tea."

Nelly didn't know what hit her exactly when the mother got going. "Do you mean to say Mrs Ewing this lad was punished for showing an interest in politics, his country even ?"

"Well" Mrs Ewing began to answer with confidence until interrupted.

"A right we fought eight hundred years for, hmm ?"

"Well," Nelly started to answer, a little more hesitant than before. Sensing she had her rattled the mother blew it further out of proportion,

"Would you prefer he sat in front of the television all day or playing with gadgets ?"

"That's no business of mine" Nelly snapped, finding her feet in the row "The classroom is no place for politics or backchat" she asserted, her brow brooding. I stood well in, crawling up the mother's skirt, fearing she might unsheathe the lat at any moment.

"Oh I'm surprised Mrs Ewing" the mother tactfully changed her tone to one of exaggerated surprise.

"And why might that be ?" Nelly enquired scornfully.

"Well now" the mother readied herself "a little bird tells me that you're fond of politics yourself".

"And who might that little bird be ?" asked Nelly flashing her yellow eyes on me.

"That doesn't matter" the mother retorted briskly, leaving her protective hand on my crown. I plunged my thumb into my mouth nearly sucking the nail off it.

"I wonder what the Inspector might make of your own political interest ?" the mother asked, taking the tiger by the tail.

"What do you mean ?" Nelly now nervous with talk of the inspector, a bible to a vampire

"I mean you sitting down there resting yourself, reading every word letter and syllable of the Irish Times election coverage as well as the sport I'm sure ...."

"Well I never," says Nelly, "in all my years, I never," bewildered at the audacity of the accusation.

"I bet you haven't" the mother suggested, "well, tell me, what would he make of it ?"

Nelly was lost for words "No, no point going down that road Teresa" she answered finally, contrite, "maybe, well maybe I was a little heavy handed" she admitted further.

"You might want to apologise to him then !" the mother said, taking her hand and leading me into the limelight.

STORIES OF A DIGITAL SPALPEEN

Nelly hesitated and harked, "he's a great boy," says the mother "never put a foot wrong or caused me a day's trouble", then I harked and hesitated. With the greatest of effort, Nelly managed to eke out a single solitary watery "sorry" just as the most eager pupils had started to file into the classroom.

After the episode with Nelly, I never looked back, I was eating two dinners a day (the mother threatened a worm dose) which was standing to me at the football, between the bin and the lamppost and the two jumpers on the other end of the street I was holding my own. It was in the throws of a game when I next met Davey, balubas drunk.

"Hello Davey" I said but he was too far gone to put a name on me. The head was going from side to side and he was talking away to himself. His face was a rainbow, from the red nose to the blue lips and tangerine skin of his jowls with two white moons shining from under his grey eyes. "Do you know me, Davey ?" I asked.

"Heerraaaa," he answered in a long drawn out whine.

"Davey" I reminded him.

"Heerraaaa uaa ga ga ga ssssh" he replied, holding up a finger and looking around having an existential moment until he spotted the ball and took off with a gallop after it. The trousers nearly came off him, slipping south till he got a good grip on the arse. The new Dunlop's weren't doing him any favours either, they looked two sizes too big and were making a loud slapping noise as he ran. All said he was determined and despite the jeers and distractions he managed to get a hand on it and that's when the pantomime began.

"Uchtrannnnn no hEireannnnnn," he called out, got on his knees and made the sign of the cross across his chest, stood, blew a pea of white spit out his mouth and threw a flying boot off the welly to start a stampede down the street, the lot of us including Davey chasing after it. I was desperate to get my hands on it and show Davey how I could be man of the match, "weesh ooohhh" Davey roared at the height of the excitement, the ball smacking off the side of his face and landing in my arms. Before the melee landed on me I drew forth the biggest boot I could muster and watched as it sail across the street in slow motion and walloped off Taylor's window smashing it to bits. The crash had scattered the lot of them as Lizzy Taylor emerged like the grim reaper with a look of disgust. Davey didn't give a fiddlers fuck of course and fell off down the street and into Mannion's doorway, leaving myself alone to face the music.

"What has he done this time ?" the mother enquired apologetically having to listen to Lizzie go on about the price of windows and basically her whole life story, on her feet from the age of fourteen. Although everyone knew that the only people that went in there were the pupils from school to steal the chocolate mice. Three cups of tea and a plate of Jaffa cakes, madeira cake and other nice things the mother finally managed to calm her down.

"You had a terrible shock Lizzie, will you have a drop of Powers ?".

"Oh never during the day" says Lizzie although everyone knew that Lizzie had a bottle under the counter. Must have been the guts of an hour before the mother had her on the threshold of leaving.

STORIES OF A DIGITAL SPALPEEN

"It's not the money but the principle" Lizzy reared up again, although the whole town knew she still had her confirmation money in a biscuit tin.

In the end, it took a gentle shove to get her out the door and the mother turned to me high as a kite from having to listen to her go on and on like the Angelus.

"Gimme that here," she said snatching a fig roll from my hand.

"What on God's green earth am I going to do with you at all ?" she pleaded "Wait till ... " and she hesitated, Nelly was on the tip of her tongue, but realising it no longer held the influence it once did hesitated for a rethink. "Wait till I call the Garda," she said to my instant shock.

"The Garda", I repeated with a gulp.

"Yes," she replied "they might keep you in the barracks for the night" with a threatening look. The thought of the cold dark lonesome cell sent a shiver down my spine.

"Ah you wouldn't do that would you Mammy ?" I queried nervously,

"I would indeed" she answered promptly "mark my words !".

I thought for a while at the proposition of being under lock and key with no football, I might not even be out for the Friday edition of 'Wizzard' and 'Chips'. After all the hard work I did for Garreth Fitzgerald and where is he ?, Taoiseach, and where am I ?, heading for prison. Well now, if that isn't enough to give anyone Election Fever.

I Want to Break Free

In our dining room, there was a large mahogany table, on each side positioned a ruby red armchair. The handles were black but worn colorless from repeated attacks, especially the one in the best spot for the tele. It was Thursday and knowing that generally anyone or anything could turn up in our house from stray dogs to Francie Cawley shouting up to my sister's window (looking for his New Order record), Thursdays had a kinda sort of consistency, mostly because of Top of the Pops at eight o'clock the one program everyone could all agree on. The battle cry would be yelled up the stairs "TOP OF THE POPPPSSSSS," and there would be a mad rush for the chair. Even the brother Pierce would down the books for turning off the desk lamp. He was studying like a madman, desperate to get to UCD. My sister Ruby back combed her hair and let her school blouse buttoned down. She wanted to be a model and was acting like one. Izzy was cool, she wore Doc Martens and black tights with ladders on both legs, she smoked in the top room constantly listening to Love Cats or Depeche Mode. They sat side by side on the dining table with legs dangling down. I lay under it next to the leg close to the halogen glow watching the records fall from the sky in a kaleidoscope of colours, exploding as they did to the tune of Thin Lizzy. I had a plate of bird's eye potato waffles with a tin of Heinz spaghetti, another Thursday favourite.

In comparison to the dining room with boxes from the shop stacked high around the piano, torn wallpaper with crayon marks and mouse holes the TOTP studio looked like the most colourful joyous pocket on earth. Blonds in pig tails bopped in candy coloured shell suits with L.A. Gear trainers, boys in their Dad's suit jackets dropped their moody shoulders to emulate Spandau ballet. The hosts Janice and Gary looked incredibly happy. With a cheeky grin, Janice welcomed everyone to the BBC Studio in White City before passing to Gary who with his right hand in his chinos close to his balls swivelled to the stage introducing Echo & the Bunnymen. "Cool", Ruby says watching the bass player strum the guitar hanging close to his knees. Pierce, yawned on the Red chair and ran his hand through his messy hair. The camera returned to Janice and Gary who were surrounded to the point of suffocation by the audience who were in a state of blind euphoria, only half believing this was reality. The countdown commenced from forty, PTY Michael Jackson, Robert De Niro's Waiting, Bananarama to the Cocteau Twins. Izzy wanted the Cocteau Twins and groaned when we went to a video, a Love worth waiting for Shaking Stevens. "Coffin Dodger" she shouted at the tele. UB40, Cherry Oh Baby's performance on stage was a good one. Under the table, I finished the last waffle and lay on my belly sucking my thumb as we navigated through the movers, the fallers and the new entries. We were close to the climax, with only the pointer sisters standing in the way of the top ten and when Gary took a pause from the panic and calmly assured us all that this was one of the best top tens ever. Suddenly he was off again and we slalomed from ten with a jazzy electro pop backdrop stopping only for breath at number three.

D. M. O'DOWD

It was the first time I saw a woman with a mustache or a man in a mini but it was brilliant. He walked up the stairs with a hoover and kept exclaiming how he'd fallen in love and wanted to break free. He moved his conical tits like weapons around the house to the annoyance of the auld lad on the chair, thrusting his hips violently to a velvet baseline. He needed to be sure but yearned to be free. The song stopped for a second of suspension and resumed with that uplifting harmony again. The harmony and vocals were a bowl of trifle with a slice of Vienetta to the ears. I forgot after that what was number one, Duran Duran in red leather and blow dried blond I think. Pierce slid from the chair before it was over and clicked on the desk lamp that could be seen from the street late into thenight. I hummed "I want to break free, I want to break free" and sure enough the following Sunday I broke free.

A heat wave had taken over. The paper was full of it, kids licking cones on the front of the Irish Times and flowers in glorious bloom all over the country. My eldest brother Ciaran worked in the shop and was mostly too busy dressing the windows or trying to make the last pound to watch TOTP but it was Sunday the shop was closed and he was ready like Rambo. His right-hand man Conway borrowed the car from his father, Val. A bright yellow Volkswagen Passat, brand new. Connolly took the driving seat, he was in his blue jeans and bare chested likewise Ciaran had no top on and fiddled with the radio searching for something to get us going. Conway slipped a fag between his teeth lit it and slapped the seat belt across his chest.

STORIES OF A DIGITAL SPALPEEN

Ciaran halted the knob and turned it up full blast, he found my favourite "I want to break free". I stood between the front seats with an elbow on each. I had on a pair of red O'Neills shorts (the round towers colours), and wanting to be like the lads I removed my T-shirt. We drove fast with the windows down, the air gushing into the car, the tires cracking on the dry road above the sound of the radio. Cows mulched happily in the fields and Conway hung the elbow out the window. A branch nearly came in at Clarks Bridge. The point was packed that day. We parked sideways onto a dune and walked down a long way to the beach, the lads were still in their jeans, Conway had a black leather belt with a silver buckle, the kind you might normally see on a pair of pants. Each of them had a bathroom towel under their arm and used it to hide their modesty when putting on the Bermudas once we reached the shore. It was still a lovely day and the sun glimmered across the wide ocean. The seagulls were having a field day on the half eaten ham sandwiches left here and there from family picnics along with bottles of lilt or Club Orange. I squished my feed into the wet sand as we walked towards the waves, stopping for Ciaran to blow the beach ball he convinced Conway to buy on the way down from one of the small shops livered from street to roof in buckets and spades. The water was Baltic but we didn't stop to ponder, sloshing further out. Ciaran was the first to plunge. He was a good swimmer and was strong as a bull from all the weights he was lifting. He had the room full of mail order Joe Weider equipment with pictures of Bruce Lee and Arnold Schwarzenegger blue tacked on the wall. Every second night himself and Cullen were up there with the stereo on full blast moaning like a hospital as they struggled to make that last rep. The whole town could hear them at it including the father who was directly below in the dining room. His chair was the other red one, beside the fireplace with the two dogs, he watched cowboy films there, (any cowboy film that didn't star John Wayne, he was only a cod) and smoked Major or Carroll's. Each thud as a barbell dropped to the floor would raise his huge hirsute eyebrows. The more thuds the more agitated he would get, until eventually he would light up and roar, "They'll send the fecking roof in on us".

He swam out for some distance, Conway stayed with me. He was lean, no muscles like Ciaran, or no interest either it looked like, which was strange because he was a soldier in the Irish army. Sometimes he would help me with my maths homework. The mother would always say he was clever and very obliging. He told me the army was full of cunts but laughed about it and talked to me like I was an adult. We threw the beach ball back and forth and he said I was a fast little fucker and one day I would be stronger than yer man Ciaran. We arsed around like that for a while and then went back to lie down and dry out. Conway went straight for the fags and smoked one and then another as Ciaran squinted to the horizon looking for women, nodding to Conway on basically anything in a bikini which was fine with Conway, who often mentioned that he would ride anything. We kicked the ball around for a while until Ciaran beckoned us on up the beach, so we walked on our feet to The Anchor. Harp Lager was big at the time and that is what the lads were after. Conway asked me if I wanted a sup. It was long and golden like the sun with a frothy head like a summer cloud. Bubbles traveled up it in a hurry. There was an ad at the time where there was a guy in the desert, 'Sure you could fry an egg on the stones,' he said before musing "if you had an egg". Well that was the approach I followed, using my forearm to clear my waiting lips as Conway tenderly lowered the rim to cover my face. Thinking I might not get another chance, I drank with the concentration of a free diver. Removing the glass Conway looks at it and paused "the little basted nearly drank it all", he screeched with delight. That wasn't the end of it either. I managed another three or four gulps as the rounds kept coming. I was half stoned when two fine looking women in white jeans and San Tropez tan entered the bar and made their way to the counter beside us. "Hello ladies" I call out. They laugh when they spot me smiling at them with a big pint of Harp in front of me. Ciaran sits up and flicks the crisps off the crease in his vest. They girls sniggered. They ordered and took their drinks to a table in the lounge, the three of us like a Wimbledon crowd watching them as they did.

Ciaran steadied himself and I was promptly instructed to make my way over to the women and ask if they would like to join them. I would only on condition of another heave at Connolly's pint and with that wobbly off.

"What for ?" was the frank and honest response from the birds (as Ciaran called them). I was dispatched with a rather boring retort,

"Because I want to talk."

"Which one ?" asked the brunette. "The one with the muscles or the one with the black hair and the teeth."

"The one with the muscles," I answered without hesitation.

"Which one of us does he want to talk to ?" She asked. I didn't know.

"The blonde one," confirms Ciaran and "Conway wants a how's your mother with the brunette". I looked and Conway, he shrugged so off I traveled again. I conveyed the request, the two girls who listened intently. The wind changed and the brunette looked suddenly serious. She placed her glass on the table, focused her face and leaned into me, "Tell him to mind his own business," and smiled nicely. So I returned with what seemed like bad news. Conway let out a great laugh and looked at Ciaran, who quickly responded, "tell her. I'm going to make her my business". All this over and back had tweaked the barman's interest . He was using the prop of drying a glass on a dishcloth to observe me stumbling over and back across the floor. "In your dreams," says the blonde, "In your dreams," I repeated heading back with more bad news. "In your, Dreams," I said to which Ciaran began to labor on for an answer. Conway smoked casually. "In your Dreams" Ciaran said again "Your Dreams," like an elocution teacher with a Mick Jagger mouth. Conway puffed out a cloud of smoke, "Ask them," he says "Would they be wet dreams ?". I looked at Ciaran, he gave me the nod and I trotted off again. That was the ice breaker. The Brunette, said they would be over in five minutes. "I knew it," Ciaran says. Conway smoked two fags in the next five minutes but no sign of the birds. Then ten minutes passed and still no sign. "Go back and check," Ciaran insisted which I would only do for a last last last sup.

STORIES OF A DIGITAL SPALPEEN

"No" he flatly insisted, that "I would only get sick in the car,". "I wont budge so," I said and he capitulated in seconds. When I got there the table was vacant but for the two glasses one with lipstick on the rim and the other stuffed with an empty packet of peanuts. "I knew it," Ciaran says and leveled his hand on the table.

By the time we found the car, dusk was threatening and the beach had thinned out. The lemon VW stood lonesome in the same spot. We rolled down to let out the stagnant heat from the day and whacked the radio on. Still half buzzing from Harp, Conway instructed me to shout out the window at any passing girl and ask "How's her mother for sugar ?". Depending on the response the lads would either egg me on further or act highly insulted and admonish me for such language. By the time we hit the back roads with only cows to serenade the game was over. I lay the length of the backseat and the smell of the new car warmed all day in the sun lulled me to sleep.

Conway poked me awake when the crows above were giving it a last lash, circling in the sky before nesting down for the night. There was a nip in the evening air and I was on the cusp of a first hangover. Passing the hall door realizing it was Sunday after spotting my upturned Liverpool bag in the same spot where I had pegged it on Friday afternoon. I would surely be in trouble tomorrow with no sums or reading done. To top it off my back was scorched from the sun and I could feel the blisters brewing but for now I just needed to sleep. On my last legs I climbed the two flights of stairs holding the banister to steady myself. I peeled back the blankets and slowly lowered myself into the bed. It felt like it was only a moment, my eyelids lifting like lead when those dreaded words came traveling up the stairs "time for school".

Thursday was a long time coming, the blister on my back was healing and the raw red replaced with layers of peeling skin. I begged my sister to peel it for me in front of the mirror. I had gotten a belt on the face from Nellie for not having the sums done but that was in the past now. Conway visited that evening and stood at the range in the kitchen, he didn't seem to be as excited about TOTP. He had news, big news, which he delivered with a half smile, he was heading for the Leb. Leaving the week after next and until then he would be in Monaghan on training. He knew it had been coming so

there you go. "How bad could it be ?", he asked but no one knew the answer to that one. "Not as bad as round here on a wet Tuesday," he laughed. He might even get to have sex every now and then. Ciaran was still in the shop, Conway went out to tell him the news. What could Ciaran say either except to joke, that he'd better save some bullets for the brunette in the white jeans. Conway came back in from the shop and joined us in the living room to watch TOTP. In his house, he was an only child, in ours there were nine, that is probably why he liked our house so much, he never had to fight for the chair in his. As the countdown began, as usual everyone participated with a yeah or a nay of the chart entry. Then a bizarre thing happened, Gary held the spongy yellow mic up to his nose and announced a new entry at nineteen from the Human League "The Lebanon". "Fuck me" he said with a muted laugh and poked another cigarette under his teeth. The song told the story of a girl that was living through the war, the colour and innocence ripped from life. A soldier also questions his involvement in a pointless conflict. I didn't have to ask Conway, to know that one day he would probably feel the same.

When we hit the top ten I was in my favourite position, under the table resting against the solid leg waiting to see where my song was, not ten, or nine or even eight. The countdown continued seven, six, five passed like cards being delt in a casino, not at four either It came to three and my sister called out with excitement, "Your song," but Freddy wanting to break free was but quickly passed over and on we went on Phil Collins in and number two with against all odds then back to Gary in the studio who excitedly introduced the brand new number one as the camera panned to the crowd. Simon Le Bon like a pop culture icon in red leather with bleached hair.

Conway said he was going to Hayden's for a pint of Harp and asked if I wanted to join him for an club orange. I looked at my brother Pierce who was heading back up to the biology book, his hair was a mess but he wasn't aware of that or the tails of his sky blue shirt hanging out from beneath his navy jumper. I told Conway I had homework to do unzipping the Liverpool bag and rummaged around for the pencil case. I found a protractor and a four coloured biro, my maths book and copy and laid them on the dining room table. There were two doors from the dining room to the street, the first a cream door with etched the second one the main door. Conway stood between the two for a moment and shuffled in his pocket for his fags before twisting the latch and pulled, he needed to do it three times as the door was warped from rain and hard to open, but we were used to that. The third time it opened and the glass rattled. I focused on the first problem, calculating the area of a farm subdivided by the farmer for goats, chickens and pigs. I liked these kind of problems, the ones with a story around it. Knowing I was good at these, I took a moment to savor the aroma of warm waffles under the grill in the kitchen and my mother humming "Oh lord it's hard to be humble," to herself as she fried the fish in flour. It was true I wanted to break free, I wanted adventure but knew that the Leb would not be the kind of adventure I wanted and returned back to help the Farmer with his problem of the goats, the chickens and the pigs.

The following month a postcard arrived, a splash of colour among the brown bills that had arrived for the shop. It depicted a long beach, lined with pastel parasols. In the top left corner an icon of the Lebanese flag with it's two red stripes intersected by a white one in the middle of which a beautiful green cedar tree. On the back it simply read, "Greetings from the Leb !!" with a p.s. "We have come because we heard about the Harp. Love Michael". Back in the home country, the heat wave was long gone, it drizzled non-stop from morning. Ciaran was dressing the windows, putting a blouse on a mannequin when he noticed a girl passing in a white anorak holding the hood. As she passed, sensing that someone was looking at her she lowered the hood slightly and raised her eyes to meet his gaze. There was a definite pause as they both tried to work out where they might recognise one another from. Who was it but none other than the blond from The Anchor "So that's the new girl in the bank they are all talking about" Ciaran thought to himself. They continued to observe one another in silence, a mischievous grin growing on her face so he responded in kind with the best

smile he could muster. She blinked, he blinked, she nodded, he nodded, she pointed to something and he wondered what at ?, suddenly realising his right hand tenderly cupping the tit of the mannequin. He removed it in a shot and stuffed it awkwardly in his pocket but in that moment like the smile from his face she had vanished again. He groaned to the point that the auld fella thought he had come down in the window, "Are ya alright, are ya ?" he poked his head in. But Ciaran was too occupied to answer having just come to the realisation of a possible redemption and that he needed to go to the bank that afternoon with the takings.

Finding Headser

Digital watches were all the rage when I was afoot the Rubicon of manhood, anxiously gazing at the dying embers of my youth. In Mikey's Electrics, a mechanical glass cabinet with varnished wooden borders housed the aspirational bounty. We watched in awe with hot breath steaming against the glass as one tray shuffled past the next, each bringing it's own delight of wobbling Chinese kitsch. From brushed metal straps with backlight display to ostentatious gold calculator models that shimmered as they bobbled past. After the watches, came the rings, gold, and silver each with a single large coloured stone of synthetic plastic, Garnet or Opel or Perl. At this point the trio of upturned arses occupying the width of the cabinet would cease debate on the watches and observe the rings, each man harbouring his own romantic notions. I had my eye on a particular gold one with a green garnet, attached a handwritten price tag of £8.49, a veritable fortune. A thousand times I re-enacted the scenario, Geraldine Sexton standing at the lounge entrance of her father's pub as she often did when I approached exuding confidence. I had seen how it worked with women in the karate kid but somehow it didn't feel the same where bog sod replaced boulevard.

Mikey had a tagline when taglines were the preserve of blooming corporates - "it's hard to make a pound". He drove a Mercedes when others rattled around in tin pot escorts, kept it immaculate as did his wife of their dwelling a few doors up. Her pendulous hips could be seen daily swaying to the rhythm of the broom sweeping clean the doorstep. Mikey started small, selling penny sweets at which time his motto might well have held true and slowly progressed until he was the electronics king of our small patch. "You have your eye on that one" he said to my surprise unaware he had come to attend. In fact, until then I was unaware I had been visiting daily and often alone to confirm the ring remained unsold while I considered how to amass the relative fortune required to acquire it. My response was motionless stupefaction as a wave of molten embarrassment rose up inside of me, lighting my face to a crimson lux of stark contrast to the waxy angular skull of Mikey. He gave a chuckle clasping his hands benevolently in jest.

"Sure look," he said, "I'll give it to you for a square eight if it suits you?"

"Thanks, Mikey, I'll be in again" I murmured and skedaddled for the door.

"See you tomorrow," he said with a wave.

I didn't go in tomorrow or the next day and when Mossy suggested we go in on the Wednesday I managed to side-track him by suggesting instead we head for Lizzy Taylors, see if we could fleece a wad of chocolate mice or a ball of refreshers. These tactics weren't going to last forever however and I needed to come up with a plan fast.

Michael the stump Mulvey didn't know what he was getting himself into when he converted the grotty windowless space adjoining his lounge bar into a video arcade. The former storage room was given a lick of paint with the mauve carpet laid on the floor almost stretching to the corners. Michael's face couldn't belie the lustre of pride as he beheld the sparkling new contraptions four of which were lined along the back wall opposite the door and one more on each along of the side walls. Bomb Jack, Bobble Bobble, Wonder Boy, Green Beret, Pang, and Kung Foo Masters are all in the same heavenly room. Personally, it proved a double-edged sword. On one hand, it distracted Mossy myself, and Bosco from Mikey's cabinet and the possibility of being called out, on the other in a quest to inscribe my initials on the leaderboard of Kung Foo masters proved to be an unrelenting drain on my finances. I was on a budget of 60p a day and on a normal day at lunch that accounted for a Macroon bar and three chocolate mice or a Wham Bar and two Refreshers or one outright Wagon Wheel, after school once the dinner was devoured a Yorkie, a Star Bar, a Mars, a Twix or a Double Decker was the highlight of the day. We had a unique technique for dismantling each of the aforementioned, e.g. Twix, remove the caramel layer with incisors, nibble carefully the chocolate veneer along the four sides of the rectangular biscuit base, retract the entire flat biscuit base into the mouth using the tongue break into two equal parts against the roof of the mouth. Mulch to a paste and slowly swallow. Repeat for the second biscuit bar. Both coins of the remaining 20p were set flat against the screen of Kung Foo masters as a marker for combat.

Geraldine Gormely happened to be the sister of Bosco Gormley who also happened to be my best friend. Bosco was as close as a kid could be addicted to video games. He spent day and night in the arcade, himself and Ulick Lawlor. In both appearance and twitchy reflex Ulick had the attributes of a nervous animal, which didn't help his credibility but facilitated greatly in the fledgling art of gaming. We watched on in awe as he controlled the figure on the screen the doppelganger of Bruce Lee. He finished Level 1 in a breeze lepping into and hammering the shite out of the big lad with the bat. Between each level he vigorously scratched the briar of hair, and nibbled a nail. Level 2 was trickier with earthenware pots falling in all directions, left and right with snakes and bombs followed by whole heaps of lads to be kicked punched and walla kicked, the odd one flinging a knife. At the end of the level, a deadly opponent armed with sickle like boomerangs awaited (this is where I would always become unstuck). Level 3 was more of the same with the addition of dexterous tom toms that could summersault in the air and land plumb on your head. Ulick was an expert at anticipating the summersault and would pre-empt with a kick one after the other. The opponent at the end of this level despite his size was handy enough, a big wavering giant that could be managed with a walla kick followed by a sequence of sidekicks until he fell with a roar. The fourth level was more of the snakes in pots, thicker and faster, it was difficult to get away without a bite or two from the little buggers even for the likes of Ulick. The wizard encountered at the end of this level was the greatest bastard of them all. Flinging fireballs, it was impossible to get in near him, and time after time he did for Ulick and the long line of others who could only get this far on a rare occasion. Time and time again Ulick's Bruce lookalike fell to his death, the big booming laugh rubbing salt in the wounds, "moo ha ha ha ha ha ha". Overcoming the wizard became the single biggest challenge occupying the thoughts of most budding teenagers in the town.

Geraldine was down after Bosco to come up for his tea. The mother had sent her. Her big light eyes like new moons patiently waited for his answer. We watched from opposite sides of the machine as he struggled to get the joystick to follow instructions.

"I'll be up after you," he said irate at having just lost a man.

She paused for a moment, sumped her mouth and made for the door knowing her mother would be annoyed.

"Hold on," I said in my bravest act to date "I'll come".

Bosco glanced a look of surprise before being drawn back to the challenge of saving Sylvia from Mr X, furiously trying to shake off a bunch of underlings as we parted. We strolled up the rock, it was dark and quiet in contrast to the fluorescent light and whirling sounds of the arcade. I desperately rummaged for something to say.

"Will your mam be annoyed ?" I asked.

"She will but she's used to it" said Geraldine not sounding too bothered.

"How was school today ?" I asked.

"Good" she replied and enquired the same of me.

"Boring" I answered.

She stopped facing me "your very clever and it's easy for you", she said implying that she wasn't.

"Yes, but you are so lovely," I thought "and it doesn't matter if you are clever or not because when we grow up and marry I'll make the money and you will make the babies".

STORIES OF A DIGITAL SPALPEEN

"I am not" I replied "It's just that everyone else in my class is thick".

We reached the door of her father's bar, she stopped, the pleated skirt of her dark uniform swayed, and her white socks pulled up to the knee glowed angel bright in the shadow of the door. "Thanks for walking me home" she sounded genuine. I didn't want it to end but pushed open the door showing her in. The lights were low, Dire Straits were playing the "Walk of life" on the juke box. It was turned right down, Monday evening levels. Mags and Julie were positioned at the near end of the bar entertaining the romantic aspiration of some old farmer while he fed them bottles of Ritz. Lilly the Pink was in for her evening puff and sucked a major deep into her mouth between her loose lips. I watched on as she made her way to the kitchen, interrupted by a big toothy smile and outstretched arms of hello from Paddy Burke to his pet Geraldine. I watched on as long as the slowly closing door allowed me.

In a moment of madness, I confided in my sister Izzy who was overjoyed with my coming of age. With the greatest of enthusiasm, she brought a steadfast focus to the project, a welcome distraction of her normal projects of adopting and feeding stray dogs on slices of turkey and ham. She started with my appearance uplifting my hair with my older brother Pierces wet look gel and arranging the outfit I would present myself in on the day I was to "pop the question". The results were pleasing but it was in terms of finances she excelled. The following Thursday was a mart day which brought with it an undoubted visit from John P. He sat in the kitchen blind drunk beside the range ranting like a madman through his porter stained cleft lip. "What's your name ?" he roared at my sister as if she was out the door and up the town "Come ere till I see ya," he said as she willing approached and out from his pocket produced a roll of notes earned from the sale of heifers and unpeeled a big green pound. "Whaaaz your name ?" he then roared at me "Yer a mighty man" he bellowed departing with another hard earned pound. We left the kitchen through the door to the dining room and re-entered the kitchen through the door from the hall. "Whaaaz your name ?" he roared again and with my mother attending in the shop not supervising the scam my sister was rewarded with another pound by giving a different name. "Whaaaz your name ?" turning to me and I became Pierce "your only a Bollix," he said but nonetheless handed over another fat pound. Another round resulted in another two pound although he hesitated with an excruciating thought before eventually dipping into the pocket. A drop of homely tea and a ham sandwich with Coleman's mustard gained the final reward the complement of being a "lovely lassie" coupled with a pair of pounds. Eight pounds total, that ring had Geraldine Gormley's name on it.

The wizard proved impossible. For weeks Ulick and Bosco fought it out, succumbing on each occasion to the relentless fireballs. Time after time the peering heads witnessing the fatal fall with groans of disappointment. Failure resulted in frustration with fists smashing screens and machines getting a kicking much to the anguish of the stump who like the wizard began to appear sporadically and throw a fireball of his own in all directions with barring orders and warnings. A rumour circulated that in the *casual corner* of Sligo town a guy with the ominous tag of Headser could complete the game start to finish with a single life. As the failure prolonged Headser's repetition grew pro rata. Rhetoric described him as tall with raven hair, a velvet suede dinner jacket, eloquent fingerless gloves adorning dexterous fingers. Despite the reputation of the casual corner being dangerous territory especially for buffs the like of us, we decided the temptation was too great and threw caution to the wind to attain the secret of the wizard.

On a Saturday morning we led Ulick to the station like a champion and boarded the train. Spud Mc Donagh was enlisted to bulk our ranks. I had agreed with my sister to be back on the afternoon train giving us enough time to dickey up and get up to Mikey's to make the purchase. I had the eight pound in my pocket occasionally rubbing my index finger along its folded spine, heady with the magnitude of events to unfold. Once settled, under the consultation of Spud we huddled in a group agreeing as a collective not to look scared in approaching the casual corner. The townies could smell fear Spud forebode. A fag was suggested by Mossy to assure a confident look. Yes, a fag was definitely required Spud agreed. The casual corner was as dark as a mine with dense shadowy outlines moving with the suspicion of inmates. Bosco who seemed always to know these things hissed "That's Headsers brother" as a tough looking kid with a ginger Mohican passed by. We fumbled onwards aware that the slightest of nudges on a stranger might set off a fight, making our way deeper into danger to the towering figure with hair rising like branches against the moon of the exit door light. He was as foreboding a figure as they had rumoured. We were encircled, speechless in attendance. Much in similar way to Ulick, he graced through the first three levels. Our tacit excitement grew as he approached the wizard halting intently at the third column a blind spot to the fireballs then waiting for the exact duration of fifteen seconds before walking on then descending to one knee and hammering fists into the belly of the wizard. It was all over in in seconds. We collectively sucked in deep breaths of dank air in order not to let out a vainglorious cry of victory. The next level, the final one, after months of effort, had never been witnessed by us. Headser himself jerked nervously.

I was startled by a poke, "give us a fag" two guys both with shaved heads, underfed and smelling of chips. I fumbled in my pocket and handed one over. "And my bud" he motioned with his head looking annoyed so I submitted a second. A touch uneasy I returned attention to the game. It was like a revelation from the Bible to see Headser take on the final opponent a dancing prancing prince of Kung Foo. With another twist in the tail, the Headser lost the battle and walked off speechless with his entourage in tow. Ulick took the opportunity and familiarised himself with the layout of the new controls, rotating the joy stick and confirming the configuration of the buttons. He had no money he claimed and Bosco sponsored him a coin. Further investment was needed and they turned to me for a pound of my eight. I watched as one after the other Ulick dropped coins into the machine until the pound and then another expired. On the final 10p to the awe of an equinox, the gazing eyes witnessed the bitter sweet victory as Ulick completed the game. The melodic music as Thomas repatriated with his love Sylvia was a reminder to me that myself and of Geraldine were growing further apart as a result of the expenditure. A second bony poke to the shoulder.

"Give us a pound". I looked around to my colleagues for support catching the eye of Mossie who looked away as if diverted to an item of interest on the screen. I handed over the pound, "and him" the skinhead pointed to the friend. A sudden nihilistic gloom overcame me.

"Do you think I'm St Vincent De Paul ?" I protested, the reply was succinct.

"Do you want a fucking slap".

I handed over the pound. The final blow to my finances occurred on the train on the way home when the conductor knocked on the toilet door – "Tickets please" and kept knocking until we finally tramped out. I stepped off the train with a single solitary lonesome loveless pound.

Izzy saved the day, "don't mention it to anyone" she said restoring my faith in human nature, watching on as she carefully unlocked her walnut box full of tattered letters and scattered notes and coins. We raced together to Mikey's. She navigated the buttons as I watched attentively to point it out to her. Endless rows of watches came one after the other. "Slow down" I requested as the rings eventually came into view. In that instant, my heart dropped like a stone. "It's gone," I said to my sister, beseeching my bottom lip not to quiver. She had given me hope with the money and now she gave me courage picking out a silver ring with a black stone. "She'll love it" she assured. Mikey honoured his price promise and we were back in the house adding the final touches to my hair. It was still wet when I kicked the stand off my Grifter and sped through the streets the pure air of evening giving me new hope. I dismounted the bike with a skid and almost stumbled over the two figures exiting the door of Gormley's pub. "Oh shit sorry" I apologised before realising it was Geraldine followed closely by Mossy carefully escorting her with an open hand on her lower back. She looked radiant. "Bosco's in the kitchen" she chirped as I dusted off the front of my cords. "Well actually... " I began before realising she wasn't paying much attention, craning backward with new found affection for Mossy who blanked me completely. Her two hands were intertwined on her midriff the fingers on her right twizzling the ring on her left. An unmistakable Gold ring with an envious green Garnet stone. The ring of my Rubicon.

Plucking Crows

Some said he was born that way, others said she made a fool out of him but they all agreed he didn't have much between the ears. Every Wednesday you could set your clock on them appearing over the top of the rock for the messages in Cullen's, Iggy Quigley and the mother, Sweet Alice. He was twice her size, the Duffle coat looked just about on him and for every step, he took she took two. The march came to a halt at Cullen's corner where he handed over the shopping bags to Sweet Alice. He never went in, but then again she warned him not to budge and in fairness to him he normally never did. Instead standing stiffly with a fixed grin across his shiny face greeting everyone who went in or out of the shop. This was no mean feat as Sweet Alice might be an hour or more probing the nice sides of bacon, fingering the leafy heads of cabbage or lifting the delicious apples one by one to her nose for examination. She paid with the pension, wondered if things had gone up from the last week and complained that you would want to be a millianre to keep the likes of Iggy in mush.

This would go on in all weather of course and weather was the one subject that Iggy loved most.

"Hello Mrs Kelly,", he says.

"Oh hello Iggy I didn't see you there," a hand on her head to protect her wash and set from the wind.

"Lovely soft day Mrs Kelly," he suggested after her.

"Oh it is Iggy," she says looking back at him trying to get in out of the wind.

The Dog Murphy pulled up in the Massey, he wasn't so worried about the wind in his hair, he was bald as an egg with a long lilting fag ash on the tip of his woodbine. He descended from the transport box.

"Hello John,"

"How ya Iggy ?"

"Soft Day John,"

"Tis Iggy,"

"Do you think it will rain later John ?"

"There's a fair chance Iggy and sure what if it does, we're not made of paper,"

"That's right John we're not made of paper John, wouldn't it be queer if we were John ?"

"Would Iggy,"

"Talking about paper, I must get the Journal,"

"Do John, lovely day isn't it John ?", to which the Dog unsure what to reply rubbed the back of his head and went for the door.

"Good luck Iggy,"

"Good Luck now John".

Iggy was now alone, delighted with himself, looking up and down the street with the innocence of a child. We also wanted to have a word with Iggy, not about the weather, no, we had a crow to pluck with him, his religion, or as reported his recent lapse.

Crouched behind an Escort, myself, Mossy and Bosco had agreed on the running order. "Ready" Mossy hissed, "steady" he continued looking from me to Bosco to the fender, "Go !" and he leapt up on the bonnet. "IGGY", he roared across at Iggy who was startled into an upright position staring intently, wondering who this surreal apparition was that was hailing him. It was my turn, I heaved myself up beside Mossy "THE PRIEST", I exuded from the depths of my lungs before Bosco joined with a stumble "WANTS YA" his voice trailing off into the deadly silence of no going back. It was hard to make out exactly what Iggy might be thinking, he was stock still with a growing look of wonderment. Suddenly the bonnet popped as Mossy peeled off to my left and fled, then Bosco to my right, in through the door of Manion's pub and to safety. Seemingly at the same time the penny dropped with Iggy and his twitching indecision was apparent as we locked in, eye to eye across the no man's land of O'Connell Street. Without warning he exploded, the pounding of his manly beats rung out, his mouth swinging open like a gate in a gale. He was increasing in size with every bounding step, readying himself to devour me. I jerked with fright and wobbled off the bonnet almost falling over with the seriousness of the situation, he was halfway to getting his hands on me before I managed to kick in and take off, the two of us off up the town, bobbing and weaving, ducking and diving, swinging and swaying.

I wasn't thinking smart, if I had I wouldn't have taken the road towards the castle. A steep straight hill flanked on either side by a hedge and a high wall making it impossible to disappear. Ironically we were halfway up but who did I see coming in the other direction but Fr Hegarty. His unmistakable clean cut outline in the distance flicking his walking cane like a metronome as he bounded along, sniffing in the summer scents of honeysuckle and fresh cut grass. What would he make of all this? I put the brakes on, stalling with indecision; Fr Hegarty in front of me had also come to a halt to admire a fox glove, Iggy to the rear still in motion like the six o'clock from Connolly. There was only one option, "Father" I bid him good evening out of force of habit as I flashed past in the hope he wouldn't recognise me. I could see his hand go up in greeting and linger in disbelief as Iggy followed unrelenting.

I steered left through the towering wooden gates of the castle entrance, into what was familiar territory having climbed each and every peak of the ruins. Up the stone stairs embodied in the main wall, poking an eye through a portico halfway up to view the broad outline of Iggy entering the courtyard. He stalled and grunted whilst deciding on my most likely direction. Instinctively he knew. I burst up the second narrow flight into a large open room. The fireplace in the middle of the back wall I knew was hollowed along the chimney breast, a kind of secret passage. I stooped under and stood up on a jutting rock, squeezing my shoulders between the two mighty pillars of cold stone. The bodhran beat of Iggy's boots followed, making dust of the small stones beneath them then scraping to a halt. His laboured breathing immediately filled the room, his searching eyes progressing over the naked walls from roof to ceiling. A further echo of a step and he was in the room proper, only feet away, if he uncovered me now only the ghost of the Red Earl would ever know what became of me. I began to imagine the blackened gaps in his teeth as he wrung my neck. Another dragging boot in the direction of my hide sent a rattling shiver up my spine. Jesus, Mary and Joseph. I recoiled awaiting the duffle coat to reach up and grab the top of my leg like a python.

STORIES OF A DIGITAL SPALPEEN

He was right next to me standing at the chimney breast mutterings away to himself. If I angled my eyes I could see the up-turned bottoms of his chocolate brown pants hover over the tops of his boots. My heart was beating like the hammers of hell, so much so I thought it was going to burst a hole clean through my chest and the wall. I tried to calm it by talking in soothing tones but no joy so then toyed with the idea of making myself known, to slip out from under the hearth like an eel, "Aragh Iggy is it yourself ? Lovely day isn't it ?". No, I would surely end up in Perry's hearse, with wreaths of son and friend with old women keening over my broken body, young ones drinking to the first of the gang to go. "Come out" he said in a low effeminate, mischievous voice. Holy Moses, he surely was mad as they said. "Come out the priest wants ya" he said again, the incantations of his malevolent tones curling into the confines of the chimney. Think of Sweet Alice Iggy I implored in my mind, think of Sweet Alice my eyes wrinkled shut expecting the worst. He paused, swivelled, paused a second time and took off down the stairs the thump gradually fading was music to my ears. Through a poke hole, I observed him pass through the courtyard his broad back exiting the ruddy gate. I thanked Sweet Alice, promising faithfully that would be the last involvement I had in her son's pastoral care.

The next time I ran into Fr Hegarty was only days later, and if he didn't have a good look at me belting up Castle Hill there was no mistaking me on this occasion. Below at the horseshow, myself and Spud Mulligan knocking seven colours of shite out of one another. It all started out pleasant enough, much to the delight of Dan Banks chairman of the committee the sun was cracking the stones. He could be heard on the loudhailer from some distance announcing the next event to the ring. He was probably sunburnt and sweaty, sitting in the car complaining between announcements of the woeful heat and could someone get him an ice cream. The reflectors on our bikes shone brilliantly as we formed a cavalcade speeding past the horses and horse boxes in an array of earthy hues, drinking in the musty smell of horse shit belly dancing on the breeze. It wasn't a day for the equine alone however and included the bovine lupine and indeed the feminine, hoisting buff bonnie babies for presentation to the motherly mugs of the judges. Mossey spotted Spuds Chopper slung against the fence, distinctive maroon with sun orange branding and tassels swaying from the handlebars. Not one to miss an opportunity he produced a box of matches removed one and snapped it into the valve. We watched on as the air hissed over the sounds of distant laughter and horse hoofs on the trampled turf. He did the front then the back, the air slowly whining to an indignant end when Bosco raised the alarm, "he's coming" he muttered from under the canopy of his hand. Out the side of my eye, I could see him stomping forward, his arms swaying defiantly, a knuckle duster strapped on his right wrist, accompanied as always with his loyal dog Rusty. He was a year older, already into heavy metal and had fingered Jazz Mc Donagh from Tubber. He looked down on the sorry state of his chopper, flicked his hair back and drew a boot on my wheel.

"Did you do that ?" he demanded.

"Did I hell" I replied with anger watching the reflector dislodged by his boot ping off into the long grass..

"Look what you did" I said getting off my own bike and giving him a good shove but Spud wasn't interested in me or my bike.

"Who did ?" he asked now right into my face and before I could contemplate grassing Mossy he swooped an arm round me dragging me into a downward headlock till I was suddenly eye to eye with Rusty. His tongue lolling from the heat, his hot breath instantly suffocating me. Understandably the dog was also confused and in his excitement barked a loud warning.

"Aagh, ya little bastard" I roared in shock and sprung backwards with all of my might to lift Spud off his heels and peg him flat on the grass.

"Wah hey," Mossy exhalted in triumph. I flashed him a dirty look as much as to say, "your a bit smart for my liking", he shrugged as if to respond "What can I do ?". The lads nearby, paying fifty pence for three goes at putting the ball through the tyre were over like flies to a shit, forming a circle of death, grappling for space demanding action, *fight fight fight*, there was no getting away from it now.

He peeled himself from the turf with a "you're going to get it now" and slanted eyes. Swung a wild left and caught me in the eye with a dirty finger. The next one landed with a crash on my shoulder and I crumpled to my knees. I wasn't sure if the welling tears were a result of the dirty finger or the overwhelming feeling of self pity that had overcome me. I surveyed the ring of faces closing in on me, gleaming with as much delight not to be involved themselves as the enjoyment of the spectacle itself. I fixed on John Bulmer Finn, he was friends with my older sister, he just stared back with a look of you're on your own boss. A pretty girl in jolpers pushed in to see what all the commotion was about. She looked down on me solicitously, "Oh he's bleeding" she said moving her hand to her mouth. At that point, the most unlikely voice spoke to me from the depths of my mind. "Get up let ya" she said. "Is that you Mammy ?, "Get up let ya ...." she repeated. So I lifted myself and hit him such a tally that he let out a withering whimper, the girl in the jolpers eeeked and the Bulmer Finn roared "Good Lad". Before I knew it I was astride Spud, raising my fist like a Guillotine, the crowd quietened in expectation, I could hear Dan in the background, he had forgotten to turn off the loud hailer again, he was talking to someone – "a fight ?" he said "that's a terror altogether". Spud grappled to get hold of my face but it was no use I was only picking my spot. The right eye looked good but then again so did the nose. Spud had other intentions of course and with the dexterity and strength of a salmon bucked upwards and sent me tumbling, both of us now flat on our backs looking upwards at the mooning faces when the dainty white hands of the young priest parted the crowd and looked down on us both with disdain.

I suppose the knock on the door was inevitable. He stood there with an upright posture back to his happy self. "Young man" he greeted me.

"Bless me Father for I have sinned" I muttered a wilful act of contrition.

"Sorry ?", he looked puzzled.

"Hello Father" I said.

"Is your mother in ?" he asked.

"She is" I said. "Let me get her for ya" turning away before forgetting my manners, in that I was referring to a man of the cloth.

"Sorry Father," I said.

"Excuse me ?" he said, again confused.

The kitchen opened, the mother was squinting to see through the burst of dusky sunlight that was calling on her. Likewise, it was a call to arms for Dana our dog, at the sight of a stranger, head to toe in sinister black, started yapping like mad. Dana was tiny, shivering and mangy when we took her in, a cross between a Collie and a Jack Russell she was ferociously loyal as a result. "Come in father, come in" my mother beckoned him buffing her hair with a hand. She often mentioned how refined he was and if he weren't a priest how he would get the finest of women. At the sight of Dana's angled head, jammed between the door of the kitchen and the mother's leg, dead eyed with drips of spittle dropping from her needle teeth, he hesitated. The mother motioned to me bruskly to let her out the back so I took her and hitched her to the visitor's rope calming her by running a line from the brindle bristles of her skull to the buff of wayward white fleece on her rump. She rolled her eyes whimpering like a child, she loved me madly, despite my flaws.

The mother ushered Fr Hegarty to the drawing room, the best room in the house. I immediately plugged my ear to the door listening to their canting mumbles, catching the odd word here and there. She would be proffering him a tea and Marietta or a slice of sponge or perhaps something to give him a lift like a whiskey and ginger. They giggled nervously. They would slowly progress to the meat of, the witnessed misdemeanours, the poor attendance at Mass and other moderate offences. The mother would take it all in of course, too coy to comment, "emm" she would say. She had her suspicions, we both knew it, almost catching me on the hop once or twice asking "Who said Mass ? ". The fighting and Iggy baiting would be news to her though and hearing it first hand from the handsome fresh faced priest would surely embarrass her. Ten minutes in, the mumbles grew louder, realising he was coming for the door I folded back into the kitchen to look for something to do.

"Oh you're still here ?" he asked.

"I am a father" I said leaving my hand on the frying pan.

"You're doing a bit of cooking is it ?"

"I am, I am."

"Anything interesting ?" He asked.

"Just a bit of steak and onions Father."

He looked at his watch and wondered, "At ten o'clock ?, isn't it a bit early ?"

I needed to think fast, "oh not for me Father, it's for the dog."

"For the Dog" he looked completely lost altogether. By this stage Dana had spotted him through the window and reared up again, back yapping like mad.

"Will you be down for football training tomorrow ?" he asked me oblivious to Dana half choking, twisting and turning every which way to free herself from the rope.

"Oh, I will Father" I assured him.

STORIES OF A DIGITAL SPALPEEN

"I'm really looking forward to the championship this year" he went on "I think we have a good little team in the making".

If there was one thing Father Hegarty loved more than God's work in nature it was the GAA.

"Oh we do Father" I replied.

I could see Dana was working herself into an awful state altogether, barking endlessly, rushing forward and reaching the end of the rope which jerked her backwards in a violent bundle against the wall.

"What about this business with yourself and Spud Mulligan ?" he asked. I wasn't sure what to say.

"I hope ye can manage to get along on the pitch" he said.

"Yes Father" I said meekly. Dana queasy and dishevelled from belting the wall croaked a few hoarse harks, composed herself for a moment and threw herself into one almighty toss forward.

"Do you want to tell me what the row was all about ?" Fr Hegarty said getting all serious, placing a comforting hand on my shoulder. I was considering where to begin when a sound of a snap from the back yard drew our attention to the window. Dana had broke free, the blue rope trailing after her in swirls. Fr Hegarty gazed at me in disbelief watching the vicious bitch launching herself at the door and popping it open with a four legged leap. He let out a withering howl of terror and took off for the hall door some fifteen metres away, Dana not far behind her nails scratching frantically across the lino. I dived to the floor making a grab for the rope but it all happened so fast it whipped through my hands. Face flat from the floor I was helpless to assist the cries of the handsome priest, he had managed to get the hall door open and was all but out except for a lazy hand which Dana with the precision of a bomb squad Doberman managed to latch on to. The mother joined in with her own wavering variations of a liturgy so that anyone might think the devil not seen since Tooreen had made an appearance. By the time I managed to peel myself up and wrench open her jaws, blood had been spilled.

I was sent to fetch Dr Hodgins, locating him as expected on the high stool in Haydens. When we returned Fr Hegarty was sat shivering on the drawing room couch medicated on whiskey (it hadn't raised the gleeful giggles of the previous offer). We watched on in silence as the musty, half drunk old doctor administered a tetanus jab on his flawless buttocks. He rose stiffly, embarrassed and out of sorts. He wished the mother a half hearted goodbye at the door, keeping a wary eye out for the devil of a dog and limped down the street. Dana spent the rest of the day under the table until the old fella arrived back later that evening. "What would you go giving him a pair of me good trousers" he laughed, "and what in the hell brought him round anyway ?" he enquired further while fiercely petting Dana as if she were the victim in all of this. The mother was none too pleased though, she accused him of caring for the dog more than humans (which he didn't deny) took a shot of whiskey (highly unusual for her), grounded me for a week and went off for a Radox bath. The Old boy looked at me with a sympathetic chuckle that meant "take it like a man" and went off to join the Doc in Haydens.

STORIES OF A DIGITAL SPALPEEN

My weeks detention was coming to an end, the good weather had managed to hold out. From my window, I looked down on the chirping sparrows happily collecting crumbs from the dusty street. I was missing the fun fair at the mart, Bosco and Mossey would be up there now, in the bumping cars no doubt, skirting the edges looking for an opportunity to accelerate into the back of a day driver and wham the head off them. The louder the shriek of surprise the better. The girls were the best.

Tobin passed by the window earlier, spotted me and shouted up, wondering why I was not out and about, did I have nits or something ?. That would be the rumour now I suppose. Anyway there was the bonfire to look forward to, the trekking through the fields to pilfer silage pits of their tyres or evenings with hatchets hacking the shite out of branches in the orchard. This year's competition with Spud and the park lads for the most impressive pyre would be all the more fierce.

The sparrows chirped, fun fair or not. Iggy was standing silently at Cullen's corner, loosening a button on the duffle coat when Fr Hegarty came along. I couldn't hear the conversation of course but imagined it went something like this.

"Hello Iggy."
"Ah hello there Father,"
"Lovely day isn't it Father ?"
"It is Iggy, it is, thank God."
"Will it rain later Father ? "
"I hope not Iggy, I don't want to miss my evening walk."
"I see Father."

D. M. O'DOWD

"Good, Good Iggy, now Iggy, I'm glad I ran into you., you see I have a crow to pluck with you about .. about, well how should I put it .... your attendance at mass ...."

That Beats Banagher

There were some mad Pats in the town at the time, Pat the Flute, Pat the Brush or Pat Mc Guiness, some bad Basterds like the Blackie Lohan or the brothers Bragan but as a pure hore altogether Michael Cahan stood on his own. I suppose in part because he was cut from a different cloth, you see he came from a very respectable family. His mother Grace was a chemist in the town a paragon of virtue and a fountain of good sense, the wooden chair in her chemist shop a sort of pew for women's problems. The shelves heaving with remedies for all ailments from heartburn to haemorrhoids, ringworm to rheumatism. She even stocked rubber johnnies but rarely dispensed any, preferring to give advice on what God and nature intended and once famously sent Bob Dunn doused in Brut back peddling out the door informing him "he was no teenager".

Michael didn't look much like Grace or his father Gerry for that matter. He was as wide as he was tall, with a Leonine head covered in thick black hair. He had the arms of a cyclops and his shirts were always rolled up to the elbows. The Father always said he was the cut of Jack Dempsy, which was a coincidence as he was an intervarsity British Isles boxing champion representing the University of Galway. Recently after a hiatus of a few years he had made a reappearance in the town, back to his old bedroom which seemed like a step back for a man of his candescence. When asked what brought him home the answer was simple "because New York was too small for him".

D. M. O'DOWD

Now from all the people that came through the doors at the shop at home, from all the in's and out's to the Kitchen, from all the friends up and down the stairs, neighbours, cold callers and hawkers there was no one that got on so well with the father like Cahan. He was like a son to him, both clever and brave, a man that let nothing get in his way, who through education had extended his horizons and rubbed shoulders equally with thugs and theologians, plebs and philanthropists. All of which he brought to life in the kitchen by the range with his heel hooked on the wrung of a stool making rollies on his knee. He spoke deeply and slowly, purposely leaving pauses to take a puff creating great suspension through the weave of the yarn, always ending with a huge billow of smoke and an understated chuckle. "Well Hang me!" the father ruminated, yet again left in amazement, at another tremendous recount of his adventures.

It wasn't long after arriving back from the concrete jungle, the sprawling metropolis, the melting pot of cultures. That Cahan managed to go missing here in the back end of beyond. Grace hadn't heard or seen from him for the best part of four days when she sent word down to the father asking if he had any contact or knew where he might be located. No, no sign of him. It was all quiet until Quinn came into the shop saying that he had seen him in Charlestown, in J.J Finan, playing 25 and winning all round him. Quinne explained there was a large stain on his shirt and he had a pile of books that he was carrying around with him. A day later we heard another report that he was in the front bar of Kieltys swaying on the stool half singing *the prodigal son*. He was on the top shelf, Hennessey and Sandeman and a wad of cash left on the counter in front of him, all in a big heap. After that it went quiet for a couple of days followed by a sighting close to home in Foxes just out the road, he was all around the place, nearly fell into the fire. The father jumped into action and went to the phone in the hall, rifled through the phone book and rang Foxes. He was gone, up to the Traveller's Rest with Benson they informed him. He handed me the phone book, "find the Traveller's Rest ". T, T, T, I ran my finger down the page.

"Found it" I announced.

"Was he there ?". "No. Not been in all evening" The man replied, and the trail went cold.

Grace was down the next day, entered the shop furtively and spoke to May Mc Fadden, who knew all about it, sure her Tom might go missing for a week, he was a terror for it. He would be off the beer for the longest time and then break out altogether, poor auld May was tortured, we must have heard it a thousand times "Did you see Tom ?". As they were sympathizing with one another, who appears but another long suffering martyr Mrs Hagen, her Sean the worst of the lot. It was so bad that she would hide all his clothes which went to plan until one day he was seen in the hotel imbibing a half one in her violet nightgown and matching slippers. Aw now, small towns and built-up areas.

Things remained quiet for a while until he was seen in the bookies in Ballaghadreen, putting a blue one on *toy boy* at the three o'clock in Fairyhouse. He fell across the pool table in the Fiddlers and then went for the fella who tried to offer him a hand up, things were getting messy. No one knows how he got down to Castlerea or why on earth he was at an itinerant funeral but he was and for the full duration according to Garda Naughton whose people were from down that area. It must have been on account of himself and King Pat having a great interest in the greyhounds. Carrick on Shannon was the next sighting where himself and Pat Mc Donagh were seen entertaining a group of American Tourists in Flynn's. The father putting two and two together mumbled that Mc Donagh was half mad and renting a pub in Tulsk so obviously, Cahan had made his way there and the two of them headed off together on the rip. "That I'd be it alright," he said to himself and walked off. As it happened somewhere along the line Mc Donagh was lost as Cahan was next seen solo in the chippie in Boyle tackling a snack box before turning left into Mattimoe's to open the taps. "Thank God he is eating a bit" Grace prayed.

Based on the map he was heading in our direction and sure enough he was back in the town and reported as above in Gormley's. His arrival wasn't without incident either and he wasn't long in the door when Marty Morrison roared "Where were you in 1916 ?" and Cahan reacted by grabbing him by the craw of the neck and had him up against the powers mirror. Gormley had to run out from behind the bar and mount him to loosen the grip. I was sent up to tell him come home, but he wouldn't of course. Helen Sweeney one of the few who didn't need to keep her distance, was a match for any man on the pints of Guinness and the rum and coke, asked "would I have a mineral", buying me a club orange which I sipped on the long seat underneath the powers mirror where Cahan had nearly extinguished the harmless

STORIES OF A DIGITAL SPALPEEN

Marty. Lilly the Pink spent hours every day on this seat, she was to my right and offered me a Major. I took it on account of me having recently mastered the art of inhaling. Ironically I half hid it from Cahan when he looked over his shoulder. He had a cut over his right eye, the blood was black, and the Guinness stain over his upper lip was the guts of ten days old. He fixed on me and steadied himself, there were tears in his eyes. He turned back to the bar, hips swaying two hands on the counter, head down. Lilly said she would tell me father I was smoking if I didn't carry her messages out home, and they said she wasn't right in the head.

In the end, it all ended tamely, he savoured his last pint, left the glass down gently on the counter and left without announcing his departure. "Hello Michaeleen", Grace says calmly as the door opened and the hall light illuminated the dark street "I have a dinner in the oven for you" she said and led him in. When I told the father this he stood still on the spot. "Stone the crows !" he quipped but not another word for a long time after that.

Now it might be said that Cahan was unpredictable and no one knew what next, but after putting his body through the marathon session the next time we saw him he was promoting health and healing. He had a tincture with him, of which he dropped six drops into a glass of boiled water which had cooled to room temperature. We watched each of the tiny drops dangle and fall into the glass. After the sixth, the father examined it, drank it and waited for the effects, which there was none. "Great for the blood," Cahan said. He then examined the father's feet, and each of the pressure points of his sole and let him know that we would need to keep an eye on his kidneys.

"O man dear !" the father said in amazement putting his socks back on, feeling a twinge in or around the kidney area. After the consultation concluded, they both sat back to have a smoke.

"Hold on" Cahan advised the father, "try one of these ones" and so the father repatriated the single cigarette back in the box. We watched him as he worked his magic again, two rizlas attached for length, three clumps of tan Tabacco evenly placed along it's length. He paused searching in his inside packet producing a little bag of herbs which he carefully opened, taking a pinch between his thick fingers and sprinkling the dry leaves along the top of the tobacco. He rolled with care then sealed with the tip of his tongue dabbing the gum at multiple points along. The last act was to rip the corner of the Rizla packet, roll it into a tube and insert it into the end of the cigarette. He offered the completed article to the father who handled it with care, placed it into his mouth and gently moved into the flame of the Zippo that Cahan was holding up. "Inhale deeply", Cahan advised, "good for the lungs". After that they more or less smoked in silence, the whole kitchen gradually filling with a beautiful sweet smoke until we were all existing peacefully in the cloud. "Good stuff," Cahan says, grinding the stub into the ashtray. The father tried to reply, opened his mouth and raised his eyebrows he had a lot of important questions to ask about the herbs but didn't manage to solicit a word. "Well T.J. I need to be off", Cahan says gathering up the pack of Golden Virginia, hooking the rizla on the inside cuff and folding over the cover. The father, still searching for his tongue managed to bleat "Right o, Michaeleen" in a feeble voice.

The father sat at the kitchen table for the guts of two hours after that, just sitting there smiling away to himself. I entered with a half excuse of opening and closing the fridge, he was smiling at me, his eyes all glassy just looking at me and smiling. I definitely knew then that there was something up with him, I could count on one hand how many times he had smiled in the last year never mind a continuous uninterrupted rictus. Should I call the doctor I wondered, I couldn't check with the mother as she was in Monaghan with my sister, at a man with the cure for Eczema. It began to get weirder. To my astonishment, he was making himself toast. To see him messing with the grill, trying to fit it in properly was a sight never before seen. He simply never cooked, the mother served him the breakfast, dinner and tea everyday and cooking was just not in his bag. Looking at the plate he was on his second batch of three slices. I watched as he slathered on the butter and bit down on the bread in slow motion. Chewing every last atom and swallowing like a reptile. I watched on in amazement wondering what or who had taken over my father. I wondered if it was Fr Hegarty that was needed and said so to the mother when she arrived home from the cure. "Where is he now" she asked,

"Gone to bed" I explained.

"Gone to bed ?", she checked if she had heard correctly. Everything was just different about him, he was usually up half the night, walking round the house, you might meet him appearing out of any door in the depths of darkness, scaring the life out of you.

I explained further, "he went with the Irish press, it took him about 20 minutes to put on the pyjamas". "I watched it all through the keyhole" I informed her.

"In bed ?", she said again as we made our way up the stairs, opening the door and revealing himself propped up by plump pillows, the paper open across his chest, the headline reading, "Record drugs hall uncovered in Leitrim". He had given up on the pyjamas the pants were still on him along with the bedroom slippers, the sheet only half covered him. A smile ran like a ribbon across his face. "Jesus, Mary and Joseph", she exclaims in disbelief.

The last time we set eyes on Cahan was a passing conversation on Teeling Street. The father was sweeping the street, getting ready for opening when Cahan who was passing stopped to say hello. They had made an agreement for no fixed day or time when Cahan would bring another pinch of the herbs which the father described as a lovely smoke altogether. The meeting never happened of course, which was bittersweet indeed. Fr Hegarty said he was a big loss to the town and would be missed by all, or a few at least. He said, he had hoped he was in a better place and at peace with the world. But he didn't need to hope at all he could have asked Grace herself who was at nine o'clock mass without fail every morning and the last update from her was that he was in Montreal opening his third car dealership, the first two doing so well. She was like a new woman. It seems it happened like this, or so the last reports go. It was a quiet Sunday morning when Cahan arrived in Gormley's, he had with him a bag which he left on Lilly's long seat and took a position at the bar. He enjoyed a few slow Hennessey and Sandeman having the craic with Bertie. It could have been any other predictable Sunday where the denizens dripped in, the jukebox would be warm before mass but to Gormley's surprise after a moderate few he raised the bag over his shoulder and said he was off to win a handball tournament. It turns out he did just that. Some hours later returning, handed the Trophy to Gormley and asked him to place it behind the bar and began to finish the bottle of Hennessey. It is still there today, the trophy, in the same spot beside the Toucan lamp and a red rosette *best in show 1988*. Before leaving for the second time that day and last time ever he threw the bag on his back and from there he was seen stepping on the train to Dublin. No one knew why, he never mentioned it to Gormley who only wondered if he saw right when thinking there was a tear in his eye, at the time putting it down to the glint of the light from the door as Cahan paused to look around for a last look. A week passed before Marty Brennan who was over and back to Anfield the whole time was expressly explaining in the post office that he had spotted Cahan with a foreign-looking blond on the deck of a PO Ferry bound for Holyhead. They were like a celebrity couple, he explained with great excitement and hand gestures and the rest is history as they say. When the Father had heard this, he was having a cup of tea at the kitchen table, listening with such intensity that the biscuit he was dipping couldn't hold on any longer and dropped to its death. Now that would be the kind of thing that would normally drive the auld lad mad but he just sat three in amazement, with the remaining half in his hand. He asked me a few times to repeat just to be sure he had heard clearly all the details and when satisfied withdrew for a moment into silence, "Well, that beats Banagher" he said eventually with a smile of tremendous pride slowly fixing over his entire face.

Marmalade I

That was one hot summer, when the majority of our long days were spent lumbering on the tapered wall along the tennis courts, like lizards, smoking cigarettes in the glorious sunshine, side-eyeing the gaps in the manhandled fence for the vision of Caroline Conway to appear. Then we would sit up and glower, as we watched her nubile body rolling freely beneath the confines of her white polo, as she hopelessly tottered to reach the net. "I'm no good at this" she would declare in a slump, "so what" we opined but ostensibly offered shallow words of encouragement. Mossey, who in the shower rooms after football flaunted his precociously hairy torso, while I, smooth as a Perl cowered in the shade of self-consciousness, was the only one to make any headway with her. He had shifted her, more than once and said without verification that on one occasion he had managed to brush the side of her left tit before she grasped and navigated his hand back to the allowable nether regions of her lower back. "Jaysus it was like heaven in a handful" he would say with random routine , his right hand wrapped around his left wrist pulled into his groin, bearing the immense burden of the testosterone throbbing through his evolving body flowering an effervescent flush to his still boyish grin. "I'm going to ride her this summer" he insisted with the integrity of a forsaken Italian waiter. If he was, then for sure it was going to be at her discretion, she would be the one to ride him, if she so chose. The thought of such cardinal bodily contact to me, who daily beseeched his body to give up a single wiry pubescent follicle seemed like reaching the surface of the moon itself - on a bicycle.

The only other topic of interest that could exclusively command our attention other than Caroline Conway was the county final. We had navigated the earlier rounds with ease, laid down the gauntlet by beating our fierce local rivals the Harps in an east divisional final which brought the glisten of tears to the eyes of our manager Johnny B. After the game he lost the run of himself altogether, hugging and kissing anyone that came within range which wasn't to be expected of a man who half an hour earlier was making shapes to run headlong for the ref and grab hold of his neck. The semi-finals took us to the north of the county and again by a similarly narrow margin we defeated St Pats. Fatty Hannon assistant to Johnny B and local GAA historian fed our growing sense of self-importance by informing us that we were the first minor team in eighteen years to reach the heady heights of a county final. "I'm giving up the fags", says Mossey with another statement of intent, they nearly had him "kilt" he reckoned and there was no way he was going to make a show of himself in the county final, not with half the town watching, especially not in front of Caroline Conway or maybe more so his father, a former county footballer for Christ sake who himself was now coincidentally an eighty smokes a day man (Mossey took equal pride in both accomplishments). We were gathered in the doorway of the community centre. I looked at Bosco and he looked at me, both taken aback. He offered me a Benson and I accepted. For the purpose of torment, we smoked them like we had never enjoyed a pleasure like it before in our lives, such luxuriant puffing was never seen. "We'll that's alright for ye lads," says Mossey, irked, "I'm off for me tea". In the void that followed his departure, I thought about his commitment. It made me nervous, outlining the magnitude of responsibility in donning the maroon and white, eighteen years was a long time in the history of an underachieving club inured in failure. Would he stick it though? I thought, knowing that he was prone to wanton disruptions of commitment and routine such as school work and football training.

It took a jolt of Bosco's elbow to shock me from my state of preponderance. "Who's that" ? he was asking.

"Who's who ?" I replied with some surprise given Bosco knowing all in sundry in our kip of a town.

"Yer wan with Nula Barrett" he says, by which time I was stunned into silence, confused, confounded and completely in love. She was everything a pasty faced teenage scut from the rain sodden Atlantic coast could possibly have dreamed of, dark and exotic, sweet and wholesome, a specimen of which like only known to us in the form of Australian sitcom transmissions aka Home and Away. Nula, well Nula was best described as ... as sound.

"Hello lads", she says stopping with a flat smile but obviously proud as punch that she could now draw endless attention from the opposite sex, but no one could blame her for that I suppose. "This is Gabriela, she's staying with us for a month, she from Seville, in Spain". Gabriella, took a step forward and spoke, her lips parting like Velcro.

"Herro juys" she said warmly, endearingly.

"Hello, Hello" Bosco spluttered. I started drawing on my cigarette for comfort, one rapid draw after the other, and blinking, blinking like McGoo, draw, blink, draw, blink, draw, blink, draw and so on until the tip was as long as a hookers fingernail and hot as a poker.

"Are you guys going to the disco in the hall Friday week ?", says Nula.

"We are, we are" myself and Bosco affirmed.

"Great, see you there then," says Nula before letting us know they weren't stopping and walking off towards the supermarket to run errands for the family-run Hotel down the town.

"Wait !" I called with assertion half surprising myself. They both halted and turned.

"Are ye going to the County final, Friday week ... it's on before the disco, well ... the disco is in fact in aid of the final, well not in aid but you know what I mean ....". I was beginning to ramble before Nula benevolently intervened.

"Yes we'll be there" she said, her eyes rolling over the rim of her Indigo framed spectacles. Turning back into the doorway I looked at Bosco, unsure if there was a hint of suggestion in Nula's response but not wanting to ask him directly implicating myself so as to speak.

"See you there", Bosco repeated, codding but confirming my suspicions.

"Shit," I thought quickly flicking the fag butt to the floor before it burnt my unsuspecting fingers.

The next two weeks were like torture. We were training three nights a week and Johnny B ran us like wildebeest over the plains of the Serengeti. We were to face Shamrock Gaels in the final, the smallest Parish in the county but one with a civic pride that bordered on fascism. It was reported that there wasn't a telegraph pole on beach or boreen that didn't bear the emerald green and saffron of their beloved Gaelic team. Much to our amusement Johnny B ranted and raved - "down from the mountain, with their togs above in the arses held up with bailing twine" or something along those lines. It gave us respite from the sweat and the flies. At night my mind ran riot, flitting between me casually lobbing over the winning point and frolicking barefooted through the orange plantations of Seville with Gabriella. Since our first meeting, I had only managed to secure her interest for a few solitary moments. We shared a cigarette and passed it to and fro as I taught her how to blow rings and she picked the tumble dryer cotton fluff from my sweatshirt. Was there a real connection or was it just me ?. Other than that brief interlude and the odd effortless smile from distance I couldn't seem to get next nor near her. Every which way I turned I seemed to run into either Nula, who was wearing more and more eye liner by the day or Mossey who had now re-pointed his hairy torpedo in the direction of Gabriella. "They were definitely going to "*How's your mother*" before the summer was out, but that was no surprise and every time she was within an asses bawl he was like a dog in heat. All this was playing out much to the annoyance of Caroline Conway who herself was uncharacteristically dishevelled being demoted to second fiddle. The drama for me didn't end there though, in those two weeks referred to I did produce my first legitimate pubescent hair, a proper manifestation of manhood, black as the night, curly as a pigs tail. Unfortunately, the heave of testosterone seemed to have had a kinetic effect, manifesting in a blocked sebaceous gland to the left of centre of my nose or so the Biactol bottle informed me. With a howl of terror that caused the mother to come flying up the stairs I stood in front of the mirror eyeballing a motherfucker of a zit.

By the time the final arrived, I was as exasperated as a mother of twins. Sleepless nights, pie eyed with love sickness and of course the zit and the looming morbid nebulous of self pity it brought along with it. Mossey had broke out and was back on the fags which gave me some little consolation. On the big day, in a rare outing his father loaded us into the station wagon, myself, Bosco, Mannion and *the terror* Taylor, all rammed into the back. On route he wheezed us through the panoply of accolades sustaining his glory years at full back donned in the very same maroon and white. "There wasn't many in the county that could round me" he articulated in a slightly affected tone as we gassed along. "Not with a beer gut the like a that" came Manion's riposte, not wanting him to get too far ahead of himself, good and all as he was reported to have been. The auld lad didn't like that of course and although we had already arrived, sitting stagnant in the Volvo he refused to let us out until such a time as Mannion was well and truly versed on who, out of the two of them, in 1980, whetted his lips on the O'Hara cup and it full of whiskey and Brandy and all kinds of foreign tack. As a result, we were the last stragglers into the hub-ub of the dressing room. Johnny B, already a high colour broke away from a hushed conference with fatty Hannon to shoe us on. "Come on lads tog out" he roared in disbelief, provoking a general shuffle. Boots were unloaded from bags, clacking hard against the concrete floor. The acrid whiff of

STORIES OF A DIGITAL SPALPEEN

deep heat circulated as Johnny B intently scanned the room, now and then returning a meaningful utterance to Fatty who would in turn remove the pencil from the marshes of his mouth and scribble the given instruction in his tattered red notebook. Fatty for the occasion had on a suit jacket which was in itself a talking point. The back of it barely stretched across the breath of him but the arms so long his fingers just managed to reach daylight. Bosco concluded it had been specially made for the gorilla in Duffys circus, Manion's theory a little more convoluted, claiming it was an old blazer belonging to Rasputin having made its way into Fatty's possession through a complex series of events involving Fatty's murky past as a double agent in the Russian Revolution. Johnny B was getting fed up with the messing and called on us to "quieten down lads" that he couldn't think in a straight line. He was set to name the team. Jokes aside when he made shapes to do so the adrenalin poured through my veins in gushes as the room hushed to a purr. Johnny B all of a sudden stoic called the names from the little book of truth. "Goals, Danny boy Scanlon, full back line, Flynn in the middle, Bosco on the left and Irwin on the right". With each name called I became more and more nervous watching Fatty hunched uncomfortably over the onion bag with a builder`s crack firing the numbered jerseys to the name called out. I peeled the number nine off of my crown, the lovely scent of Lenor telling me Mrs Cullen had washed the Jerseys, the eight crash landed at Mossey's feet. Midfield partners again but much to Mossey's annoyance my name was called as Captain, the thought of which evaporated all remaining moisture from my mouth, all I could taste was bone.

Mossey was right about one thing, half the town showed up, most of them gathered en masse round the dressing room door, in rambunctious mood. Older boys for the sake of devilment hoisted younger ones to their shoulders to rattle the window. Each such rattle Interrupted Johnny B who was in full flow with heartfelt outpourings reflecting on subjects such as passion, sacrifice and *"making a name for yourself"*. On the cusp of his crescendo, about to call on the story of his addled grandfather's deathbed, the jolly face of a youngster appeared in the window like the vision of an angel, we erupted in laughter and Johnny B in turn lost the rag altogether. Without request Fatty nearly leapt through the door and ran the lot of them, scattering them like cats at a crossroads. It took Johnny B some time to work himself up to that state again and by the time he did, we weren't far behind him. There wasn't going to be a Shamrock bastard left on the pitch by the time we were finished with them. Only the tattered remains of garments and the odd dislodged tooth buried deep in the earth would persist for the Archaeologists putting it down to the site of a great battle. Fists flying the dressing room door was unlatched and flung open, we bundled out like animals escaped from the zoo, into the livid light of summer, through the slew of backslaps and onto the freshly shorn flag-lined pitch.

Warming up we booted balls in towards the goals as young lads scrambled in bunches to be the first to return it. All the while I scanned the sideline for sight of Gabriella, but not sight nor light of either herself or Nula. A roar from the dressing room signalled the emergence of the Gaels, flashes of brilliant emerald green in all their glory amid the pedestrian blur of frieze. We stood and watched as they made their way to the far end of the pitch, each man spotting his opposite number. There was no sign of baling twine or mountain goats not even the usual one or one or two lads with the jocks drooping below the shorts or opposite socks of random washed out hues, not today at least, not for the County final it was Sunday best. Due to the nerves I wasn't sure if I needed a piss or not but wasn't given the choice as we were signalled to join the parade. A kind of morbid march round the perimeter of the pitch, both teams aligned, plodding to the drone of dancing Larry's bagpipes, jangling hands, stretching necks, unsure where to focus our attention other than the patch of Larry's marble white legs visible between the tops of his stockings and the hem of his Clan Kilt. As the last dreary gasps of the national anthem dissipated from his beloved instrument the crowd erupted with roars of anticipation. The umpires, white coated intently took their positions at either post. The ref, another well fed individual was well known and liked throughout the county from Harry's pitch and putt on the coast road, people knew him as Harry even though they'd also known he wasn't the proprietor but all the same insisted on calling him Harry. Anyway, Harry not having officiated for a few weeks nearly choked on the whistle calling us in to toss for ends. Their captain had to run up from full back position. Watching him come was like watching Omar Sharif in Lawrence of Arabia, it felt like a week or a fortnight before he would materialise at all. Not knowing what to do with meself I looked coyly along the jagged line of supporters, my heart jumped, I spotted both Nula and Gabriella, propped up by their arms sitting legs stretched along the grassy verge. Gabriella looking truly delicious, tanned ankles radiating in her Daz white plimsolls her faded blue jeans turned up at the ends. She tilted slightly and raised her arm chest high and discretely made the motion of a wave with her clasped fingers. Trying to hold my smile I winked in reply, not knowing if it had reached her or not. Their captain grew ever larger the closer he got, the thuds from his boots on the sun baked turf growing more pronounced, the controlled snorting through his flared nostrils used in transporting his impressive bulk. The coin was flicked, our three heads coming together, peering down at the result. "Tails" announced Harry straining to get down in order to repatriate the coin to his side pocket. "Stay as ye are so lads" he says and just as he had arrived Horsebox turned and was away, his every movement enough to set off his supporters with roars of encouragement. With one last definite look, Harry raised his right arm and gave a shrill blow to the whistle signalling the immanent battle. I flashed a look at Mossey as the weatherworn leather O'Neills was lifted high into the still air of evening as we grappled for a territorial foothold on the hard turf. For a solitary moment on that summer evening, everything stood still as night silently approached day, boyhood slipped passed manhood, bodies coiled, waiting for the optimum drop on the ball as it hung suspended on the farthest outreaching branch of the tallest tree in the orangery. My body's every sinew ached to hold its perfect smooth flesh steadfast in my unwavering hands, to thumb the dimpled flesh, to taste the sweetness of the sun-ripened fruit in my desperately dry mouth.

Marmalade II

Imagine O'Haras bread van coming round the hairpin at Clark's corner and SuperValue about to open, that was the measure of force he landed into me with, the Horsebox. Levelled on the flat of my back, in the odalisque, with the wobbly look of an Egon Schiel muse, a sickening dull pain in the pit of my stomach. "Don't get sick, don't get sick", I babbled like a pardoned pagan finding it hard to concentrate on anything other than in-out breathing, my free arm left limp across my belly, "not in front of half the county, the family, extended family, councillor Perry and most of all my beloved Gabriella". I spoke strictly to myself while watching through a grimace the Horsebox waif in the distance, gone as far as the forty five, flanked on either side by their two midfielders Curly and Carrot, each labelled according to the ebony and russet heaps of hair. Horsebox laid it off to the latter and with two quick solos taking him ten yards further Carrot rolled the ball off of the palm of his glove dropping it to the toe of his boot and rotating it soundless over the bar.

Mossy shadowed over me and hissed – "Get your finger out,". It was all very serious now, five points down fifteen minutes into the second half. He was panting like a camel with a covering of salty sweat reflecting the golden sunlight off of his fearsome face. His hair was wet and dark and flat and stringy on his forehead, his crown a solitary dry clump. He didn't wait around for my excuses. Truth is I didn't have any to give and more-so didn't blame his frustrations, for too long in this game I had been a pedestrian, my opposite number, Carrot had the better of me. At half time Johnny B had taken me aside, grabbed my arm and insisted I "make a name for myself", his big bulging liver yellow eyes crawling over me. Taking his advice, at the throw in I landed a sharp elbow on the Carrot but to my dismay, it didn't knock a stir out of him, instead backfired with a flying fist of bone and buck ignorance that rattled me good-o.

"Fuck off Moss". I collapsed on the broad of my back beholding the serenity of the blue sky, the freshly shorn grass prickly against the back of my head, fingering the stump that remain of the near conquered spot (toying with it had become a habit). Summer swallows chirped, swerving sharp lines in search of crispy exoskeletons. In and out from under the eves they darted, oblivious to my cataclysmic predicament.

"Will ya get up ta fuck up". Johnny B's unmistakable screech tore through the cheering and jeering popping my reverie. "Here tog out" I heard him say then, "Was he subbing me ?", "the final blow of indignation, the walk of shame, in front of my betrothed and Councillor Perry". I limped to my feet, for a moment considered capitulating altogether (fake an injury). Sure enough, Johnny B had a hold of Sean Mc Donaghas's arm, spilling instruction into his ear, Gallagher was making his way to the line, his head hung, unfastening the Velcro on his gloves. "Thanks fuck," I said to myself.

That moment of redemption brought me hope and It was at that point I decided I was going to squeeze it all, every last drop of salty sweat from the core of my body and bone.

I was going to run like Forrest, contest every lost ball, attend every dog fight and run and run and by Jesus did I run.

Point. Vincent managed to get his claws on a scuttery ball I had driven into him, turned with his rotund arse and whipped it over the bar. I was liking my newfound engine, covering the hard yards. Back into the middle to meet the kick out, Mossy got an arm to it and managed to ping it from the rumpus, who was there to meet it ?, yours truly, solo, solo, solo, bounce, solo bounce, solo with Carrot and Curly both hanging on to me as if I were the last bus out of sing sing, solo, solo and I was within range, no time to steady the ship before shooting, on the inside of the boot an in-swinger, slowly curling, curling in, and in further and over. I turned and caught a glimpse of Gabriella, she was on her feet with Nuala and Caroline Conway, Gabriella holding Brendan the bear, our mascot, dressed in the round towers Jersey with white shorts, his torso covered her face as she struggled to hoist him, her T-Shirt rising to reveal her petite navel, perfectly positioned in the centre of her caramel tummy. Nuala and Caroline each held a flaying arm as they jumped for joy.

We knocked over another two. I managed to play my part (thank God). One of them a block down that had the crowd going mad altogether (if there`s one thing they love more than a score it's a block down). I caught the cornerback off guard and had him running backwards like a rabbit into the headlight, till trapped and in desperate angst he drew a scrappy leg on it. The deflection off my hand fed Bosco who secured it and popped it over the bar, no fuss. We were back to two between us, the Gales not registering a single score in fifteen minutes. It got better. Clawing back the deficit to level the game (Mossy and Meehan with one apiece) then another from the in-dominatable Vincent took us into the lead for the first time in the proceedings. The intensity on the pitch was mirrored on the line with Johnny B finding it difficult to remain within the confines of the dug-out and wandered half way out onto the pitch, gabbing instructions like a wireless, Fatty not far behind scribbling each and every detail in the red notebook with the literary ambition of a match report for Thursday's edition of the Champion. Not to be outdone however his opposite number, who, although not a big man was a fearsome enough candidate with tufts of hair sprouting from all cups and saucers of his swarthy face, an aquiline nose, a Cobalt suit paired with pea green Dunlop's completing the look. It started with a brief exchange of handbags.

"Quieten down,"

"Quieten down yourself,"

culminating in an interlocking of elbows. The crowd weren't sure which of the two contests to focus on and with the force of a high tide swept out in pursuit. It wasn't till a ball cleared the lot of them Harry blew up in a frenzied attempt to regain control, admonishing each of the guilty parties, running the line length moving every stubborn toe and boot behind it, including Gabriella, Nuala Teddy and all. It couldn't have gotten any more tense than this, then it did.

Hop Ball to restart, Curly managed to poach it from Mossy. He hoofed a hail Mary. Falling short of the posts Scanlon stepped out to meet it, reaching skywards with open arms ready to cradle it comfortably. It dropped and dropped and dropped, we watched, it was in his arms, we were at the point of turning when suddenly, silently, unbelievably, it wasn't, slipping through the gate of embrace to the ground. You couldn't even say it rolled, more so and dribbled over the line. The wateriest goal you will ever see up and down the length of the country. Scanlon dropped to his knees like a dog of shame, wailing and bawling. "What's he saying ?" Bosco enquired, sliding in beside me with his hands slipped down the waistband of his togs like a toaster (a bit too laid back for my liking).

"How in the hell should I know ?" I answered, taking off to find Harry.

"How long ref ?"

Harry's stoic gaze returned a total of "Three mins," to all within ear-shot.

"Come on lads we're not dead yet,". Scanlon had managed to stumble to his feet and toe a mount, carefully finger-tipping the ball to its summit. A spikey glance at Mossy, his shimmering dark eyes flickering the fire from his belly below, both his fists clenched, white tight. The ball was in the air now, the thump from Scanlon's meaty boot still echoing when Mossy coveted it in the air and landed safely. The crowd afraid to breathe for the kick out now bubbled like blood, the roar following Moss like a burning bush as he strode the length of the pitch. He was just outside the big square. I wasn't far behind him, continuing to track his line until the goals were within range then halting, as we all did, me the world and his mother, he struck it, hard and true, "AAAGHHH," the emission of angst and anger and exhaustion as he willed it on. It flew past the keeper as all heads witnessed, hard and true, nothing could stop it, except for the crossbar, smack it wobbled, surely to the point of snapping, the ball shooting north like an arrow. A switch flicked in me, a light lit, a deep bemoaning voice in the depths of my innards cried out "Up she flew," and off I went through a bushel of bodies left standing spellbound. It gave me a yard or two, having a clear run until the horsebox (just my luck) materialised in the pinch of my eye, he jerked and snorted into motion. Seconds later we were converging at full tilt, that familiar snort drawing nearer. I cocked my shoulder and hoped for the best. We met square on. A burst of his buttery breath blasted my cheek, I shuddered then wobbled about to crumple but somehow through luck or the gentle intervention from God alone I managed to find footing. I didn't have much time to consider however as he was coming again with the ball almost hanging within reach. Wham, the collision poked every organ in my body, his sweat sopping head whiplashing against mine then falling off. I could hear the clip of his boot as he crumbled. The sheer joy to see him collapse to his knees pitching an arm to prop up. "Give her woskey," Johnny B roared out and as he did I rose up like Nijinsky (either of the two) my fist pure steel. It was now or never. And what happened ?, I missed it, fluffed it, duffed it, made muck of it. The crowd gasped barely able to watch as the clip I did manage to get on it sent it spinning. Landing on my feet I was in despair, the horror show in my head, the eighteen year famine, the what ifs, the gloom of the dressing room. In all honesty, I felt it more than I had actually seen it, the ball, ricocheted off my left shoulder wrong footing the keeper completely as it crashed against the back of the net. The umpire instantly snapped the green flag. I dropped to my knees, no one more surprised than me, gagging with tears, gasping for breath, grunting, just grunting. The crowd streamed onto the pitch bearing bears and bunting, flags flew and arms were outreaching, freewheeling with unbridled joy. The lame threw down their crutches and walked again, the clouds parted and a double rainbow of the brightest hues stretched across the bluest sky, that's how I remembered it at least.

We could have listened to it all night, the story of the Glorious Goal. "You could hear a mouse fart", Fatty commenced again referring to the moment the crossbar was rattled to within an inch of its life. Now, post-match Fatty was talking to us like men, fags were flicked in full view, pints paraded about without the fear of a scolding or the threat of laps. We were in the front Bar of the hotel Johnny B mellow as milk, hoarse and half cut nodding his head with great modesty at each passing pat bestowed upon him. "You'd want to get a burger into ya" Fatty advised to keep him steady on the pins. I'd had three pints of pleasurable porter myself, and could feel it on me, the chest puffed out as maybe it should have been after scoring the winning goal but at the same time, there was a nagging niggle. Try as I might but not able to prevent myself from glancing at the door wondering where Gabriella might be and why she hadn't joined the celebration just yet. Surely still in front of the mirror upstairs in Nula's room, stepping in and out of outfits, unable to decide on the perfect combination on a night where it mattered oh so much.

STORIES OF A DIGITAL SPALPEEN

Back to the burgers, we were called into the celebration meal, oh the beautiful Burgers, buns like pillows, soft white fluffy Irish flour, the meat firm in the hand friable in the mouth. The chips, heaped high as the tower of babel on the plate, each a golden yellow baton of crunch. Just what the weary body needed and all arranged thoughtfully on tables with criss-crossing covers of red and white, each glass stuffed with either a red or a white napkin. The whole affair was a credit to Mrs MacGowan and the hotel whom Johnny B thanked and thanked a thousand times. It's no wonder we broke out into song, "ere we go, ere we go, ere we go". Mossy rose, he hammered the butt of the knife into the table top and roared he was going to shift Gabriella below in the Loftus Hall tonight. At hearing this the bite of the burger nearly lodged way back in the umbra of my throat. I wasn't done for the day yet, maybe a bigger battle awaited.

The front bar had filled to elbow room only with visibility blinkered due to the bodies beneath the blanket of weaving blue smoke. The amber side lamps were illuminating to bolster the squares of fading summer light filling in from the windows. I glimpsed her through a parting of the crowd, the gap quickly closing again. She along with Nuala and Caroline Conway were occupying the nook at the bend of the bar, a gaggle of giggles munching on Tayto. It seemed they had not ventured home, not to doll-up at least as she was wearing a borrowed fleece of some sort, man-size by the look of it, much too big on her, but like the proverbial black bin bag no garment could purloin her beauty, not a tom-boy fleece nor the chipped bubblegum nail varnish or the smell of cheese and onion.

D. M. O'DOWD

She stood to greet me, all doey-eyed and cupped my ears wither her hands. Oh how well I had played (well, really), she expressed with ebullient joy, how she didn't really understand the rules (oh let me teach you), how everything was so new and exciting for her. I wished it would never end, at least continue till Christmas leaving my hand on the warm arc of her back, like a tiller together navigating the undulations of the high seas. Without warning Nula whipped an arm around my naked neck and landed a kiss on the fat of my cheek, hooting in my ear – "Go on ya good thing ya,". A little more reserved Caroline Conway rose also congratulating me, said "I played great", smiling across the table and reached out to shake my hand. Rather awkwardly she was left in limbo as I was jerked North – "Mrs Cahan Cough Mixture is here" Mossy says, let's go.

Mrs Cahan Cough Mixture was code for Linden village mixed with Whiskey, Vodka, Rum, Gin, a dash of coke a squirt of Sherry. Dishwater stirred with a dog's dick. You get the idea. Bosco removed it from the bag as if it were a museum piece, Mossy spun the cap, gave it a nod of reverence and sprung it in my direction. I needed all the Jungle juice I could. The gable of the hotel, next to the car park provided the setting.

"Where do you go ?" Gabriella asked solicitously as we were leaving.

"I'll be back" I assured her with dolorous eyes, delighted with her interest.

The trick was to flick a switch, block off the brain, refrain from breathing and swallow like a machine. Letting the suction pop as it departed the upper lip.

STORIES OF A DIGITAL SPALPEEN

"What's it like ?"

"A bit like cherry coke".

There was an after taste, made worse by the fag which made the stomach nausea slightly better. At first, we stood around chatting, smoking much as we had done in the pub, Mossy was still going to try Gabriella as his number one, Caroline Conway his number two, he also had a number three but refused to divulge. By the second iteration of the nefarious concoction, we groaned. Mossy had me on the stand "Who was I going to try for the shift?".

"No, one," I insisted, Gabrielly remaining tenuously tethered in the stormy secret harbour of my heart. By iteration four with only the bilge in the bottle, Bosco had his arm along the gable holding back a burp that had threatened to liquidise into vomit. Vincent on leaving the hotel, heading for the hall came around wondering what we were up to. He insisted he wouldn't touch the top shelf not to mention the shite that remained in the bottle. "Where are the girls ?" I slurred, my eyebrows rising.

"Gone down ahead" was the answer "long time ago now".

My legs were spongy, trying not to look drunk, a gurgling nausea in my stomach. I was going all "Pat the Brush", one step forward and two steps back (it could take Pat a solid hour to make it from one end of the bar to the other in Mannion's). By the look of Bosco and Mossy, they weren't much better, the three of us moving apart then coming together in the shape of a Mongolian folk dance. Laughing at our fingers. Vincent's patience drained, he walked on. Despite the state of inebriation my confidence remained a Swiss cheese of admonishing self-doubt and at the door of the hall accepting a slug of a can proffered by Meehan resulted in him tearing it back off of me with a golden glug of it landing on my shirt. I grunted, wiped my mouth and made off, an echo from Mossy followed – "Hey", he called, thinking I had the run on him with the women.

I took a moment to compose myself, Whitney Houston came muffled through the double doors. Concord was deploying the new smoke machine to good effect, a winding hiss immediately obscuring my view as I entered. Gyrating bodies everywhere. Diamonds of lime and lilac and peach tick-toking round the disco screens lined along the stage. I clawed my way a few feet into the sinister shadows playing out the slow set questioning how I would make it as far as the harem normally positioned on the top of the right by the stage door. Surely she would be there waiting for me, patiently plucking the petals off a daisy (gathered pitch-side and stored in her pocket as a souvenir). I stumbled forward, made out Vincent and Nuala, slowly circling, her head cradled on his shoulder. His self-same arms which had so competently grasped the O'Neills were slowly clawing towards her arse. A second shocking volley of smoke nearly choked me. I couldn't budge another step afraid I might get sick, one hand slapped across my mouth the other extended as a balancing pole. "Last set of the night" the honeyed tones of DJ Concorde announced the lights up and we were all waiting on a prayer. How the hell were we so late in arriving. I must find her, Gorgeous Gale seeks Gabriella. I was not about to give up, not after getting this far, bathing the bastard of a spot for a week or more under the instruction of my older sister, TCP and lukewarm water in equal parts administered carefully by cotton from egg-cup. Not after my single hand heroics on the football field, quashing the hoodoo of county titles. This was it now or never, I plaintively peeled the hand from my mouth, in hindsight a bad thing, paying more attention to the gut than the foot and as a result with the next stride the left knee folded like a hinge and the body followed in a heap. The remainder of the night follows a staccato of polaroids, a brief conversation with Mick Mc Cann from the handball club who was bouncer for the night bundling me to a bench asking "if I was alright and had I been drinking ?". A squirt of projectile vomit found its way through a gap in my fingers, Mick jumped back sharpish checking if I had got him and I ran for the jacks. The whole world spinning. The piss from the floor slowly seeped into the knees of my jeans. The Carrots, oh the ubiquitous carrots.

Carrot orange turned to crimson shame and gun metal gloom. I hadn't left the house all week. I nearly fell through the curtains when I seen her coming to the door. She called to say goodbye, standing with a sloping shoulder, the Sienna skin of her neck glowing against the dew still lingering on the lawn. I motioned her to the good room, struggling to look blasé. As it turned out the owner of the fleece was Colm Conway, the older (much older) brother of Caroline Conway.

"I just want to thank you for being such a nice guy," she said in her ever effortless way.

"Not as nice as Colm Conway I suppose ?" had departed my gob before I could call it back.

"Yes he is a nice guy too" she answered sheepishly. "I am leaving for the airporto soon" she stated and I melted with grief, simmered in sorrow, died in part.

"The best of luck," I said. What could I do if she couldn't love me? I could only put it down to the alpine spot and the lack of body hair. The squeaky hinge on the good room door alerted the mother of her departure and with the speed of an apparition was on hand to let her out. Gabriella paused for a moment staring through me with an intensity I had not witnessed before in the plunge pools of her eyes.

"in Seville" she pondered "we say, the bitter orange makes the sweet marmalade". She twisted her lips to the left, a gentle ripple on her forehead awaiting a reaction of some sort but I was still snagged on the bitter barb of Colm Conway. She shifted legs, "Caroline was wonder where you went the other night at the disco" She expanded further raising her eyebrows a tilt, turned and was gone up the town to Nula's, myself and the mother tracing her sensuous strides, a half arm raised in a half goodbye. Suddenly visions of Caroline filled me, her standing in the hotel to greet me, the joy on her face as I was shouldered to the terrace and presented with the Nestor Cup, the gleam of her smile as I hoisted it into blue and lilac sky. Her solicitous arm comforted me as I lay a broken on the bench in the hall, Mick Mc Cann at a loss to explain my condition as Concorde packed up, the blinding bulbs revealing my sorrowful state, her gentle assurance to Mick that she would see me home when I cam out of the toilets. I closed the door on Gabriella, light as a lark, greeting the gaze of the mother.

"Would that be one of the Flynn's out the Gurteen road ?" she queried.

"Mammy," I said, looking at her with an intent that gave her a start,.

"Yes" she replied,

"Mammy," I said again my big red heart all a flutter.

"What is it ?" she sounded concerned,

"Mammy,"

"Yes Mammy here,"

"Mammy,"

"Are you raving or something?"

"Marmalade Mammy,"

"Marmalade ?" she wondered.

"Yes Mammy, sweet sweet, oh sweet Irish Marmalade,".

Peig Sasta

It was leaving cert year. "Out with your Peig," said Miss Evans, her voluminous buttocks familiarising itself once more with the edge of the desk. We must have been on page forty-seven for what felt like a decade or more. *Peig* was settling a dispute between neighbours on the ownership of a young clocking hen. To listen to this day in day out was a torture worse than the Saturday night bath. Lending in no small part to the torment we put Miss Evans through. A few sentences in Mossy instigated the craic.

"Arse !" he modulated low, out the hole of his mouth.

"Who was that ?" she demanded looking up.

"Mossy Callahan ?".

"No, not me miss" he protested like a wounded animal. That was the prompt for Durcan to unleash. He had a new addition to his arsenal.

"Mutton Dagger" he educated us was a euphemism for *blow job*. And so it received its first air play "Mutton Dagger".

"What was that, Mutton what ?" she asked standing up a little dishevelled. Nobody offered an explanation. Miss Evans sat down again and resumed with a notably feeble voice.

"Mutton Dagger".

"TOMMY DURCAN" she wailed, recklessly lashing down the book on the desk.

"Not me miss" he stood up instantly raising his hands in outrageous protest. She fell silent already a withering mass of defeat, lifted the book as if it were Big Ben and continued on.

"Cock", she looked up with a grimaced but ignored the expletive and furrowed on.

"Balls" was followed by "hairy balls" followed again by "big hairy balls".

She closed the book without having managed a paragraph and sat in a silent slump, a wet tear sliding down the side of her face which set off a Jubilant cheer of victory. She ran from the room.

"Mutton Dagger" Durcan roared at her trailing stiletto.

"Don't think ye are doing this for me" she carefully intoned. It was now the following day, Miss Evans presented a more composed figure. She wasn't unattractive for a middle aged un-attached Irish teacher. In recent weeks she was notably dolled up on a Friday setting alight the rumour mill that she was dating an old bachelor from Roscommon. "It's YOUR Leaving Cert in two weeks time not mine" she clarified, giving ample time to allow it sink into our thick skulls. In the moment of silent reflection, a paper plane projected from the back of the class glided gracefully through the air. Enola gay penned on the side, it came to a sudden stutter halted and nose-dived square onto her left breast. The class erupted with euphoria. "Mutton Dagger" Durcan roared and we were off again.

The unofficial class committee largely composed of future ICA members confronted the trouble makers, encircling Durcan in particular. "Just because you don't care if you pass or fail David Durcan", Patricia Walsh directed the accusation.

"Just because you don't care if you pass or fail David Durcan" he echoed in a voice he imagined Peig might have.

"You'd better stop all this messin" she threatened.

"You'd better stop all this messin'" he was now had a hump on his back.

"Ya big Child" she concludes and turns away from him.

"Well Mossey ?" Patricia says "What about you ?", all Mossy did was return a dry smile.

Cara Hamilton, one of God's most beautiful creatures west of the Shannon glided up like a swan. "Tell him Cara ?", Patricia requested. Cara was about to endorse the sentiment in her laid back effortless way but before she could utter a word in comes Lancelot (without the horse).

"Ya Durcan" Mossy blurts "Don't be such an ejit and treat Patricia with some respect" he demanded, looking to Cara while speaking. Durcan straightened up confused and started to pick at a boil on his neck. Cara smiled, her ice blue eyes twinkled as she twizzled her straw hair and paddled off again.

"And you as well" Patricia directed at me "I thought better of you" she punctuated and turned on her heels. I was about to retort stating that I was a lover of the *Coupla Focal* and had an Aran jumper in the wardrobe at home, not to mention desperately worried if rise to a D in this subject or the inhumane treatment of a decent woman Mrs Evans who's people never missed a funeral.

Instead, my attention was caught by the corner of a folded paper envelope jutting from my bag. I waited till the group dispersed before reaching for it. It emitted a great whiff of flowery perfume with the letters S.W.A.L.K written across it in swirls. Could this possibly be a Love Letter ?, had the Lynx Ice finally worked? Ensuring there were no prying eyes I carefully set about opening it :

Hello Sexy

It started. This most certainly was a love letter. I continued to read.

You know me and I dream about you.

Can you guess ?, I'll give you a clue :

My hair is blond and my eyes are blue.

P.S I'm in your class

P.S.S Are you going to the disco in Balla Thursday week ??????.

P.S.S Write me back – put the note in the fuse box in the hallway.

P.S.S.S Love Love Love your new fingerless gloves

Love

Bubbles

Hello Sexy if you wouldn't smile. *Bubbles* I wracked my mind for a reference to *Bubbles* but came up short. Thursday week, the disco, I violently swung from dream to reality, Thursday was the day before the Irish exam. "Oh no". I had promised myself faithfully I would give it a decent go. The mother's voice sang in my head "You'd better knuckle down now" her finger wagging a warning. *Hello Sexy* if you wouldn't smile. There was no doubt I had to go, despite the self restraint and me telling the lads twenty times or more "*nich, nein, no way*". Destiny wasn't in the picture at that time, however. What man could stand in the way of destiny ?.

I had the pen in such a grip that my fingers nearly went blue but finally at the expense of all other revision homework managed to eek out a reply :

Hello Bubbles

What a surprise, I feel alive

Your eyes are blue, mine are two.

P.S Who are you ?

Love

Fraggle

The *nome de plume* proved the most challenging aspect, I had no bearing or relation to a fraggle except that they looked cute from the Sunday afternoon show on ITV and from a limited pool of knowledge I was aware girls lined them on their sweet smelling plump pillows to cuddle for surrogate warmth and affection. The response was placed in the requested location, ferried on a falsified request for the toilet.

Miss Evans relished the silence of the classroom as the story of Peig unfolded from one disaster to another, floods, famines, repeats on the television. The threats of the young ICA women had effect and Durcan spent most of his time lolling his head on the desk picking or picking at the boil. I was happy with the fact that I was beginning to get a handle on Irregular verbs in between the flights of fantasy involving myself and bubbles supping *tinkers champagne* under starlight. Miss Evans even remarked after class one evening on my continued improvement. This spurred me on of course, "flattery will get u everywhere Miss Evans" I agreed. It being Friday she was donned in the glad rags ready for a night of *how's your mothe*r with the reputedly wealthy farmer. On the topic of reputed romance, the question of the identity of who the mystery girl bubbles might be, I had whittled down to three, largely on the basis of the blond hair and blue eyes but also on recent past experience:

Cara Hamilton : Best case scenario. And did she give me a look the other day when Patricia confronted the upstarts ?.

Double D Marie : Due to the sizeable cleavage. Not a bad booby prize (pun intended). Not something I would consider long term but without disclosing to Mossy or Bosco there was little doubt in my mind she could make a man of me.

Ramona Nora Finn : More mousy than blond. Her brother Luigi had approached me in his family's chipper saying his sister was doing his head in talking about me and would I him a favour and shift her. Christ sake I was only in for a chicken burger.

The letter was gone, a Memo and a note returned in its place :

Hello Fraggle (so cute)

Sign my memo (be honest).

P.S You haven't said if you are going to Balla Thu night ?

Yours Always

Bubbles

The memo was covered with a Tim Wheeler (Ash) centrefold from Just 17. It took me most of the night but I replied to the questions as follows :

Name : Fraggle

Age : 17

Star Sign : Virgo

Favourite Colour : Blue

D. M. O'DOWD

Favourite Teacher : Miss Evans
Favourite Subject : Irish
Favourite Food : Chicken Burger
Favourite Band : Thin Lizzy / Ash / Stiff Little Fingers – too many to mention
Favourite TV show : Home and Away
Dream Girl : Bubbles (a distant second Samantha Fox)
After school what you want to be : Rock Star
Secret Desire : To meet bubbles in the grave yard behind the hall in Balla on Thursday night.

I reviewed the answers running my hand across the page. I had thrown down the gauntlet fixing a potential meeting in the graveyard where the groups of teenagers would meet to drink flagons of Linden village before the slow sets began. It was, I felt, cleverly suggested as my "new" secret desire, replacing the former, a naked jaunt roller skating the Florida boardwalk with Samantha Fox. The memo was returned carefully to the fusebox.

On the Wednesday the Leaving cert papers arrived. Two abrasive delivery men dropped the secured boxes to the floor of the assembly hall with irreverence. The innards withholding the hopes and aspirations of a generation. On the same day, two further significant events concluded. The first, we turned the final page of *Peig*, the proud unshakeable old woman stood on the stoop of her Blasket island cottage reflecting on life, the trials and sorrows, the hard-won short lived pleasures. Her journey on the remote outcrop was coming to an end and she was preparing for the *Long Road* with great acceptance of mortality at peace equally with the world and nether world beyond. The second event, a response was received, the date was confirmed, the tallest Celtic cross along the back wall. I knew that cross exactly, it rose higher than the rest, the thrushes loved to perch on it, searching the wall for snails. In response to the question I had directly posed, *Who are You ?,* she replied, *Who am I ?, only the girl of your dreams.* I pulled the letter close to my chest and shuddered with a heady mixture of lust and excitement.

On the run in Miss Evans grew in stature from day to day, she was firing out the revision lists, the pitfalls and quick wins, timings for questions and other pearls of wisdom gleaned from her years of experience. On the Thursday, our last class ever, she thanked us all, said we had been a great bunch of students (Aw now …), to remember to always do our best and whatever happened she was proud of us. On a final note she said not to overdo *it* at the disco as she knew there was temptation to let off steam but please don't throw away all your hard work for the sake of a few hours fun. The ICA women lined up misty-eyed, throwing wet kisses at her. When the bell went I hurried home to throw on the AC/DC T-Shirt and run a clump of wet look gel through the hair.

Disco nights were a cash cow for Christina, the only place in town where we might be able to gulp pints without question as we were the only ones would gulp her questionable pints. Mossy might get a drink in other spots, he had a moustache in the making and a tactic when ordering.

"Say it fast and never with a please or a thank you". The point being, if you are in a hurry and have no manners you expect to be served, just walk up.

"Two Guinness". I tried it in *Shoot the Crows* and was told to come back in 1995.

Christina bestowed a great welcome for us, "hello lads" she says laying a few beer mats on the counter, "What can I get ye ?". Aside from us along the counter, the only other person was the mournful Cry Baby Shannon, her one and only regular. A rash of randy teenagers invading his nook was not complimentary to his nervous disposition.

After a settler or two Mossy says "Watch this", "Shannon" he calls to him "Your mother was a Tattie Hawker in Texas."

"Ha ?", Shannon replied not being great of hearing.

"Your mother was a Tattie Hawker in Texas", he spoke louder.

Shannon said she "was not, no Tattie Hawker in Texas or anywhere else."

"And you father a pint swiper in Zanadus !" Mossy spoke louder again.

"A Wha ?" Shannon roared back.

"A Shirt Lifter" Mossy roared.

"Fuck off would ya" the Cry baby called back, "me poor auld mother, she worked hard" he said to himself and the tears began to roll down the old man's face from drink and memories and the confusion of being overrun. With the budding ICA women well out of sight a grin of malevolent delight swept across t Mossy's face.

"Your some cunt" Bosco says.

STORIES OF A DIGITAL SPALPEEN

"The Bus is outside" Meehan stuck his head in the door to let us know so we drank up before ordering another and skulled it. In fairness, Mossy bought a half one for the Cry Baby and sent Christina up to him with it. With the few quid I had left, aside for the money for the bus and the hall I bought a flagon of cider with the plan to share it with Bubbles. I had taken my parka jacket in anticipation of a long night under the stars, just Bubs and me. Meehan stuck his head in again. "The bus is leaving, now...." so myself, Mossy and Bosco finished off the dregs and left the Cry Baby with the last two cure heads who were sitting in the corner, too cool to be seen on a bingo bus.

Ramona Nora was the only one of the here shortlisted candidates I could make out in the dim light. It wasn't unexpected, Double D was walking distance to the hall from home and I had heard talk in the pub Cara would travel in her brother's Volkswagen Golf GT with alloy rims or as Bosco called it, a gleaming gold fanny magnet. The atmosphere was buoyant on the bus. It hobbled along to the usual banter of bands and boys and who fancied who. "Are ya not talking to me ?" Orla Scanlon interrupted my reverie. She pushed in beside me, fixed her loose cotton blouse and dabbed a drizzle of perfume on each on each of her wrists then to her neck. It filled the air.

"What's that ?" I asked an effete referral to the odour.

"Opium" she answered showing me the bottle, inviting me into the shade of her neck for a sniff. "My sister brought it back from London" but more to the point she wanted my opinion on a serious matter, she was intent on doing nursing in England but was worried about her relationship with Cormac not going the distance.

"Well, I said, if he really loves you he will understand".

She was satisfied with that reply. We smoked a fag together when we arrived and discussed the lighter topic of Blur v Oasis. "They're both crap" I stated. On the face of it I was the epitome of cool, my parka hanging hangdog off my shoulders, a rip in the left knee of my jeans but in the still summer night, my stomach was twisting into the shape of a pretzel with nerves.

"Want to head in ?" Orla enquired taking two quick puffs and dropping the butt to the tarmac.

"You go on ahead," I said "I need to meet up with the lads".

"Ok so" she responded rubbing lipstick on with her finger, looking into a petit makeup mirror. "How do I look ?" she enquired, her face askance.

"Mighty" I assured her staring at the gate to the graveyard over her shoulder.

I lifted the latch beseeching it not to squeak too loudly as if some class of clandestine operation were commencing. The two cure heads we had left behind in Christina's were on my right, talking in low voices passing back and forth a bottle of wine. "Lads" I nodded and marched on holding the Linden village by its ruff. Halfway down I stopped dead. I could make out the outline of a figure in the shadow of the cross. *My Bubbles*. I swallowed a gulp of air and walked on, my DM's crunching the chipped stones on the path, my fingers tingled. I had come this far and didn't care who she was or what she looked like, I had fallen for her, my love uncompromising. I watched her ghostly movements and an instinct inside of me rose up, I needed to get to her, to protect her from the dangerous night. I cut across the verges of the ancient graves through patches of untamed grass, stumbling to where she waited. Just a few more meters and we would be conjoined as one. She turned and came towards me cloaked in a scarf. "Bubbles" I hesitated as she took a step "Bubbles" I called again with a croak of nerves, my heart rattling in my chest. She raised her hands unleashing herself from the scarf, "Fragglleeeeeee" she cried in a voice less poetic than the one I had imagined from her writings. Her face and body now free from bondage she fled towards me with the enthusiasm of a Labrador while a second body appeared at a height on the wall behind her. "Fragglleeeeeee" they called in unison in a derisory tone, my face meeting the impact of her stale smokey bussom taking me to the ground with a thud of passion. "Mossey you bollox" I groaned in pain.

"I knew all along" I protested, "you did in your shite" Mossey says.

"You should have seen your face" Bosco still in a fit of the giggles.

"Come on," Mossy says "I just seen Hamilton pull up, I have more important things to tend to, if you know what I mean" he says raising his eyebrows.

"Go ahead" I said "I need a piss". It gave me a moment to consider the I had been. It wouldn't be long before the story was out. The burble of Bosco and Mossey dying Amadan out as they moved on, the brilliant stars looking down on me with earthly pity as I besmirched the wall. The Flagon I thought, I must have dropped it with all the excitement and went to rummage it out. It was a consolation of sorts in the whole dirty ruse. I Fizzed it open sitting with the Celtic cross towering over me my legs prostrate along the body of the occupant below. I zipped my parka to the neck and slugged back a deep pull and lit a fag squashing the empty box and tossing it on the grave next to me. The haze of coloured lights in the distant windows of the hall flicked Violet then Green and Amber then back again. The whole of the moon was playing, echoing tinny from the hall. I rocked my head against the Granite headrest mouthing the words "You saw the whole of the moon". I was still in love with Bubbles. I gurgled another sup of cider morose but at the same half enjoying myself.

I awoke from the dream with shiver then a shock. My head was soupy, my eyes squinting to see the hand in front of me. I was still in the same position back flat against the cross, the top of my parka a wet mass of drool. I pawed the damp dewy grass around me trying to figure out my escape route, the high pitched squeaks of bats, car crashing overhead. Their outlines black against the big moon. The lights were off in the hall, the bus long gone. The Irish exam. Fuck. The Irish exam I thought unfolding myself. I was seven long miles from home. Fuck the Irish exam and I tucked my jeans into my socks and started running for what my life was worth, pounding like a paratrooper the dark roads in front of me. My breath heavy husks of anxiety working in unison with the jungle drum of my boots. A car passed, travelling in the opposite direction. I could hear the swoosh from two miles off, then the headlights in the distance growing stronger until it became a blaze of light and noise. It sent me into the hedge for protection, where I hunched until it had passed, the tail lights fading into the distance, the encapsulating silence of the star strewn universe slowly taking hold again. The thump, thump, thump of my boots resuming. I was still a long way from home.

The mother woke me with a jolt of the broom handle on the ceiling. "Wake up" she roared from below "Are ya alive or awake up there ?". I wasn't too sure. She fed me buttery toast with Jam and milky tea, blessed me with the holy water for the start of the exams and sent me on my way. The sun was threatening to make an appearance as it always did at exam time. The birds chirped gaily in the horse chestnuts on the lane leading to the sports hall where the exam would be held. In the limited time I had, my engine still running on the adrenalin and cider I powered through my revision notes in my head and then in the doorway of the hall. All thoughts of Bubbles or Mossy and the moon-lashed graveyard had been throttled. There was a great buzz of excitement. Miss Evans was floating around handing out final modicums of advice, the nervous faces around her absorbing willingly. I snaked by, taking my number and finding my desk. The basketball court had been transformed with neat rows of tables. The invigilator was already seated reading through a gossip magazine. Slowly the room filled as students dripped in, in ones and pairs, cramming furiously, smiling nervously. The invigilator checked her watch and asked for silence before taking the stack of folded pink and blue papers and walking slowly along the rows sliding them one by one under our noses. ARDTEISTIMEIREACHT toping the page in bold.

I folded it open, my eyes devoured the questions. I began to write furiously, fuelled by the frustrations of the night before, I lost all sense of time.

"Time up" the invigilator called, "finish what you are doing please" she continued. She stood over me as I completed my last sentence. For a long time after I sat at my desk as others filtered out. Each time the door opened I could hear the gurgle of excitement. The post-mortem had begun, comparing and reviewing answers. The ICA women declared one and all that they had failed for sure. Durcan was the first to leave, after the mandatory half hour of lolling his head on the desk, he grabbed his sweater off the back of the chair and made for the door. Most stayed till the end. Cara H, close to the end. I watched her walk past her cheeks berry red from endeavour. She left and streaked off in her brother's Golf. Mossy and Bosco were gone for Christina's after a hard day at the office, it was a Friday. I remained at my desk, taking Peig from my bag, reviewing the text against the answers recalled from memory.

Just myself and the invigilator remained when I made shapes to leave. She was collecting the papers strewn across the desks or dropped on the floor. I bid her farewell and she returned a friendly wave. Outside I took a moment to commend myself, breathe in the fresh air and watch the first swallows of summer swoop for flies. It was more or less a tradition to defile, destroy and bin old school books once exams were done but looking down at Peig in my hand I knew I hadn't the heart for that. The door opposite opened and Miss Evans emerged. "Oh there you are" she said "I had been hoping to see you". "Well how did you go ? " she asked, a bluster of wind catching her hair which she hooked back with a long finger.

"Not too bad" I responded and went through the questions in detail. She paid great attention.

"I'm really pleased," she said with a pursed smile.

I wasn't sure what to say but it was at this point that it dawned on me that being a Friday she wasn't made up for a date as she normally might be. Maybe her line with the old farmer had come to an end, I hoped not, the thought of Bubbles still a fresh cut.

"What would she have made of all this ?" I asked Miss Evans.

"Who ?" she enquired.

"Peig" I said holding up the book.

She chuckled. "I suppose she might have thought better here than sitting in a Curragh with a cold".

"I suppose so" I concurred.

"At the end of the day", Miss Evans continued "she was content with what God had granted her", "she was," I said "and she loved the old language". "If we followed those simple principles then I guess we would all be the happier for it".

"It's true for you Miss Evan" I agreed fixing my school bag on my back. The only thing left to say was "goodbye", but I hesitated and we stood for a moment on the stoop of the sports hall door, enjoying the echo of birdsong. In that moment, the football pitch had become a lush green pasture, the smoking tree a noble Oak and myself Miss Evans and Peig Sayers a trinity of martyrs with a common cause.

Sigmund's Men

Vincent had the makings of a politician, just about the size of Napoleon with a well-oiled jawbone. It was April and he had another of his brainfarts, calling for a committee meeting in the lounge in Tighes. Not entirely sure why he needed to call one because we would all most likely have been there anyway on this regular damp dissolute Saturday night, same as any other. He commanded our attention, positioned against the mullioned window, a dead arm flat along the lacquered counter, he wanted to talk to us about the business of hurling. We listened like a bony-arsed band of savages i.e. mostly in one ear and out the other. The gist of it went like this, in these modern times of fizzy water and stay-pressed denim there were only five hurling teams left in the county, even Iggy in the Duffle coat could extrapolate that reward in overcoming any one opponent meant a semi-final berth. From there on as Iggy might also explain in the course of a knock out championship anything could happen, save the thought of holding the cup itself aloft, high into the ebbing summer skies of late August.

In the beginning, there wasn't much of a response, "I'm telling ye lads, we'll look back on this in the years to come and recount it as a missed opportunity" Vincent affected his speech with a Belvedere accent to add kudos to the stew but all in all there was little in the way of signatures. It didn't help that the sing song theme tune of 'match of the day' sounded in the background and he lost half of the crowd to the big screen. I was on the fence, loving the idea of resurrecting the team but none too keen on exposing the Lilly white legs to the elements or indeed the scrutiny of public gaze after such a prolonged period under the cover of darkness. Some of the lads were looking nervous, there had been a lot of Smithwicks under the bridge since the Feile in Ogonnelloe, when, although losing three in a row were commended locally for fighting tooth and nail. Only two among us were dead certs, Nails Shanahan five foot six with the temper of a terrier and Kelly, six feet five (if counting the hair standing on his head) with a shorter fuse again, more like a snake charmer`s Cobra, both lit up at the prospect of off the ball incidents with a weapon in his grip.

Vincent wasn't feeling the love and the night was at risk of slipping into the obtuse panacea of porter until from behind the bar Harry appeared with a well-timed chug on his Hamlet and announced that he would sponsor the jerseys. The tide turned. Jo Jo said, "Indeed Ogonnelloe was a mighty time altogether, so it was, so was, so it was". Vincent was about to jump on this one when Harry again interrupted declaring that if we won the county, he would put up a free bar for the night, hands down, no codding. That let the animal out of the cage altogether, by the time the outstretched arm of the zoo keeper on the of the Guinness clock reached ten minutes to official closing not only had the aches and pains of old war wounds evaporated but the appetite for hurling was reaching fever pitch. Duggan who had hung up the boots when Gola was in fashion was now on his feet ready to tog out on the spot. Lang, a Yorkshireman never having held a hurl in his life split the arse of his Farah pants going down for an imaginary sliotar. Kelly let some class of a roar from out of him, something about DJ Carey sleeping soundly in his bed tonight, Vincent had the notebook out, busying himself gathering signatures until it reached the grand odd number of legs eleven, myself included.

In the lulling light, Vincent and The Horse went through the names in the copybook. A committee needed to be elected and sure who better than themselves as one two of chairman and vice chairman. It was agreed with a handshake in the shadows of the small hall. The hurling talk concluded with the last shouts on the street drifting skywards into the swirl of drizzle around the Halogen head of the street lamp. We had walked on ending up in Jo's bedsit for a hand of poker and Bruce Springsteen on the record player. Harry was left to close up, waiting only for the Hannon brothers to rouse from the vacant stares and finish up their sup of comfort.

They say Freud didn't know what to make of the Irish, at times it's clear we don't know what to make of ourselves. Who else would subject themselves to this? Six lonely pale figures distant shadows of the previous night serried along the gable wall as the rain came down in plip plops along the length of the everun overhead. I had spent the most part of the morning rooting aimlessly round the attic to locate the old hurls. Uncovering string plucked tennis rackets and the doodle adorned covers of old school books. TK + AC forever, Love and Rockets, The Buzzcocks – "What do I get ?", "Maggie is a bitch". I glossed over the ink art with the newfound nostalgia of a first year University Student returning from the contrast of the clipped lawns of Trinity

STORIES OF A DIGITAL SPALPEEN

College and the greasy walled bedsits of Rathmines. I would have spent the morning there in a slovenly slouch flicking through the scrawls of Hot Press had it not been for the mother shouting up that the Horsebox Candon is at the door for me. Back under the everuns, we waited for the rain to pass, the bright tips of cigarettes looked alive against the gunmetal sky, one after the other the buds of orange glow flicked into the loose chippings waiting for it to pass listening in silence to the rain overhead, plip plop. Someone put out a hand to see if it was passing but wasn't sure till enormous low mass diverged revealing a buttery evening sun. We made a burst for the pitch in celebration, a glistening candy green shimmering with delicate droplets.

For a hand full of weeks we persisted with what might be best described as a half arsed sort of effort. Laps to beat the band, pulling and dragging out of one another, fellas knocking lumps out of the pitch trying to pull on the ball and if he managed to get the ball in hand it was fresh air swings all the way. After what was about the fourth week or eight or ten sessions Horesbox slid in beside me along the low bench of the dressing room. He removed the cap and rubbed the head. Interest was waning, Vincent was nowhere to be seen, we were heading for a crisis. "No sign of Vincent again today ?" his voice heavy. He stood up and paced the room, about to speak again when, speak of the devil, in arrives Vincent, buoyant as a bubble with an "evening lads and how are the hurlers ?". The horse only looked at him, just looked at him, that is all that was needed for Vincent to know that he was sour. He let us know with discernible pride that he was not long off the phone with the chairman of the county board confirming the date of the first of the month for the opening fixture. "And what about the poor turnout ?", well there was an answer for that too a recruitment drive. "Recruitment drive ?" wondered Horse, hanging on the thought.

The recruitment drive was documented in the notebook by Vincent's deft hand as so :

1. Flannery's – The four Flannery brothers were the backbone of the Ogonnelloe which would have won the feile were it not for the three losses. Could we tempt them back ?.
2. The Tinkers – Had settled in the town in Harmony Hill only recently. Reports confirmed that at least two of the lads were mighty handballers and the hope was that their talents extended to the clash of the Ash.
3. The Germans – Had bought an old cottage out the Ballinascarrow road. There were about four of them, strong looking bucks that had long hair and often seen wearing nothing but a pair of shorts while renovating the cottage. We would visit them after the previous two.
4. The Hannon brothers – worst came to the worst one of them would stand in goals.

We would call to each of the locations in the listed order, all to be conducted on the following Saturday by myself and the Horse, Vincent was unavailable due to family commitments.

STORIES OF A DIGITAL SPALPEEN

It was a fine day come Saturday and the recruitment drive commenced at Flannery's, the end house of the terraced row with a grey garden wall enclosing an un-kept patchwork of Doc leaves and Dandelions. Nine strong were reared in this three up two down, four boys and five girls. It was herself that let us in with the warm welcome of a milky tea. "Hurling !" exclaimed old Flannery, wondering had he heard rightly, forgetting the glory years of his own sons, he had never witnessed hurling in the area but went on to extol the virtues of some of the finest footballers known high and low the length and breadth of Connaught. He mentioned a few, Walsh, Mc Murrow, John Andrews, as the story goes brilliantly talented, incredibly gifted, terribly undisciplined and following the height of their glory their inevitable decline, the daemon drink, a hore for the women and a mad gambler altogether, Walsh, Mc Murrow, Andrews, one, two, three. In relation to his own lads "not tat tall, John doesn't play at all now, you know yourself", "Padraig is in England", the youngest Luke, maybe the most talented of them all was reduced to the rubber ring factory. "He doesn't play much either since he started going with the one of the Mc Loughlin's" was the sad conclusion. "Have we any drink to offer these lads ?" he wondered to himself then found a six pack of Guinness bottles in the press under the sink. Down the hatch with a couple and the horse gave me a let's leave look and we were just about to get up when the mother appeared with the pan in the hand and wondered would we have a bit a breakfast. Horse gave me another look.

"Well, well, go on then, sure why not" and we sat again. It was mid-afternoon by the time we had the last sausage washed down by the soft Porter, Mr Flannery let us out looking up and down the terrace for any signs of life, he would be sure to tell Luke that Training was Tuesdays and Thursdays below at the pitch.

We weren't too sure approaching the Tinkers camp what kind of reception we might get, they could set the dog on us and if they did we wouldn't get too far after the feed we just had. I ducked behind Horse as he knocked on the first caravan, it shook. "Hello" a muffled voice called with a clobber of feet following, the door swung open. A suspicious teenager with the scrub of a beard and half a sandwich in his hand, his mother a big woman stood in behind him and wondered what could she get us lads. She figured it was Pakie Junior we were after, that he was handball mad and he would be back soon, "come hon in" she said. It was a cosy fit that got tighter again once Packie Junior arrived back with the cousin Charlie. "ye lads from hup the town ?", he wondered, they thought it was a joke altogether when we let them know about the hurling, the laugh still going when the door opened introducing Packie Senior and the caravan sunk an inch with the weight of him.

"Ye wouldn't be Garda ?", he wondered narrowing his eyes. If it was tight before it was now a full house, arranged mostly in around the main table neat as sardines. Packie Senir apologised for his suspicions but you can't be too sure and when more relaxed informed us that they were Mc Donagha's related to King Pat Mc Donagh buried out beyond in Blossom Hill. He produced a bottle of Poteen and watched intensely as my eyes watered, one glass after another, tough stuff altogether. We fell out of the Hobby.

STORIES OF A DIGITAL SPALPEEN

"Tuesdays and Thursdays" the horse reminded them as we did.

The German's place, a stone cottage in the process of renovation was located four miles from town at the end of a boreen, south facing, gagging for whatever sun they might get. We were again met with such a welcome that it couldn't be refused. In fact, as foreigners, they outdid themselves assimilating into a part of the country fabled for hospitality. The evening was drawing in, the cottage enjoying the last gasps of light when we got down to the business of hurling. The horsebox, sensing he was representing not only the parish or the county but maybe the entire country began at source with Cu Chulainn, describing excitedly the puck that did for the feisty hound, the young Sedanta's remorse and his committal to undertake the expired hound's duty. He went on detailing the progression of the game from ancient oral tradition to faction fights at crossroads, much to manufactured awe of our Teutonic friends. Their concentration levels were aided by the magnificently constructed joint that carouselled its way round the room. Home grown of course making use of a perfectly serviceable bathtub. The bock style beer was another testament to the cottage industry we drank from big brown bottles with fitted corks. It flowed like the river Rhine down the Rhur valley. As the sun slowly sunk the light dwindling through pokey window the candles were lit. The haze of fragrant smoke enveloped the outline of the Horse who was up to the Gaelic League and Douglas Hyde its poetic founder. The more I looked at him the more he began to look like Cu Chulainn, a fantastically wild thing, with the eyes spinning in his head.

D. M. O'DOWD

With the sun cosy in the clouds he was still going but at this stage more so as a side show, parked in beside the dresser as the room seemed from one moment to the next fill with a gaggle of girls from the town. This was much to my delight of course being suddenly surrounded by the preponderance of pretty girls within circulation of the Champion, drawn no doubt by the allure of the handsome Bavarians. The only lump in the porridge seeing my own sister Izzy among the bunch, perched on the edge of the same worn dresser. She was engaged in flirtatious conversation with the dashing Sven. Semi aggressive thoughts of Fuck it who does he think he is coming over here taking our jobs and our women slithered into my mind but as luck would have it just at that moment a big smouldering smoke came my way, I took a huge toke and concluded that Sven was a sound man. My last recollection of the night was the horsebox attempting to mount the a carefully restored Monot Guzzi with two perplexed Germans trying to coax him off, "take him please home" one of them suggested to me. I confirmed I would, holding him up with one arm also reminding them training was Tuesdays and Thursdays below in the pitch.

All things considered, we put the drive down as a success not only bulking the number to a man in every position which I must also point out included one of the Hannon brothers wearing the jersey over the jumper and standing in goals. Come the day of the game, adding interest a nice little crowd had gathered, consisting of:

- The hurling enthusiasts – totalling two – Paddy Brogan from Clare and Joe Beggan from Kilkenny.

- The Schandedfreud – The majority in attendance, all eager to see the prevailing chaos.

- The hurler-ett's – The most exuberant in attendance – mostly here for admiration of the Bavarian Bodies on show. Again this included my younger sister who remained hot on the heels of Sven.

- The Garda – Who attended all GAA matches in this parish and other neighbouring parishes as a matter of duty.

- The Travelling community – they support their own.

Vincent used it to great advantage, eyeballing man for man each man with equal intensity. His hands were joined in a reverent bundle. His face slack with the compassion of Christ. "Listen to them" he finally uttered profoundly, "they're here for us". The Germans looked obliviously jolly having exchanged the army surplus Kaki for the Maroon and White O'Neill's. They smoked away on a big reefer which Vincent requested they extinguish, manifesting genuine concern that we would all be taken up by the Garda. Kelly and Shanahan gave it a try.

"Powerful altogether" Kelly commented holding it beyond the end of his nose appreciating the curls of smoke.

"Ya power in that" Sven echoed.

Packie Junior and Charlie were interested to see what was taking place, "wha dat ?" he enquired to Sven.

"Try !", Sven offered it to him, "Go ahead".

It went from Packie to Charlie who both sucked on it until it was within an inch of it's life.

Shortly after Packie leaves for a moment and returns with a gleaming bottle of Poteen wrapped in a dish cloth. "Here you go boss take a mouthful outta dat" offering it out. Always willing to experience the local cuisine Sven took a nice slug, nearly lost his breath.

Packie Junior hit him on the back like a proud Uncle, "good lad" he said as Sven passed it to his German neighbour to share in the unmistakable experience.

"Tog out", Vincent was calling through the dense smoke but no one seemed to be passing any heed, "Tog out lads" he pleaded again just as the Germans unwrapped and shared around the homebrew that was supposed to be for post-match celebrations.

"Wha kinda tack is dat ?", Packie asked and was straight over again to get his gob on it.

The craic really started when Flannery turned up with the stereo, the two Tinker boys were going hard at it pucking the sliotar to one another in the showers. Flannery hit the play button and suddenly Bruce Springsteen echoing off the walls. The trousers nearly fell off Vincent who was walking round with the belt open trying to calm things down. Flannery knotted the Bandana around his head and we all joined in on the chorus, everyone was on their feet and the noise levels were like Whelan's on New Year's Eve. The Smoke along with the noise all escaping out the missing pane in the window. The spectators attentions drawn to it wondering what in the hell was going on.

By the time the knock came, it was too late. The knobbly Ref flanked by two Garda, one of them Sergeant Mullen who stood patiently for minutes waiting for a response before putting shoulder to the door. Panic ensued with Mullen reaching for the notebook. A dog rushed through the demesne of legs gathered in the doorway and began yapping irreverently at the stereo speaker. He was quietened with the full force of a naked foot. Ignorant to the seriousness of the situation Bruce was still putting on a hell of a show full tilt with *dancing in the dark*. The yelp from the dog prompted an almighty roar from the imposing Mullen – "Who's in charge here" ? he wondered, which quietened the cabal who wondered the same. All eyes searched for Vincent and failing to find him rested squarely on the horse whose sudden hangdog countenance bore the look of a guilty man. Gerrymandering, plaumasing, and soft talk ensued resulting in Mullen returning the notebook to the top pocket, nameless but sorely aggrieved as a staunch GAA man at the shame brought on the parish. The game was disbanded of course, the opposing team making a rearguard action for the minibus. The ref left to figure out what to include in the match report. The dog left licking his wounds. The horse much the same.

The fallout lasted for a few hours in Harry's. A deep dive into the root cause analysis resulted in Vincent being bestowed the moniker of Houdini. Harry had located a prominent position over the fireplace for the team photo. We watched on in silence, a collective representation of failure as he carefully placed it on a wobbly nail. We beamed with pride. A tremendous, self satisfying, unadulterated pride. An unfounded, unjust, unmerited, unexplainable pride. Now put that in your pipe and smoke it Sigmund.

The Tripp to Tipp

Friday evening just off the train, along with a handful of others who had another week done in the big smoke. We stood still in Mullingar for over an hour, the usual shit. It was worse when moving, camped between the carriages, the toilet door swinging and banging. You couldn't make it up. The last hour was always torture and if it wasn't for the Walkman I might have jumped out the window. What to do with the last fiver to me name ?, I mulled it over watching daylight on its last legs, black crows danced out the last waltz before bed down. Luminous white lichen stood out against the grey granite of the station wall. I would head for Harry's, trailing my finger along the wall as I went. I hoped the horsebox might be in. If he was, he would surely stand me a pint or six, he was good like that since he got the start at the steel fixing, he might also have brought along those Punk albums he was always on about.

No sign of the Horsebox says Harry, should be in later. It was quiet, Patsy and the wife at a far table, her looking east, him west, one sighing the other groaning. Leonard and Black Mick at the bar, drunk and dirty in a half embrace with Leonard drifting in and out, attempting to pull the Black in close and tell him all his darkest secrets. With a leathery cloud of Condor smoke slowly drifting in my direction Harry gave a rye smile and with pearls of wisdom let me know that there were many different kinds of love in this world.

D. M. O'DOWD

There was indeed and maybe the greatest love of them all the love of the bed. For a solid year, I hadn't t managed to rise up for a single nine o'clock lecture – Electro-tech, Digital Design, Maths and Models had slipped like tiny inky eels, one by one, into the slipstream of my morning glory. Yes, most mornings started in the afternoon. A beady eye opening to confirm the bed opposite was vacated and Bosco had left for college, the quotidian chore of masturbation followed, a fag in the horizontal and a bowl of cornflakes (yellow brand) smothered in hot milk and banana. The telly, rented from a man on Rathmines road got a good run during the day, right up to the Dail debates and ten or fifteen useless minutes of the droning test screen. Most days I emptied my bowels at eleven followed by a run to Spar for a ham salad roll or some item of poorly disguised offal, unwrapped and incinerated in an oven. The Sullivans's, Cagney and Lacy, Hart to Hart all captured my passing interest, the black and white midday movie my full attention, If I had to name one of the many then Danger mouse would have been my particular favourite come children's TV time, which also indicated the pending crank of a key in the door as Bosco (Engineering Bolton St) or one of the girls, Nuala (Optometry, Kevin Street), Caroline (sociology UCD) arrived home. By that time I would be well fermented on the couch, their passing fascination always prompting the girls to enquire if I had moved at all for the day.

One couldn't say it was the laid-back demeanour, pure laziness or the torrents of hormones that subdued all other industry. They were strange creatures to me these Trinity students, they listened to Chopin, had a deadpan interest in

STORIES OF A DIGITAL SPALPEEN

DOS, one of them a tall blond with ivory teeth and facial moles (two) intended to travel to Stuttgart for research in their third year. They were from Kildare and Tramore and Swords and Skerries and spoke with clarity and levity. They challenged lecturers on theorems and the impacts of computing on social norms. I could only manage to challenge them on my whereabouts. "Oh Trinity," they said at home, you must be a brainy bugger and I'd be lying if I denied that I smiled on the inside, but the truth of the matter was it didn't take a genius to lie scratching their balls to the tremulous clock on countdown. Alas, it was no great surprise to see the report card come June, a tumble of fails, a heap of disappointment, a car-crash of catastrophe, a long sour list of repeats. Five out of the Seven to be precise with only two modern day wonders, computers science in society and programming part two (C language), where a margin of a mouse hair took me through. Goes without saying of course the mother was like a demon, making the subject of Feile all the more of a challenge to broach. So I didn't, instead coming up with a plan B.

Plan B – "What kind of book ?" she asked.

"Well a book" I said, "Advanced Mathematics for Electric and Electronic Transactions .. by Berkley press" I stuttered on. She swallowed it (the story not the book).

"How much ?"

"Fifty five" delivered with lashings of lassitude's and a hung shoulder.

"Jesus Mary and Joseph" her only comment as she folded out the livers, the pangs of guilt clawing my conscience as she did so. The claws were clipped, however, lasting only so long as it took to me to foot it to Melody Maker where Bosco, Mossy and Nula waited with a hand on the door. Effete Nula, cool in the John Lennon specs, both lads in Bermudas and Doc Martens, burnished from the sun. It had been the first day of summer with real warmth, the air tepid at best, the light Lemon, the crows still circling. "It'll be some gas" says Mick Melody splaying the tickets on the counter, hitching his thumbs to the side pockets of the leather waistcoat. We were too busy to chat, noodling over the names of the bands each in a typeface aligned to record sales – the radiators from space, never heard them, Therapy ?, ya will be at the front, Something happens, puke music. Anyhow, the music was almost secondary, the potential ride and the booze, the real headline acts for us. Well with the exception of Nula of course who was going strong with Vincent. A tent was required, Bosco's brother had one – some kind of a yoke last taken out of the bag for the FCA camp in Finner. I had a tenner left over from the purchase which wasn't going to take me far, the cost of the Bus being eighteen snots. We would need to thumb as far as Athlone and take the bus from there.

The following week two events occurred that were to have quite a positive bearing on my unfurling fortunes, one relating to personal allure and the second to financial standing. For some time Nula had been impressing on me to bleach the hair and with Feile confirmed by the purchase of the tickets, it suggested the time was now. Down with us to Cahney's – honey blond, brilliant blond, platinum blond, her tapping finger passing them one by one then halting on the lid of a predominantly blue box the front façade sporting a healthy specimen with a sun-kissed bob, a denim shirt tied across her lean honeyed midriff. "Needs to be the permanent one" Nuala said with complete confidence. The deed itself, a timely affair took place in her bedroom we listened to her impressive corpus of blank tapes, from A House to Led Zeppelin, each song and artist meticulously transcribed from the original with biro, some of the cheap casing artistically doodled. We drank red wine, her attempting sophistication, me to get drunk. Occasionally she gently peeled back the bag to inspect proceedings, carefully clearing a strand before confirming I wasn't ready yet. Only with my scalp burring like a curry did she agree to the bag coming off and in I went for the shower, Nuala after me, talking through the door and looking for updates, as I crouched into the mirror, staring at my unfamiliar self, big bird hair with big burgundy gums.

The second event was an impromptu visit to the Uncles drapery & haberdashery shop on Emmet Street. At the time, as was usually the case, it started more so a soliloquy than a discussion. Uncle Eddie's moustache flapped like a gulls wing, nostalgically commenting on how people in the old days had great loyalty to the town but the youth of today didn't give a Hi-Diddle-Dee-Dee. The quiver of the bell knocked him off track, he lurched forward at the thought of a customer. A traveller in a navy blue suit emerged from the half-light, a briefcase in his hand approaching confidently. He was selling "high quality" ear piercing equipment. "I dunno now," said the Uncle in procrastination to my bid to invest, reminding him of his family being a great line of business people. He spent a long time pondering that one, sucking the gums, running his hand down the belly of his cardigan. Anyway to cut a long story short – the gun along with a strip of twenty four studs, a batch of antiseptic wipes and a donkey jacket went into the bag for Feile that night. All along with the book – Advanced mathematics for Electric and Electronic somethings – the original one, also bought and paid for by the mother. After some consideration, I said to myself I would surely get an hour here and there to cram a bit.

We set off but weren't have much luck with the thumbing, car after car after car leaving us standing, laden with rudimentary camping apparel, high hopes and delirious desires. After a stretch Mossy ordered me "stand in behind the hedge", putting it down to the hair. I complied and no sooner had Bosco joined me for a fag when the first passing jalopy squealed to a halt. A Mrs Heaver who on seeing myself and Bosco clambering over the gate got a bit of a jump and was about to take off again but for the rapacity we bundled in, that and the winsome assurance of Mossy. She was pointing for Athlone, all the way to visit her mother in law laid out with bunions in the General Hospital. Mossy at least did all the talking, myself and Bosco squeezed in along with the two kids. The Larry Gogan *just a minute quiz* was on the radio. I knew one or two and mouthed the answers to the kids who were in awe of my golden bun, "is it real ?" the young one asked his older sister, pretty in her pink dress and Peyton white sandals. She didn't answer but took her hand and wiped the bubble of snot from his nose, half ashamed. Eventually, Larry said to Eileen from Kells that they just didn't suit her today and Eileen took it well but who the hell thinks an astronaut uses a shuttlecock.

STORIES OF A DIGITAL SPALPEEN

Mrs Heaver tore along nicely, taking air from talking only as we reached the outskirts of the town. No longer enamoured but completely besotted with the young gentleman to her left, she insisted on driving us to Bus Eireann, reaching across and rolling down the passenger window with a bellow to be sure and to let her know if ever he was passing Calstlegarry. Even the auld ones loved Mossy.

A scene from platoon awaited us in Liberty Square Thurles, with bodies strung everywhere, arched in pain, or passed that point having entered the purgatorial bliss. We took the first opportunity to camp, Mossy having noticed the hurried handwriting on a rudimentary sign offering a square of clipped lawn in the front garden of a squat bungalow with oversized arching windows and a terracotta tiled roof. A second available plot was already occupied by a suitably neat tent, a modern domed-shaped one. A group of girls from Birr, Mrs Maher said, not sure where they were at that moment, out by the looks of it she observed peering down at the door. Bosco gave me the nudge to pay up for the three nights.

It wasn't until the next morning we caught sight of the women, Bosco spotting a probing blond head. "What's she like ?" I croaked.

"Not bad" he said.

I elbowed across a snoring Mossy to get a look. It was still early, the air crisp but with the promise of Sun. I blinked to focus, she was now fully outside the tent, her arms clasped skywards behind her head, arching backwards to stretch. Her cotton tie died pants hung low on her hips leaving some distance to the seam of her crop top. A second head appeared in the doorway, a criss-cross of knotted auburn, less enthusiastic to make an effort to salute the sun.

"Stay back" I warned Bosco, watching her slowly emerge from the tent in the stonewashed dungarees and white vest with one strap open, she was a nine out of ten. Mossy had resurrected by now and wanted some action, both himself and Bosco lined up behind me, we mumbled and grunted, the FCA tent wibbled and wobbled.

"Hang on" I pleaded, "there is a third".

"A third" Mossy grew excited "What she like ?" he asked.

"Not bad at all" I replied. The girls conferred in a group, took a combined look in our direction, giggled a bit, weaved their arms around one another and skipped off with breezy freedom. We were left with a pan and a pound of sausages.

Mrs Maher was no slouch when it came to making a few spondulics, not only were the front and rear lawns serving as an impromptu campsite but by noon she had a roaring trade going on the barbecue. The wall along the house was lined with hairy arses, a permanent plume of smoke coiling above their heads as they slurped sauce and gnawed their heads off through a fair percentage of Quinnsworth frozen meat section. She wasn't the only local making hay while the sun shined – "warm beer, warm beer" another swarthy local beckoned us to purchase a crate of duty-free Carling from the boot of his Transit. We sat back and supped from the shade of the tent observing passing traffic. Mossy had gotten the shift the night before we learned, a stunner from Dublin, Blackrock or Foxrock, Anna, Ann or Anette. He was pissed off he had lost her number, rifled through his pockets one last time to make sure, he was planning a mission for later to Hayes Hotel where he had run into her. All the while the tent opposite remained untouched. Maybe they were gone for the day and we had seen the last of them.

Maybe not, about an hour later we watched them return through the gate, made their way to the tenant and collapsed on the lawn. It brought a halt to our banter. I studied her warmed beauty flourish like a flower, releasing a puff of breath from her bottom lip to billow the hair on her fringe. They all seemed relieved to be back at base, organising things. The left strap of her dungaree remained undone. "Was she older than me ?", bearing in mind Danger Mouse was still in my top ten, I probably had no chance, she looked so mature. Earlier, while they were away we agreed the plan of attack, Bosco would shift the blond, I would try the brunette and Mossy would tackle the redhead. He agreed that only after some debate, as a personal favour to me, only for so long as Ann or Anna or Annette materialised out of the fortune of nightfall. "I won't stand in your way" he says laying back clutching a can.

Now push had come to shove, he loved it of course, Mossy, to see me suffer, "go on for fucks sake" he reminded me, "or they'll be gone again" he urged as if I needed reminding. I could call his bluff, and say "go on himself", but knowing him, he would, leaving me to a weekend, no a lifetime of remorse. To buy some time I went into the tent and mooched in a bag. I could wear my candy red, coal black, horizontally striped Kurt Cobain jumper, it was pretty cool, but it was too warm and Mossy would tweak the change of attire and use it to ridicule me. Lifting the jumper *Architecture and software design* was uncovered, its coffin black cover reminding me of my responsibilities. I quickly covered it up along with the ear piercing kit, which hadn't come to much yet either. "Are you not gone yet ?" Mossy called out half pissed off. I sighed, there was no getting out of this.

It wasn't till I eclipsed the sun she looked up with a wrinkled nose. Despite my procrastination, I hadn't come up with a single seductive sentence, instead stood standing. I could hear Mossy up my rear gasping a smarmy laugh, pulling the rug from under me to the brink of stage fright.

"Do I know you ?" dribbled from my mealy mouth. She took her time to respond.

"No, I don't think so" she said, "I don't recognise you at least" she confirmed.

Well, that was that then, I turned slowly to leave and faced Mossy in the distance.

"By any chance" I asked "would you know how to pierce an ear ?"

"Are you serious ?" she asked.

"Ya," I replied and offered her a smoke.

She jumped up and in seconds we were eye to eye over the naked flame of a bic lighter. Minutes later sitting cross legged in a pow wow encircling the crate of Carling which Bosco had ferried across along with the ear gun, positioning himself in close to the blond. Mossy also joined, unusually mute.

They were indeed from Birr, just done with the leaving cert at St Brendan's, down to their last tenner and saving it for the night. We were older, in college and richer, just about in all three cases. The Carling was drained, Bosco and the Blond nominated to venture to the off-licence for replenishment, sensing his opportunity on the way back Bosco stopped her at Mrs Maher's burger stand and they shifted. I could just about make them out in the distance through the mass of bodies, separating from a kiss and looking at one another in that half embarrassed dreamy sparkle. The redhead wanted to study English and Philosophy in Trinity, the brunette wasn't sure what the future held but might travel to America for a year out which made my heart sink.

Mossy stood up and roared across to Bosco to "come on with the cans".

Our last money went on the burgers.

Mrs Maher wouldn't give a discount, "I'm not charging for the use of the toilet" which was hard to argue with given the queues for the port a loos. With evening setting in the Kurt Cobain jumper made an appearance. Mossy and the redhead had fractured from the group eating the face off one another. Myself and the brunette sat in silence smiling. The street strewn with litter. The noise levels increasing to rowdy.

"I like your hair," she said.

"Thanks" I replied and leant slowly in, she came halfway to meet me with those beckoning Babylonian lips.

The idea of the ear piercing was "mad", she said, fish in a barrel as it turned out (bearing in mind I was well cut myself at this stage). One after another they lined up, blind drunk and brimming with bonhomie. We soon had a process in place, she swabbed the fleshy lobe, I buried the bullet, she collected the cold cash, the fee for which varied from free to a fiver. A pixies fan from Kildare insisted on the ceremonial necking of a Bulmers before I popped the pistol. Two lovers, just met, wanted to mark the occasion by adorning with matching red ruby studs. A lad from Donegal, just come out of the closet and had travelled liberated to Tipp, he had both ears decorated, pop, pop. By ten o'clock drunk as Bacon rich as a Roman I wrapped her in the Kurt Cobain jumper, kissed her and held her softly. We took the two remaining cans to the tent and jettisoned all bags and baggage, laid out my mouldy blue sleeping bag and lit the lamp. I unhinged the remaining buckle on her dungarees and we met skin to skin. Her low muted moan signalled a sensation of warmth reaching as far back as my furthest molars, my mind a mingled mix of manliness and childish delight as we had full consensual adult intercourse. No more could Mossy recount a night of fumbling at second base or Bosco bray about his latest conquest without me skulking for a fag or a joke or some other crutch to deflect the conversation.

Eighty three quid was the final count, a small fortune she rolled through the gaps of her fingers with shivers of delight. We spent it all, every red cent, every black penny through the slow course of a luxuriant lazy day, sitting on barrels of beer in the gangway of Hayes Hotel. Mossy was drunk since daylight, swamping pints and talking the hind legs off anything that moved, the red head sick of his carry-on. Bosco was still holding tight to the blond for fear of losing her in the packed pub, music lilted in the background, I love this song she would say from time to time and I would strain to hear, see if I could name it. At some point in the afternoon, Nuala and Vincent located us. By which stage I was hoarse from talking and laughing and roaring. The girls hit it off right away. At some point, now that I remember, all heads turned to the piercing posh call of "Mooossssy" from the doorway, it was Ann or Anna or Anette from Foxrock or Blackrock. Like a loudhailer she spoke while holding him up, her long cold nose catching the side of his face as she tried to do so. The red head turned in disgust and began to look more glum than ever before but me I was in a place called heaven. That Sunday night, my arm coiling her waist, her head on my shoulder, we fell from Hayes, making our way to see the closing act, the Wonder Suff.

The father greeted my arrival home with a doff of the newspaper, his eyes following my trudge from the front door to the butt of the stairs, "aw now" he remarked raising the paper again. At first I thought I had missed it, surely it was in there somewhere, but it wasn't, it was gone, the book. I tipped all the sorry contents from bag to bed. The remaining studs sprinkling downwards like gold-dust, single socks and dirty jocks but no book. I would have cried why me, but that would have indicated madness seeing as it was me flung the bag in haste from the door of the tent across Mrs Maher's lawn. I collapsed, legs tangled, on the duvet with a hollow in the pit of my stomach, drifting off into one of those awful clammy dreams, with thoughts of heading to the station in the morning, returning to a flat that smelled of damp briquettes and a fly frantically buzzing between the net curtain and the window, and the sour milk in the fridge, that bloody sour milk.

The following Sunday I could go no further without the book and so took my place along the serried wall of the Rathmines Inn waiting for the phone box, rehearsing my lines – "Mammmy, ya know that book ?" in my best *sonny don't go away* intones. With a final clearing of the throat and lungs in the hollow box, a butterfly in my belly, I bit the bullet. She ate me alive, from head to toe and by the time she had done with me I had but two units left on the call card, the receiver slippery with droplets of my pleading but at least I had secured the book for the third time, no mean feat. Feile seemed so so long ago, did It happen at all I hesitated for an instant. I took a breath as a hairy hand on the Perspex window knocked and enquired if I was going to stay in there all night, "ya ya, five minutes" I said, tensely unfolding the precious rag of paper with her name and number. It rang, my heart was thrumming.

"Is Aine there ?" I asked.

"Hang on" – the boy said about to run off before pausing to enquire "Who's calling ?" the little shit asked.

"A friend" I replied (a response the sister had learnt me), which seemed to satisfy him. After a torturous silence, punctuated with the slamming of a door, her familiar voice, warm like a cuddle.

"Hi" she said, as my heart tumbled round the place.

"Hello" I answered, "remember me ?", I asked and just as the call card went beep beep beep ...

Some Tulips

Everyone loves chips, a widely known fact, nothing new there but if you ever had the pleasure of working in Sizzlers after the pubs close then you will know the true meaning of Love and Chips. Chips and fights were the preserve of a Saturday night. Chips buried in salt or afloat in vinegar, burger and chips, chicken and chips, nuggets, onion rings, battered sausage, all with chips. They came three deep at the counter all shouting at the same time. Alphonsus Quirk, the owner of Sizzlers was the only one brave enough to open after closing time. His tie would be fishing in and out of the grease and skidding along the hotplate as he went from order to order. The chips in garlic sauce were one of the most popular and you could tell after ten pints was as addictive as smack, they would nearly drink it from the carton. Curry sauce was another narcotic like elixir but didn't come without possible side effects. With the consistency of yoohoo glue, the sauce and the chips clumped on the white plastic fork could drop like a lump and stick like a leech to a shirt. For some it didn't matter for others disaster, I'm talking about those who hadn't gotten the shift up to that point and were still holding out hope before or after the buses to and from the nightclub would pull in. The stain on the shirt, made worse by grinding it with a serviette more or less meant game over for another week. More often than once a night an excruciating screech of one swear word or another would soar above the general shouting and roaring, the smash of a container as it hit the tiles of the floor, chips and sauce, everything everywhere. To the victim, it was like losing a leg, in a half trance looking from the mess to the melee at the counter wondering if they had the strength to go through it all again.

When you are an entrepreneur in a small town, as Quirk was, it often meant subjecting yourself to these smaller indignities, chips and vomit and although he was making it hand over fist it was hard to know if he or for example the Bragans were having the last laugh. Where the brothers Bragans without fail would turn up with a bag of Bulmers and turn it into a sort of free disco but then again John was making the lolly and let them at it. In all fairness some nights, with the Music going full blast and the dancing it was like the last night of Lisdoonvarna in there. Luckily the fights would mostly happen outside and if they did break out in the chipper itself the trick was to get them out fast. The fights were the scourge really because, myself or Johan A would need to drop everything and kick into action where he would swing the door open as wide as possible and I from a running start would get behind them and surprise them into a goose tip to the exit. Alphonsus Quirk, always said the same thing as they were passing, "there's no need for the like of that". Some nights he would need to lock up after that but the mob would be knocking and tapping and as we let one out another would push their way in. The funny thing is, is that after all the hysteria, all the panic when we finally managed to wake Mc Muck and wipe his drool from the Formica table, on plates and in bags, on tables and chairs there were enough half eaten chips that we cleared into big black refuse bags to feed a small nation. It was a zoo altogether.

Talking about zoo's, Vincent approached me with an offer to join him and his student union buddies, Mervin and Ryan both fourth year Med who were planning a blowout, interrailing, "Amsterdam and beyond" he said. It was about this time that I was coming to the home straight in my final year and kind of turned a corner with the Computer Science. It was a lecturer, Sean Baker that more or less saved me at the start of the year. From the labyrinth of C programming, linked lists, malloc, calloc and alloc (commands to save and release memory), pointers and pointers to pointers I was beginning to see the light. The penny dropped on the day, wanting to make my last year count, I plucked up the courage to go and speak with him. He explained that programming was an art as much a science and that each program can be judged based on its aesthetics, how it is shaped and written as succinctly as a poem. Me, a poet, would you have thought ?, so I started to play the part by smoking more, speaking less, looking moody and putting my head in a book. A week on the continent fitted in perfectly with my artistic ambitions even if the money earned by dishing out singles wasn't particularly artisan. So the answer to Vincent was a beatnick, "sure".

Amsterdam, we went all in, Vim and vigor. The two other students along with Vincent and myself were Ryan a Limerick man and Mervin and a Dub (Southsider). If Mervin was a boy, Ryan was a man, a seasoned campaigner, he was slumped in the chair with a hump on his back, the shirt an expensive one but somehow not the right fit. It was our first beer which he handed back.

"The head is the size of a fucking cloud" he explained to the big boned waitress who in countered that "A five finger froth is expected in Amsterdam".

He was having none of it "Not in Clancy's of Bruff" was the reply and sent her on her way. He was more willing when we moved on to the smoke, "give me your strongest" he declared and the guy in the coffee shop who arrived down with a plant the size of a geranium, "No effect" said Ryan until we stood out into the fresh air and bang. We spent the next two hours holding on to a bike railing, Ryan's face was as red as a cranky baboon's arse.

Coming down from the geranium, hands raw from the railings we were in the depths of night and the meat market was in full swing, from blond to brunette, leather, Peyton and red rubber all round.

Ryan was still not steady on the legs asks Mervin "Are you, going in ?"

Mervin looked confused "Are you ?" he retorted.

"I fucking asked you" Ryan complained and turns to Vincent hoping to get a sensible answer "Are you ?".

Vincent baulked and turned swiftly to me "What about you ?".

Ryan shook his head, I didn't answer, to be honest, I wasn't sure if I was coming or going after the geranium which Vincent took as a tacit no and turned to Ryan, replying "No, no".

Mervin blurted, "Nah, no" looking apologetic."

Fucking useless" Ryan says.

STORIES OF A DIGITAL SPALPEEN

We walked on for a bit and Vincent stopped suddenly.

"She's nice", he whispered looking up.

Not my type but handsome with skinny legs in high heels, her breasts were huge, peeping out over the top of a tight French maids uniform. She had picked him out and he was slowly melting. The bumping, gasping, groaning, hooting whooping, cling clanging, wham babing thank you maming all around him hushed into the distance as her artful stare rendered him useless. Only his fig leaf and a few hundred Guilders separating them.

The new poetic me stood in. "Think of Nuala", I whispered into his ear which rocked his socks.

"Of course" he protested and jumped into motion.

"Think of Nuala" he muttered to himself half annoyed with me.

We kept going, the French maid fading into the distance, the glow from the window enveloping her but just as she was reaching out of sight he stole a furtive look over a sloping shoulder.

We ended up in Molly Malones down by a canal and drank Guinness and ate chips. Ryan reckoned the Guinness was muck but was sick of the other pissey larger and Mervin said there wasn't much difference between the chips here and the ones back home but they loved them with Mayonnaise instead of red sauce, weird. Vincent started us on the Jägermeister and that got us drunk enough to mingle with the locals but eventually, the language barrier left us friendless and Mervin fell asleep on a table. Ryan wouldn't go back to Mollys (cunt of a spot) but we continued the theme (home away from home) at O'Reilley's and St James gate. We spent the best part of three days there as Ryan wouldn't entertain the idea of going for a walk in the city or the Van Gogh Museum. He reckoned that we would only get mugged, he based it on a fella he knew from Croom that had to hand over the father's watch, that was in Frankfurt but all the same, he wasn't taking any chances.

It could have been any one of the given days Vincent went missing. It was Ryan who clocked it."

Did you see him ?" he asked Mervin who asked me.

"Was he with you ?"

"No" I replied and nothing was said after that until there were four Jägermeister stacked for him.

"Where would he be gone" Ryan enquired suspiciously.

He was getting agitated for no particular reason and I noticed a heat rash covering a considerable portion of the left side of his neck. Six stacked and Vincent strolled in. Ryan gave it a few minutes before casually enquiring "Where were you ?",

"Phone call" Vincent answered without hesitation, cleared his throat, threw back one of the shots and focused strangely on Ryan.

"What's that on your neck ?" he asked.

"What ?", Ryan replied with exaggerated denial.

"Is it a love bite ?" Mervin wondered.

"Fuck off" Ryan snarled.

Munich and the Old Irish bar. Ryan had acquired a cut on his forehead but didn't seem to know from where. He kept the rash hidden behind the shirt and seemed always to be in the standard issue College of surgeons chinos. Despite the heatwave, he wore a vest, he said "he always wore a vest".

STORIES OF A DIGITAL SPALPEEN

Mervin reckoned it was very similar to Keoghs and decided to go local on the Weiss beer. I wasn't sure if it was the right move for me, I wasn't a hundred percent myself between the beer and the bread I hadn't had a bowel movement for the past five days but this wasn't the environment to declare weakness. The Germans were friendly enough but it was with an American in a Boston Varsity hoodie that we finally broke the deadlock of each other's company. Mervin kissed her under the television and the three of us turned to look.

"He better not fucking bring her over here" Ryan says but he did and there was no getting away from her until Munich Hauptbahnhof where Mervin left her on the platform. As it turned out that she wasn't American at all but a Moldovan who watched one too many episodes of friends. The night she was shouting down the phone to the father in Romani gave the game away. That didn't extinguish Mervin's flames of passion however, they blew kisses to one another from the moment he set foot on the train until somewhere east of Interlaken. Ryan was on the verge of puking, with serious aversion anxiety and the rash was growing rapidly. He screwed his eyes as we took off, the light of day was blinding him. Mervin on the other hand was walking in the Sun.

Salzberg, the Shamrock, day eight. I had two bananas for breakfast and that suggested a bowel movement but despite all the heaving, it didn't happen. It's hard to face another pint of Stiegl after that but I soldiered on and by evening I had numbed the pain. The heat rash on Ryan's neck was creeping above the collar. The Shamrock was a cosy spot with a good mix of regulars and tourists, on the first night I acquainted with a local by the name of Magnus, he told me about his comprehensive record collection.

"Have you been to the Schiele museum ?", he asked and was astonished,

when I told him "I wasn't, I mean I hadn't"

"Where have you been ?" he asked simply dumfounded when I informed him.

"Murphys, Mollys, The Dubliner .... you know, and now the Shamrock of course".

"Not even the Salzburg Museum ?"

"nich."

"Home of Mozart ?"

"nein."

Magnus as it turns out was a regular and arrived in a second night as we were well into it.

"Your boyfriend is in", Ryan commented matter of fact. For the past two days, his face had the yellowy sheen of butter and I thought earlier I had noted a facial twitch developing. As for Magnus's it wasn't his fault that he was the typical Aryan, that he blew his nose in public with a cloth hankey or opened his jeans to the maximum when tucking in his T-shirt. Could he be held responsible for the doc Martins with white socks, or the double denim. Surely he was merely a product of his environment. Appearance aside academically he outshone the lot of us, it was the subtle understanding of the sarcastic undercurrent that let him down.

"Your round", Ryan informed him and bullied him up to the bar.

STORIES OF A DIGITAL SPALPEEN

I was beginning to enjoy the less hectic life in Salzburg. Magnus was very eager to hear about life in Ireland, the history, the literature and the music. Sometimes he knew more on a subject than me, the Joyce statue in Trieste or Che Guevara's Irish temper, all told to me without a hint of hubris. We were getting on so well that Magnus showed up again on the third night. I enquired did he come to the pub every night. He answered frankly that he was here only to see me and brought me a book *Stephenwolf*.

"Oh I said" as he handed it to me embarrassed.

"Beer ?" he asked the group, "Stige?"

I turned back to see if Ryan was watching, he was of course giving me a sarcastic nod of the head. With the beer Magnus ordered some pickled sausage, here try he said offering the fork to my mouth.

"Later Magnus" I responded recoiling at the misplaced intimacy looking round and sure enough there he was again Ryan.

"I'm telling you", he mouthed quietly, "he's after your sausage".

Mervin was eager to try, "Bierschinken wurst" he repeated after Magnus.

"Ja, it means, beer sausage".

"Beer Sausage," says Vincent, "now for ya".

"I'll stick to the chips" I said and ordered a plate. Magnus went to the toilet, another trait of the Aryan, keeping bowel movements regular.

I watched him walk back to his seat, Magnus, I remember he was wringing his hands when he gave me a delicate wink which caused the chip to go down the wrong way and shut like a trap door in my neck. I couldn't breathe. Gripping the table I eeked a wisp of air, in total shock, eyes watering. The boys beside me didn't notice a thing and were laughing away at a German television advert. I looked at Magnus and could see him marching towards me, a cloud forming over his normally pleasant countenance. His pace increased from a hurry to a rush, reaching the table and roaring loudly in German. I was at the point of passing out when he took me in an embrace and lowered my head into the cradle of his elbow.

"Oh right" says Ryan sitting up thinking the romance was finally underway. Magnus opened my mouth and stuck his finger in and swished it around as my eyes began to circle and I wondered if this was it for me. Failing the stir about, I was still hanging in by a thread, gasping, he lowered his mouth onto mine and blew deeply, once, twice then a third time.

He lifted his head and said "It is not verking" in a plaintive voice.

At the sound of that I thought it was curtains for sure, the indignity of dying on the upswept tiles of a barroom floor. As quickly as he lowered me he hoisted me again to a standing position, I wasn't sure what he was planning next. As I fluttered on my feet an almighty thud landed on my back and sent me stumbling forward wheeling towards the bar, all eyes focused on the chip that had dislodged itself and sailed spinning through the air landing splat on the mirror. I steadied myself on the counter, gasping mouthfuls of sweet air listening to Vincent congratulate Ryan on a job well done.

"Christ almighty, sure, it was only a little chipeen" Ryan replies.

I need to go to bed early after that, the lads stayed out. Magnus insisted he walk me to the hostel. I couldn't even look him in the eye after the surreal mouth to mouth episode. He would come to say *auf Wiedersehen* tomorrow. True to his word he arrived early doors with two girls, one he introduced as his sister and the other as his girlfriend.

"Girlfriend !" Ryan exclaimed with his eyes fixed on the sister, a healthy looking blond with hair as far down as her waist, she had a type of unguarded innocence about her that made him want to be a better man. If his sister was a good looking girl, the girlfriend was a stunner. They were childhood sweethearts he explained, maybe why he didn't mention. They were all going mountain biking, there being some perfect routes around Salzburg. Maybe next time he suggested and threw his arms around me for a hug.

We had a job to get on the train, Mervin turned Green on the platform and Vincent was comforting him. "Come on" Ryan demanded roughly and at that point.

I had enough of him and told him to "shut up".

He narrows his eyes and squares up to me pushing forward with his chest.

Vincent intervenes, "Aw now lads" feeling responsible that it was all his fault for bringing us together in the first place. Other, normal people boarding were taking a wide berth.

Mervin says "Oh God", bent over, hiccupped and let a lump of bile out on the platform.

Unaware I gave Ryan a good shove back for himself, he not only slips but slips and lands in the vomit then skids half off the platform. The soles on his standard issue college of surgeons deck shoes not moulded for vomit spills. Shocked at my own outburst of anger I grabbed my mouth. Ryan he let out the screech of a banshee heard throughout the whole vestibule of the station. People were stopping to look, aghast and amused. Vincent was now also very excited and started a jig.

Repeating over and over that "security were coming, cut out the shite hawking or we're all fucked".

Ryan did the best he could with the chinos in the small toilet but there remained a faint stench of sick. We sat in silence for the guts of an hour till Vincent said "The sister was a fine thing" and ushers us to go to the bar carriage leaving Mervin to sleep it off and mind the bags.

Ryan asks "Can I share her phone number ?".

We were in the bar by this stage. On the inside cover of Steppenwolf, it had listed Magnus's name, number and address. I opened the book on the table in front of Ryan, then closed it and handed it to him. He must have thanked me fifteen times as we rocked over and back heading west.

Prior to the trip, in my mind's eye, I would have been so fresh on arrival home, the sun would surely have done me good, instead, I was a crippled wreck with bloodshot eyes. I had pictured myself bouncing up the steps of the O'Reilly Institute to receive my final exam results but it turned out to be more of a crawl. Now that the chip money was blown on the continent and the lads had all split for Connolly, Heuston and Rathgar I was alone on Grafton street. I managed a coffee in Bewleys offering a few coins to a busker and then went to Tower Records to pass an hour on the sample albums. Results will be displayed in the afternoon by 13:00 the notification had said but the morning went so slowly, it was worse then choking on the chip. Entering the O'Reilly there was a buzz in the air, everyone focusing on their own thing which suited me perfectly as I wasn't in the mood for small talk. I wanted this to be over quick smart and got my head in somehow to search down the list of printed surnames, veering right to see the associated mark. There I was, I panicked, wondering did I see correctly ?, "is that a second class Honours a II.1 ?". Wait, calm yourself and take a breath to confirm. Yes there was no doubting it, I had done it, what was Manny going to say to this (won't be long till ya have ten men under ya). The relief was a tremendous feeling, not since I caught Caroline Conway in kiss catch had a sense of exaltation like this extended from top to toe. To celebrate I went to the Long Hall, ordered a lovely pint, found myself a snug and watched a tear slide delicately down my cheek and drop into it.

Normality took shape as I woke in my own bed, one booze free night back west of the Shannon. Out for a carton of milk for the cornflakes I ran into my old teacher Mr Cohen, he did his best to teach me "September 1916" for the guts of two years.

"Oh you were in Salzberg, the birthplace of Mozar", he began to get very excited, "I tell ya one thing I do like" he opined, "Schiel, now he was Avant Guard" and giggled before adding "on a serious note, any culture over there ?" he focused on me, the turtleneck and sports jacket elevated him from the average Culchie of the parish.

"Oy yes", I say as Vincent flashed through my mind fiddling with the buttons on the French maid outfit in Amsterdam. "He liked his nudes", I said to Mr Choen

"Sssh, Father Hegarty might hear you", he warned laughing before getting all serious again, "so tell me", the Leopold, I was there in '87, is it still magnificent ?"

"Oh, it is", he waited for more, I paused, then changing subject "Steppenwolf", have your read that one Mr Cohen ?", he took a huge breath to get all he knew on Steppenwolf out in the next passage.

I was saved or interrupted whichever way you might look at it by my old employer and owner of Sizzlers, J. J. Quirk. He was delighted to see me and wondered would I be back to Sizzlers. I told him that to be honest I had seen one chip too many. He didn't blame me, after Burns went out through the window two weeks ago he didn't have either the heart or the time for it anymore and had decided to get a woman in. Thanking him I slipped away with the Milk, passing the flowers in the buckets I couldn't help notice that the sign for Dutch Tulips had been tampered with, some smart arse had stroked out the Dutch and added the word "Some". I thought of the trip which it more or less summed up nicely, "Some Tulips".

The Two Paddies

Looking for a job was a shock to the system. After the failed attempt to make it in the music business as a bass player in Fibber Nix. With two gigs under our belt, one in the Leitrim Bar and the other in Kings which even included the advances of a groupie named Róisín it all came crashing down when the drummer Benny announced he was off to Australia and the mother wondered, when are you going to get a job ?. The bleach needed to be cut out, the earrings removed and respectable attire in the form of a suit required for the interviews. The tie officially strangled any individuality but I had to lie back and think of the money, welcome to the real world.

Thursday was the day that the Evening Press came out with the two-page spread, the job section. It was carefully laid out on the dining room table and a finger ran through the listings, Account needed, Senior Civil Engineer, Chef for well established business, none applying to me, Experienced nanny needed for part time position, I was still a child myself. This went on for weeks, where the Evening press went into the bin crumpled and I was spending more time on the guitar than the computer which in hindsight might have been a good thing but at the time it was becoming a critical situation where I was facing the growing scorn of the mother. Most of the positions were Dublin based and most were requesting experience, the few I applied for, Ada Programmer, Senior C Programmer, COBAL

D. M. O'DOWD

Engineer, Systems Architect all ended in deadly silence or template rejection letters.

Plucking the acoustic in my room one evening when a knock came to the door, the auld lad had the paper folded under his arm. "Here have a look at this" he handed it to me, circled in biro. "IT Graduate positions x 2", I looked up at him, "now for ya" he said.

"Where is it based ?" I wondered "Donegal be God".

I sent the CV and me brother Pat helped me with the cover letter, detailing the enthusiasm of a Labrador, work ethic of a Yak and communication skills of Lord Haw-Haw. The real truth laid bare in the interview conducted in a very official room, where Magee the IT Manager interrogated me. The place had a history I'll give it that, with adverts on the wall from a time when smoking was seen to glamorise any merchandise, when knitting was the old yoga, when Hush Puppies had their heyday. I was sure that at any moment, the butler would emerge from the wardrobe in the corner and shake some sense into me. It was during this critical hour of humming and hawing and at one point the loss of my voice altogether that I thought it was game over. In a vain effort to get back on the horse, under the scrutiny of a bemused Magee I grasped the glass of water on the walnut table but unable to control the quiver in my hand thought better and repatriated it to the table. Magee peered at me while I did. There were no further questions. You might imagine my surprise when the offer letter arrived, apparently not many from the Pale would relocate to the hills, the mother nearly danced around the kitchen. Start date two weeks.

STORIES OF A DIGITAL SPALPEEN

If the job hunt was suffocating, then the job itself was like seven years in Tibet. Venerated Priests have sat in confession boxes for shorter periods of time. Chained to the desk for a solid eight hours per day under a vow of silence while myself and James, the other graduate from IT Athlone went through our training which was a series of recorded cassette tapes. The adenoidal tones of the instructor gently rocked me to sleep daily.

"How are ye getting on with the training ?" Magee would ask.

"Great altogether" we all agreed.

"Great" Magee would say and snap his heels and walk into his office which was next door, now with two graduates he could really say he was managing an innovative team, the two of us along with Bernie, a soft spoken Donegal woman who had recently returned to Donegal form London with her husband and Artist of Irish extraction. I learned a lot more from Bernie than the tapes at least about Life and the adventures that lay beyond these four walls.

I will say however there were some pillows of relief (from the tapes) through the day, the two tea breaks at 10.30 and 3.30 when Joyce came around with the tea and coffee and digestive biscuits (there was an electric kettle in the kitchen upstairs but it was frowned upon to be so brazen and make oneself a cup of tea), lunch in the canteen (which could end up as a stressful interview if we were invited to sit with the managers) and meeting Eileen Gallager for a smoke after work, Eileen had started on the same day as me, the shared experience giving us a lot to talk about.

D. M. O'DOWD

"Well" Magee says handing me the first envelope, "Go easy now" he says and all I could do was bow and look creepy. The quaver was back in my hand tearing down the perforated edges and slipping out the rectangular chit, my eyes burning on the figure on the bottom right, £1090, all for me, every punt and penny. I held it to my lips ensuring that no one else was around and gave it a delicate kiss. I was now a self made man.

I showed it to the mother who was delighted, it didn't cross my mind that I owed her a box of dairy milk or a bunch of roses. It never entered my thoughts that it was all down to her endeavours that I had made it this far, her poking the ceiling with the broom to get me out of bed in the mornings, her putting the money together for my digs in Rathmines, her insisting that I was well able for honours maths. I was too heady in the head with the thought of going straight into town to buy a new pair of corduroy drainpipes and the Converse high tops that I had spotted, then down to Shoot the Crows with the swagger of a casual drinker before heading to Harrys where I met with Bosco and Mossy, both of who were as delighted as me at the windfall, both of whom I give a sub of twenty followed by another top up to bring us to Cleos. With the windfall a new confidence flowered, so as any woman within an asses bawl was offered a Pernod and Black. I could even afford the taxi home, thinking of all the nights I walked the roads or slept on the bushes of family bungalows. "Keep the change," I said with a knowing nod of the head, pre-empting the taxi driver having to root for the change. At Mass the next morning I reached new levels of philanthropy and put a fiver in the basket. Back in Harrys for a Sunday session where we met the Horse and Spud, Bosco and Mossy joined later and needed another sub to keep the craic going, the hours melted away and suddenly we were landed back in Cleos on the Pernod. We must have had half a dozen when the national anthem started, Bosco was across from me asleep with this head cradled in his arms. He was at the end of a long table next to him a group from Frehchpark. What about work ?, the sudden thought of it sent a red alert to the brain to straighten up but me body somehow miscalculated attempting to lay an elbow on the table and missed it completely, crumpling to the ground, the socket of my eye landing squarely on the ball of the knee of the girl from Frenchpark whom Mossy had been trying earlier. She screamed, everyone jumped up (except Bosco), glasses crashed from the table to the floor, my head along with them and that is the last I remember.

The morning broke with panic, I stumbled to the mirror. My head pounding like a Lambeg drum. I stood for a moment grasping the sink my eyes firmly closed while I prayed to God that it was all a bad dream, that I had somehow imagined the whole collapse. The vein to the side of my eye pumping like the Kronk. On the count of three, one, two, three, I opened, oh no, I didn't recognize myself, it was like a different person staring back at me, someone feckless, hopeless, worthless. It was already nine o'clock and the mother knocked on the ceiling with the handle of the broom.

"Are you up yet?", she called, just like she used to do when I was a schoolboy.

Magee looked at me and didn't say much for a long time, "it looks bad" he proffered finally, "I think you better take yourself down to the doctor". I stood carefully to do so wondering if I should make one final effort to convince him the eye was not the result of a fight. I decided against it, he was obviously making every effort to be as stoic as possible and to apply the same principle and leave as soon as possible was the wiser option. I might only light the famous fuse.

"You know that this means that I have to give you a warning also", he added further catching me before I had gotten out the door.

"Ye, yes," I said ashamed of myself for not having the courage to even look back.

The doctor proposed a hospital admission.

"You are badly bruised," she advised "and need to have a scan to be on the safe side".

Going through the form as she spoke. Before I knew it I was on a public ward, Optometry, in a hospital nightgown that covered everything but my arse. To my left, Paddy from Ballyshannon eighty four with cataracts in both eyes and to my right Paddy from Ballybofey eighty six with a scratched cornea from a stubborn blackthorn that rebelled back on him two days earlier. We quickly built a brotherhood with the understanding that we were all in this together and to get to the smoking room we needed one another for the purpose of navigation. I led Paddy Ballyshannon on the left arm and Paddy Ballybofey on the right both in the Pyjamas, nightgown and slippers me in hospital issues. We walked at the speed of an Easter Mass. At one point we taking a turn into Xray but who cared because we had no appointments

STORIES OF A DIGITAL SPALPEEN

to get to or places to be and once we got there we would spend a couple of hours smoking and chatting about the Black Bread, the Blueshirts and Banjos and as long as we were back for the three scoops of instant spuds and the bowl of trifle nothing else mattered.

As a result of the pedestrian days, at night I lay awake, listening for sounds from the nurses station not able to sleep. Paddy Ballybofey did a savage amount of work in his sleep, dipping sheep and bulling cows and cocking hay, once or twice he got so excited he leapt out of the bed and gave me the nudge to head out with him, that the brows cow in the back field was calving. It took me twenty minutes to get him back into the bed only on the promise that the AI man and the Vet were above with her. Paddy Ballyshaoon snored all the while, it was a kind of sonorous snore of a man that once played up and down the country in a showband, Dickie Rock, The Miami Showband, Big Tom, not to mention Philomena Begley he knew them all.

Three days later my eye was beginning to resemble its normal self, the CAT scan revealed no lasting damage and the blurry vision was normalizing. The spuds didn't taste any better but the stories form the Paddies kept me entertained. They were both married young, both lived in England for a while but that's where the similarities ended. Paddy Ballybofey worked the land, met his wife Katleen in the Galtymore in Cricklewood, built a house with the money he saved in a sock and, they had four children together. He liked a pint and loved a smoke. Paddy Ballyshannon never really had a real job except for the thousand jobs he did over the years. His real was vocation music although the showband scene was in decline from the eighties. He loved a pint and ate the cigarettes. His marriage didn't last but he did have one daughter, Katie.

"There were too many distractions" he said with a big chesty laugh.

Paddy Ballybofey remembered the showbands, "Sure they were great times" he recalled although there wasn't much money in the country at the time.

Mossy had visited a day earlier, on request he brought in a pair of track suit bottoms and a few bottles of Guinness, The Farmers Journal and a Hustler tucked in between the folds. He joined us as we sipped on the Guinness in the smoking area and continued on with the discussions.

I should have been delighted to be discharged. I had my Magee bag with my few bits ready to go but feeling sorry for myself as I watched them both inch down the corridor to the smoking room. I should have been right there with them heading for that smoke and chat but instead, I had to go back and face the music with Magee. Before leaving I had one final task, under each of their pillows I slipped some reading material, Paddy Ballybofey The Farmers Journal and Paddy Ballyshannon The Hustler magazine. I could picture the confoundment on their faces when they put the two and two together. I was down to my last eighty quid and was sure I would end up in the same position in the following weeks where I would meekly knock on the mother's bedroom door, get her out of bed and mumble a request for a sub of twenty quid. Except this time it would be even harder because I was supposed to be the young gun, big earner. Work was a peaceful penance, keeping as low a profile as possible, delighted at the thought of being bored in the one place for each of the eight hours of each of the five days, the tea never tasted so good and the digestive were crumbly heaven. The monotonous voice on the cassette tapes was now like a fatherly comfort to me. I learned as much as I could and before I knew it another month was done, the eye was healed, the incident was history and Magee was round with the pay slips.

He handed it to me and said nothing but raised the eyebrows as a kind of warning. I needed the complete privacy of the bathroom to open it, slipping in the latch on one of the stalls and sitting on the plastic lid. Thinking back to the talk of the formal warning and what it actually meant, were they docking my pay ?, would I actually have to pay them? Slipping out the chit, a flower flushed on my face realizing the figure was an even greater amount than the last one, £1,118, did they make a mistake? or what was it that thing Magee had mentioned about the emergency tax? I was back in the pink, my head spinning with the torrent of thoughts and lessons of the last month, the austerity facing Paddy Ballybofey when raising the family through the hard times, the practised patience of my mother, the wisdom of Magee who was obviously delaying any formalities to give me a second chance. Yes, this time I would for sure show more maturity, certainly I would be more responsible to my employer, absolutely I would forego the ephemeral pleasures of pubs and pussy (as the hustler called it) for my future self and the people around me. There was however that leather jacket that I had in mind that would go so well with the drainpipes and Caroline Conway's twenty-first was on in

D. M. O'DOWD

Harry's on Friday night, with a band, a DJ, cocktail sausages and a gang down from Dublin. Oh then there was the big one on Sunday, the day of my previous capitulation, the day of the County final. Phew, it was all too much to contemplate. The huge decision of which of the two roads, which of the two destinies, which of Paddies I actually wanted to follow.

The Three Marys

Vincent and Nula were always going to be the first to settle down and make babies. By talking to her you would think the sun shone out his arse. "A mountain of a man", who wouldn't be stopping short at the Beef or Salmon, no no, "the prawn sandwich was travelling west of Roosky". That was only the start of it, ever since the lorry-load of neat magnolia envelopes were dispatched to the diaspora a fortnight earlier, the rumours were bubbling like blisters. An invite list as long as your leg, if you weren't on it you might as well be straightening bananas in Ballyhanius, from the political elite to the piss-ant on the street, they were all scrambling for hotels and B&B's, chronologically listed on the accompanying information sheet in posh order. The fake tan was flying off the shelves in Cahan's Chemists, unless you were coming pre-cooked from Brisbane or Bangkok, which they were, by the jumbo jet with Cousin Cornelius Cardinal of California flying in especially to say the mass. Mention of a free bar had them whipped into a frenzy till it got out of hand altogether, with word coming from the midlands of an all-night vigil by the grave of Joe Dolan in Ballynacargy[1] following reported cries of "oh me oh my"

---

1. https://www.google.co.uk/
search?biw=1536&bih=760&q=Walshetown+Cemetery&stick=H4sIAAAAA
AAAAOPgE-
LSz9U3MCwoyrNMUeLVT9c3NEwqL04zs0wr1FLMTrbSL0jNL8hJ1U9JTU
5NLE5NiS9ILSrOz7NKKi3KTE0BADcu7W9AAAAA&sa=X&ved=0ahUK
EwjUjau6t7vTAhVNZVAKHdTrDvUQmxMItAEoATAY

heard emanating up and would shortly be followed by an eruption for the wedding of the decade. A bit far-fetched says you but you wouldn't put it past the influence of the pioneers, weren't they praying day and night the sun would make an appearance for the photos. As it turned out, by luck or divine intervention, it did, the rehearsal mass, the big day itself and the afters beamed bright with a bountiful golden sunlight, unheard of in the West even for June. Some said the turlough in Lisananny had evaporated overnight but I suppose that was just another one with legs on it.

For me the sunlight is recalled as a grainy explosion through the side window of Shanahan's Golf, slowly warming my crumpled coil. The stagnant smell of tepid dog and lukewarm porter farts roused me from slumber, head like a crockpot. Reaching out, I remember fingering clumps of hair and calling her name, "Mary, is that you ?". No response other than a heavy panting. "Mary ?" I uttered again in the voice of a child, reaching and searching for her, unbundling myself to seating. A lonesome whine echoed close to me and I began to wonder was she feeling ok ?. Apparently healthy, I was jolted by the prodding of a wet spongy tongue to the base of my neck. "Oh Mary," I said turning round to get down to business but met by muzzle, "a fucking sheep dog", I was now fully awake, in the car park of the Woodside Inn, "how did I get here ?". Mossy's mooning face appeared in the window to my right of me delighted with himself. My new best friend was drooling at the mouth and looked on in wonderment until Mossy started knocking on the window which set her off with a volley of barks like maracas, no the Gypsy Kings in stereo, no worse, closer to the gunshots of a Mountbatten pheasant hunt, my head was mush.

"Mossy you cunt", I croaked.

He laughed, pretending not to hear.

"You're a pure cunt" I roared.

"Wha ?" he said.

The outlines Bosco and Shanahan I could make out, standing further off, Bosco with the collar of the jacket half up half down, still half cut by the looks of things, Shanahan cupping a fag, releasing ragged plumes of smoke with a spring of the elbow, impressed by his own strength. Bosco made a move towards the pub window and with a coin or a key and tapped quickly three times, shortly after the barrel lock rumbled, a lower latch snapped and the key cranked, the poke of Angela's bed head as she looked the stragglers up and down, checked for Garda before clearing the way. "You're some Mary" I said and out the two of us got from the car making our way to join the others.

Where to start, where to start at all ?. I remember the church, wasn't it lovely ?, fresh flowers in big bunches, neat white roses and dried Gypsophila tied with mauve ribbons. Threads of tart incense drifted from the parapet and filled the nave with heavenly fragrance. Bright banners from the national school hung gallant on all pillars. Despite all that we were no sooner within than we were off again, down for Harry's, clipping the footpath. You knew it was going to be a good day when your half cut at half one and Cardinal Cornelius of California giving the final blessing. We were on the high stool before they burst through the door like the animals let off the Ark, Nuala and all in the wedding dress.

D. M. O'DOWD

Let me tell you about the fashion, it was everywhere, Ralf Lauren had made a killing, the little man on the horse was galloping on every second shirt, not to mention the women, goose skin in latticed chiffon or Tangerine loins wrapped in polyester noir, the essential clutch bag ubiquitous, replete with overpowering floral scent, administered liberally and often. The bonhomie rose to a seven with hands grabbing me left and right as I tried to make my way to Councillor Perry, "howya now" and "Who taught you to tie a tie ?". It was still only half eleven in the morning.

Back in the Woodside Mossy enquired, "If I was alright ?" observing me in my quasi catatonic state folded over a dirty pint. In contrast, he seemed sound as a pound swirling a brandy and port in a half one glass.

"Great for the stomach" he claimed, and with a scrape of the stool on the tiles he stood and went for a piss.

"Where did we go after Harrys ?" I asked myself and just as I did she flashed into my conscience, standing Amazonian in her little black number on the edge of the dance floor, undecided whether to join in or not. I was back in the moment recalling the sight that had sent surges of molten lust through my veins. That was my Mary. "The Thatch !" we went to the Thatch after Harrys, and the kaleidoscope of images focused momentarily again on a different time and place. The front bar of the thatch and all its colourful halcyon artefacts from the days of cocking hay and riding in the hedges. We bundled in with Marty and downed another scatter of pints before Marty's phone went off wondering where he was and off we were again with two additions, Fagan and Flanagan who we ran into earlier. It was a tight squeeze with the six of us. Fagan was known as Ferrari Fagan and was very particular about the suit not wanting to crease it, it having been bought new with the tag still on the cuff, the hair greased like a man from Eaton who spent summers in Verona or cycling through the Swiss alps, yodelling as he went. Speaking of the Swiss Alps, didn't we stop for two German back packers at the bridge in Ballysadare ?. Marty sponged the clutch glided into the grassy verge and hung the elbow out, "Which way are ye headed ladies ?". Looking in they wondered where they might fit, oh but they fitted alright.

Shanahan shouted a round and Angela left down the cloth she was wiping down the bar with.

"You`re quiet" he remarked impressed with his own resolve.

"Sick" I replied.

"I suppose you are" he repeated composing himself for a pull of the pint, impressed with his own resolve and capacity.

Truth was I was busy trying to recollect my first vision of her, the when's and where's. It came to me, slowly through the course of the pint, she was seated some five tables away chatting with Mary, Marty's sister, she was folding and unfolding the white linen napkin as they chatted. It didn't take the boys long to put a name on her, Mary something or other, a friend of Marty's sister who was also a Mary as mentioned. They had studied physiotherapy together in Manchester. All through the dinner, I couldn't take my eyes off her, all through the conversation with John Cawley and the wife asking about the job and how was my mother. I couldn't just help it, every time I went to answer John or the wife my eyes were drawn in her direction. She went to the toilet, I followed her every footstep, I went for the bar returning to make sure she had remained in position, a thought of slim hope she might have noticed me gone entered my mind but wishful thinking, she was yapping away still to Marty's sister. All through the speeches, I was glued to her, watching the ripples of laughter flowing across her face as Marty's speech went from the story of Vincent's day on the bog, uncovered asleep in the transport box after twenty minutes footing to the time he joined the boxing club and tried to talk his way out of a fight. Nuala's at the top table radiated happiness, surrounded by her family and friends, food and drink. Of all the times in the flat in Dublin as students and Nuala smoked fags and ate Tuc biscuits and talked of Love , "it was only for women and soft shites I used to say". I was only rising her of course, I wanted to tell her that now.

The band started up, "Four Roads to Glenamaddy" and they were all out throwing shapes but dancing just isn't my thing unless of course there was a mosh pit involved so I brooded at the bar. And that was where the most poignant image emanates from, her remaining on the outline of the dancefloor, Akimbo, Amazonian as mentioned before suddenly she was taken away from me as Mary, Marty's sister catapulted from the crowd, latched on to her and gobbled he into the sweaty Forrest of freewheeling arms and twirling ties. Marty was in there too, the sweat coming off him in buckets, Fagan and Flanagan churning arms like a pair of new Romantics. I feigned interest in conversation with Mick O'Donnell as a ruse to stalk her. Mick complained about the terrible gas in the Carlsberg after a feed of pavlova. I grunted, he went on and on and on about it and let rip a terribly smelly fart but what could I do ?, what could I do but endure it, I didn't want to lose my spot. In fact I must have remained rooted to that spot for a good hour, tearing the collar off the shirt with frustration when they arrived, both gasping for Gin and tonic after the fast set. My heart tumbled between them and dropped on the floor, along with my jaw. I straightened up and side-eyed them up and down, left and right, true, her jawline a little more angular than from afar, her thighs a little stouter, but there was no doubting she was all woman, accentuated by her heaving chest which I was now fixated on to the point where I'm sure Mrs Clancy had noticed. As the drinks landed on the counter I made my move.

"Let me get these ladies" I interjected with a pair of folded fivers extended between my fingers.

There were no complaints from the ladies while the Gin kept coming they weren't budging until close to completing the third, Mary Marty's sister said she would be right back, leaving me alone with my Mary. "Mon Dieu" the moment I had been waiting for, ordering another and indulging in flirtations conversations, I slid a hand on her hip and wasn't sure which one of us was more surprised by this act of audacity, either way, her chest was heaving heavily again and we creaked in towards one another, the rose water scent of her skin wafting closer and closer. We were on the cusp of a kiss until a voice rung louder than the church bell.

"Didn't I know it" she said "I can't leave ye for ten minutes", exclaims the other Marty's Mary.

Our bubble of bliss burst but it got worse, my own sister Izzy happened to be passing at the time.

"Oh" she says, "is there anything I need to be telling Mammy ?". "As they say, it takes one wedding to make another."

Then Marty's Mary pipes in and the two of them had a laugh out loud moment. I didn't find it so funny and wouldn't have minded so much if we actually had shifted but all this was making me go red as the tomato soup so I quietly reminded her of the time she landed home with the beard rash and the love bites but alas all in vain, she laughed it off introducing herself. Fagan appeared on my shoulder his panache still intact, held her hand with the care of a jeweller imparting a delicate kiss left of centre and says "Enchanter", I nearly got sick. The game was up I assumed with sight of Mossy and Bosco rounding the pillar wondering if I had any interest in a venture up the town for a pint, a ride, and a bag of chips, to which I insisted "no" and "no" again. Where would it end ?, The Bore Mc Bride appeared, Towie roaring not talking and the Terror Quigley after me for a half one and a pay day loan, which incidentally I handed over with a fake smile not wanting to look cheap in front of her. Standing back, I was surrounded, every man in the parish, all talking at the one time. I wouldn't mind but Quigley never worked a day in his life and hadn't even been invited to the wedding.

Now Angela might have the look of a plate of porridge but as they say, never judge a book, she made up a dozen of ham sandwiches, "I hadn't eaten the whole day yesterday had I ?". I didn't remember, not even a prawn puff that they were all talking about. I thanked Angela and called for a round, and she obliged. I was beginning to warm up, so was my brain and my memory, which led me to the Chez long in the lobby of the hotel her my Josephine me Napoleon returning from Africa or Russian or some similar unforgiving terrain. The Staff were starting the routine of the day, the hoovers hummed, Windolene squeaked against the glass. The sing song had finished up only an hour ago and only a handful of guests remained bent over chairs. After the interruption from Marty Mary and me sister, it took several hours to get in position again, till everyone got so drunk eventually it didn't matter but once we started there was flowno separating us, she could kiss like she could talk, at international level. So much so her chin was blushing now. I noticed that she was coming for me again, like a great white, it made for an awkward moment as I was trying to sit up and compose myself at the time. "A cup of tea in the breakfast room" I suggested and we made our way across the lobby arm in arm the laces on my shoes open but what did it matter? She was chirpy as ever and while I couldn't face a thing other than the tea she handled the full Irish taking great care to mop up the last of a runny egg with the boxty before leaning across the table to kiss me deeply.

"Mammy will be in to collect me soon" she said as she peeled away and I was in two minds.

By the looks of things, It didn't matter what I thought as she spotted Marty Mary and Fagan at the far end of the room. Fagan was leafing through the Times, taking care to dab his thumb each time he turned the page, the ladies were highly excited to see one another and picked up where they left off with me left wondering where they got all this energy.

Mammy arrived and Mammy got a big hug and the three of them sat in the high back chairs beside the fire which was kindling nicely. Oh call me Mary" the mother said as I brought her first Gin. Another Mary !.

"If she had known she was staying for one she would have made more of an effort" she said.

That went on for an hour with myself and Fagan up and down to the bar replenishing Gin and coffee with dainty hotel shortbread as they warmed their legs. On the odd occasion, Mary would let the other two at it for a while and turn her attention to me wondering "if I was alright", and might I be so quiet before launching into me for a Frenchie.

"Oh Mammy doesn't mind" she insisted noting my reluctance.

At one point they were on the verge of agreeing a departure until Fagan unfolded the legs and offered another libation to the ladies which didn't require any arm twisting. Mammy was thrilled with the spontaneity of it all insisting she was dressed like a tramp in the leggings and a cardigan. She had been doing the housework when her daughter called.

"Right," I said to meself asking Fagan for the key of the room to let me at least have a shower.

I stayed in there long as I could bear it, till I was half scalded but back down at the bar they remained in position and I caught them with fresh empties which I was obliged to refill. I was beginning to wonder if this was some kind of sick joke but bouncing back on the wagon helped mellow my resentment and by the end of the first couple I was even participating in trivial conversation. Mammy loved me of course, why wouldn't she, her daughter was blooming and I was keeping her going in Gin. Fagan folded the paper neatly and quietly enquired.

"Did I ride Mary ?", which I didn't answer instead retorting with my own enquiry.

"Did he ride Marty`s Mary ?".

Now heading for the afternoon the hotel bar was filling steadily, Mossy and Bosco landed, they were heading into town to watch the game.

"Would I be interested ?"

"When was I ever not ?"

Was there the assumption that I was now attached at the hip ?

Angela put up another round and lifted the money from the bar without a word. It was such a pleasure to be in her company, she understood men, knew when we wanted conversation and when to steer clear. Shanahan, Mossy and Bosco were carefully dissecting the whole affair, most closely the fight, the free bar which lasted only an hour but a good hour and Cara Hamilton who was home from England and looking fine but was off limits because she is going with an English toff. The prawn puffs even got a mention, Shanahan had never seen, never mind eaten a prawn before, "a bit like a sausage roll" his headline.

"Where did your woman go in the end" Bosco fired a query.

"Wha?" I responded trying to buy some time which annoyed Shanahan.

D. M. O'DOWD

"Do you want to go back out with the dog? he queried, impressed with his own wit.

"Where did she go in the end ?" well that was a good question. She was definitely watching the Liverpool game with interest, Mammy alongside her, Fagan and the other Mary cooing at one another on the high stool. Marty, Mossy, Bosco and the boys were further up the bar.

"Great craic going on up there" Mammy remarked. Oh there was, great craic indeed and here was me stuck with the likes of you and just then the final whistle sounded and all the boys along the bar drank up and made shapes.

"Where ye off to ?" I grabbed Mossy.

"Up to Molloy's."

An so to Molloy's with myself and the three Marys and from Molloy's to Corcran's, Cosy Joes, and onto the West where Mammy played pool with Fagan and the lads. "Where was this going to end at all ?". I was flagging as Mammy and the Marys went from strength to strength. With a flurry of jackets and a generous squirt of white musk and we were on the move again, from bad to worse, we were in the queue for *the Limit*, a light drizzle starting to come down, it was dark at this stage. "If I had known" Mammy remarked fixing the hair and mentioning the leggings again.

"Oh your grand Manny," says Mary, the little black number serving her well, I wondered "Would she be in the leggings tomorrow ?". The club was hot and sweaty and dark, the music was loud and unnerving but didn't intrude on the Gin consumption which continued at a pace funded by myself and Fagan who at this stage had an uncharacteristic look close to weary. The chat didn't end either, it continued but at an increase of ten decibels as Mary and Mary`s Mammy took turns to bend my ear, left one then right and that's where my memory ebbed, soon after I went on top shelf to help me see out the night.

When I woke in Shanahan's car, smiling away to myself in the golden silence, I thought it was heaven till the lick from the dog. She was here beside me now, man's best friend, I was enjoying a pint she was cracking away on a bone. Bosco ordered another round and Angela was on it like a racing snail. I was going to turn into an all-day session and tomorrow I would drag myself home. My sister would be mad for all the news, annoyed with my terse grunts. She wouldn't give up though wondering where was that lovely girl I met, "what was her name again, Mary?" "How did we get on after that ?" I would look at her, and wouldn't know where to start.

The Life of Lobster

The decision was made based on a phone conversation which progressed as, "I have a job and all for ya" he yelled down the line his words almost drowned out by the background Rí Rá.

"Where are you calling from ?, I can barely hear ya," I said straining from the deadly silence in the small hall in the house at home.

"We're in Sean Og's" he said as if I should know where that might be.

"Mossy is banging one of the bar maids here" he roared over the music that had just started up in the background.

"What's she like ? "I requested urgently.

"Ah don't you know Mossey, she's a fucking ride" he said coming back to me eventually.

"A ride" I said in dismay pacing up and down the hall bristling with nervous energy. "Any other craic over there ? " I asked.

"Savage craic altogether" he said struggling to find his mouth with the receiver.

"Are you still there ? .." I said, "hello ....." "Bosco", I could hear him in the background ordering a double JD and coke when someone let out a wild cackle of devilment. "Hello" I repeated but to my disgust the line was dead as a doorknob.

"Who was that ?" the mother enquired from inside in the living room, as usual wanting to know the in's and out's of everything. I didn't have the will to reply.

"Savage fucking craic" I repeated to myself.

STORIES OF A DIGITAL SPALPEEN

I gave a knock on Magee's door and entered. The air was stagnant with particles of dust dancing in and out of the shafts of daylight squeezing in through the kinked blinds. Magee was initially composed but went mad from behind the desk, his face lighting as red as the hair on his head when I told him straight out I was leaving. After all the investment in training on Programming and Database design at IBM Ireland (Ballsbridge) he implored. Not that I had learned much mind you, other than the nightly harangue from the auld barfly on the virtues of coddle.

"Are you sure this is what you want ? " he enquired maybe initially more so for his own good than mine "Harin off to New York without a proper job or a visa ?". There was a silence. "Hmmm ......" he prompted " Is that what you want ?" he repeated, placing his hands in the side pockets of his tweed blazer.

I twitched, I squinted, I questioned, and then I answered .... "it is" I confirmed.

On my last day, I waited for the Bus. The hill glistened with a weak sun perpetually drying the rain-soaked street. There wasn't a sinner to be seen other than the odd customer in and out of Maggie's for bread or milk or something to shut the child up. The old stalwart building where I had spent my days looked peaceful after the flurry of excitement instigated by the weekend clock out. I felt bad for Mc Gee he wasn't a bad skin and eventually managed to talk himself up to a hand shake and a man hug. I left my head against the window and followed the road folding home, the afternoon sun swaddled the verdant slopes of Benbulben, the silver barks of birches reflecting at its base, a solitary gull heaved through the mackerel sky. It would be the last time I'd sit half drunk on this old cunt of a bus. The world was my lobster. That much I was sure of.

She was a ride alright, a handsome sensuous brunette with Angelina Jolie lips.

"She kept birds all over her apartment in cages" Mossy explained, "she lets them out to frit and frolic when we're in the throws of passion" he uttered quickly before she had reached us. "Hey Megan, meet my buddy, he's just arrived" he said giving her the dolorous eyes.

She extended her smooth arm across the bar "We'll, we will have to drink to that'" she said with a smirk and plied us with bottle after bottle of American beer with chasers of Tequila and Goldslager, Zambuka and baby Guinness till the legs were bending beneath me from drink and jetlag and hunger.

"Jaysus, you must be starving" Bosco says finally a revelation coming to him and off they took me to the diner directly across the road for a big feed of Biscuits and Gravy, Salad with a choice of seven dressings as well as coffee and flapjacks.

"You can get anything here" Bosco exclaimed referring to Woodside, "even a bottle of Buckfast if you know the right man".

In fairness, the feed indeed was a tonic but the glare of the lights nearly blinded me and the ebullient waitresses whizzing in an out between tables packed with punters left me light headed.

"Top up sir ?"

"Ye, ye, yes please".

STORIES OF A DIGITAL SPALPEEN

With a full belly, my head was flagging slowly in the direction of the formica tabletop when suddenly we were off again. Mossey had me by one arm, Bosco by the other.

"Surley were not off for a hair cut lads" I protested, heading in the direction of *blazing blades* "Not at this time of night ?", "Surely not?"", I'm too fucked" I groaned half in disbelief.

Sure as shit the Salon door belied the low light, it open. I slipped from their grip horizontally into the long low lazy boy. Not knowing if I was awake or asleep, I watched emerging in a shuffle from the dusk of the doorway the silhouette of a beautiful woman. Her white silk gown draped open exposing her wholesome cleavage, French knickers and washboard mid rift. Her ebony hair fell in caramel cascades as she strode towards us.

"What will it be fellas ?" she asked confidently flashing her bleached white teeth.

"He's just off the boat" Mossy beamed as Bosco blushed looking down at his high tops.

"Got it boys" she nodded knowingly and turned to me dragging a long crimson nail along the length of my cheek. I groaned in final helpless protest.

"Is it yourself Magee ?" I said instantly recognising his dulcet tones.

"Just said I would give you a call" he said almost nervously "See how your getting on over there ?".

"Oh mighty" I said half lying.

"Oh, that's great to hear" he responded sounding genuinely pleased for me. "what about work ?" he enquired, "Did ya get the start ? ".

"I did" I assured him "just a bit of labouring to keep me going, a warehouse build in New Jersey, hard going at times, but sure a bit of hard work never did anyone any harm" I spewed, excusing the cop out of getting a real job.

"I suppose it doesn't" he agreed only slightly suspicious "but don't lose sight of your ambitions" he suggested.

"Oh not a tall" I assured him, intoning surprise.

"I suppose it's a great city to be young in" he mused, heaving a sigh "With the ethnic cultures and museums and all of that", I agreed it was a cosmopolitan metropolitan but not so in Woodside where us culchies were falling over one another.

"I have always wanted to visit the Guggenheim" he continued on an artistic theme, "Warhole, pop art and all that".

"I'm more a Walt Disney man myself" I joked, trying to keep it on a light-hearted level, steering him away from the realities of the rat race. The nights I lay flat on the mattress holding my shredded hands in the air profusely apologising having put them through the torment of the breeze block. The physical torture was a cross in itself but having to dance across the half arsed scaffolding at the command of the Ape Connolly a nefarious bastard of a Mayo ganger was pure unadulterated untapped psychological torture. Swiping strools of greasy hair from his face he screeched at random, "What the fuck are ya at ?", "over here, muck quick, muck", "Jaysus Christ, did they not learn you that in school". The list was endless. The thought was pointless.

Magee politely concluded the call, "Anyways sure I won't be keeping you" he said, "just a quick call to say hello is all".

STORIES OF A DIGITAL SPALPEEN

On a normal day he might be taking me to the Castle or Mc Caffertys for a quiet pint and a plate of oysters, I could almost taste the sea and the gushing waves of creamy porter but resisted the meanderings thoughts of home, I wasn't about to give up just yet, I didn't want him to lose faith. I had a plan, I was bringing Kelly over.

Why the professor liked us was hard to know, he was educated in the English public school system, was ten years older and earned a good wedge. The theory was simple, we kept him young and drunk. He was fine with an addition to the apartment the lease of which had his name on it. Mossy on the other hand was reluctant, "Kelly was a loose Cannon" he said. Bosco was fine either way. Kelly was mad he agreed but he was a good laugh along with it. Mossy was outvoted, Kelly approved and we resumed normal activities smoking a big reefer while he took me apart in a game of chess. Not my usual frustrated self having played into the professor's Italian game I soaked it up content that the Kelly plan was in motion. We were ramping up in NJ and there was the demand for a labourer, Kelly would fit nicely, any shit from the Ape and I could call on Kelly to sort him out. The other string to Kelly's bow was that he was a pugilist of boundless talent but like many a flawed genius it was hard to keep him on the rails. I had spoken to the Boss man Whitey well known in boxing circles along with the brother Eddie for running the *Hibernian* stable. I had Kelly talked up to such levels that Whitey agreed to pay his fare along with the job, "he can't be any worse than some of the duds we've had over in the last few years" Whitey said with little hope. "You won't be sorry" I assured him.

D. M. O'DOWD

Kelly stepped off the seven train, the village voice tucked under his oxen, striding forth with the confidence of a wall street trader. We made straight for Sean Og's where he lashed back a dozen bottles, the Biscuits and Gravy in the Copper Kettle didn't touch the sides. In Donovan's, he popped a button on the shirt saying he could get used to it over here. On to *Blazin Blades* where he embraced Emmanuel (previously known as the dark commanding shuffle) with the confidence of Hamlet, her submitting willingly, his Ophelia. They slipped into the night through the *private entrance, and* after that we lost track of him, for days.

"Do I look stupid to you ?" a dangerous question from Whitey "Haa, do I ?" his voice growing harsher.

"No Boss, no" I responded in an appeal to his reasonable side, which didn't work.

"Do you think I'm some kind of a dumb ass eejit ?" he went on working himself up, drawing his big paw through the thick floss of cotton white hair.

Not a time to be facetious I gave him the specifics only, "I'll have him here tomorrow."

"You fucking better" he replied.

"I fucking will" I assured him.

"You fucking better" he replied.

I was feeling the hot flush of desperation just before the phone rang. It was Megan with a message, Kelly was above in Sean Og's, Emanuel wrapped round him like a cobra, Kelly the consummate Gentleman attending to her every need.

"They're a really cute couple," Megan said innocently before passing over the phone.

STORIES OF A DIGITAL SPALPEEN

I gave him *cute* for a solid ten minutes till I got tired of listening to the sound of my own voice. Kelly the living libertine laughed it off telling me I'd be dead by thirty three if I didn't learn to relax. I told him he'd be fucking dead by Tuesday if he didn't show up for work and hung up the phone. He rang back. He said for sure he wouldn't dream of missing work and would never under no circumstance let me down. I told him he had already let me down. He corrected himself, saying it would take effect from Monday and invited me for a drink to clear the slate. I felt a bit better about that and said I would accept the peace offering. He said he knew I was a reasonable man and while I was it could I manage a sub, to bring it along with me when I was coming.

A sub I enquired, "How much are u looking for ?"

"Five hundred should cover it" he said without knocking a stir out of himself.

I told him to "go fuck himself" and hung up.

He rang back. I told him "I hadn't a pot to piss in never mind the five hundred greenbacks".

He asked me to "ask the professor".

I told him to "ask the professor himself."

He said "he and the professor had not established a relationship of trust like he and I".

I told him to "trust me sister" and hung up.

He rang back. He said "he would need to leave New York, that he hadn't a penny to his name with outstanding debt needing immediate attention if I knew what he meant".

I hung up, confused, "did I know what he meant?" "No, I didn't know what he meant, loan shark, drugs money, mafia ?"

D. M. O'DOWD

The professor book marked his page, removed his glasses and listened to my plea with patience. He rose slowly opened his underwear drawer and removed ten fifty dollar bills from the ball of a stripy sock, no questions asked.

Kelly was good to his word and once he started to work he worked like a Trojan. Whitey on finally meeting him wrung his hand like a skipping rope, eyeing him up and down head to toe, reach, BMI, orthodox / southpaw, glint in eye, fire in belly. "We'll see" he concluded with a pleasure he found hard to hide. Not only Whitey but all the lads took to Kelly greatly. It was obvious to them he was one of their own having cut his teeth on the German autobahn's as a modern day spalpeen as well as the sites in Kentish Town and Luton airport. Even the Ape Connolly regarded him with something close to affection, the two of them often seen thick as thieves exchanging gambits over past experience. I on the other hand remained an object of ridicule only one rung above Dog Shite Joe on the pecking order of things. I mumbled grievances but Kelly's response was always the same, "sure his bark is worse than his bite", or "Give it back to him why don't you ?". Not wanting to sound like Mrs Rabinowitz Cockapoo I shut my trap. The sub due to the professor was paid back in full along with a chateaux neuf de pape of a good Vintage. If he weren't at work or unlocking a sparing partner in the GYM under the tutelage of Whiteys brother Eddie (the corner man) he was proving a competent adversary to the professor at Chess. Magnanimous in defeat, humble in victory. They smoked a nightly joint over a game and discussed Ibsen and Yeats and Keats while sipping green tea. I chipped in where and when I could. At the weekends he allowed himself to imbibe with moderation enjoying sumptuously the reward of endeavour. Sundays were reserved for his no-questions-asked relationship with Emanuel, taking her to dinner in a restaurant of her choice, concluding in the confluence of her bed, the rocking moans drowned out the trains overhead. All told, he was a man in total control of his destiny.

It was the day of Kelly's first fight, I should have seen it coming. In fact I did see it coming but could do little about it. The Ape had just unsettled me with an earful of abuse. The poll was hitched to the hoist, suspended with a strap allowing it to swing freely. On a slow steady trajectory the bucket of bricks made contact with the crown of my nose sending me flat onto my back. I felt the gurgle of blood in the back of my throat and knew it was more than a scratch. Fair play to him Jimmy Jimmy one of the brickies was straight down to me.

"Are you alright ?, are you alright ?" he said. Four big googly eyes swimming above me. I could only manage a groan. I thought I was hearing double as well as seeing double until I realised it was Jimmy Jimmy who said everything twice.

"Lift him, Lift him" he motioned to Kelly and they straddled me to the Van dropping me at the door of St Jude's Hospital punch drunk. It wasn't until the nurse came to see me in the waiting room that the thought of deportation entered my head.

"What's your name honey ?" she asked holding the clipboard.

"Pat" I said as a first thought, "Surname ?" she asked bending a Wrigglies spearmint into her mouth.

"Molasses" I answered.

"How you spell that ?" she asked.

Twenty minutes later there was a call on the tannoy for Pat Molasses in room five. I limped in, the doctor seated me on the bed.

"Emm" he said pinching my nose, sending a jolt of pain that rocked my entire head. After a few more "emms " and "aws" the Doc took a step back.

"I think Mr Keating, we will have to see you back for an x-ray".

Facing the harsh reality of leading a double life as a Mr Molasses an illegal immigrant, I pushed for a resolution.

"Doc" I petitioned, "what are the chances it's broken ?".

"Strong chance" he replied.

"Could you give me a percentage ?" I clarified.

"Emm .. about ninety nine percent" he said with certainty.

I looked at him knowingly, he understood that if I left I weren't coming back.

"Do what you need to do Doc?" I said gallantly.

He took a solid foothold on the tiles and a stern handhold of my nose. I crinkled my eyes like a child. A loud grating noise was followed by the crack so loud it echoed.

"You're all done buddy," he said as I dropped to my knees yowling like a banshee.

Deeply ensconced in a shroud of self pity I split my time in equal amounts between following the cracks on the ceiling to reviewing my dishevelled features in the mirror.

STORIES OF A DIGITAL SPALPEEN

My eyes had risen like foxes puff pastry, half closed and all the colours in the Dulux catalogue. I couldn't stand without the room spinning and I wasn't going to make Kelly's big bout. They were going to make a night of it, Bosco, Jimmy Jimmy, Mossey, Megan, Emanuel and the Professor. They had booked a table at Rory Dolan's in Yonkers for the after fight party and asked me a thousand times if I would join. Word had spread, that Kelly was the next big thing and the Celtic army would be there in force to cheer their man against the prodigious Puerto Rican, Sixto Gomez who was four and zero. The professor had a tri colour, Bosco was planning to get there early to hang it prominently where Kelly couldn't miss it when entering the ring. Kelly himself didn't get caught up in the hype sticking staunchly to the training routine. He had only one objective in mind – to repay the faith I had shown in him.

Kelly came to see me, I blessed him with the holy water the mother had sent over from Knock. He wanted to get to me early before they got in from work and made a fuss of him. He was right about that, when they arrived one by one they were all over the shop looking for shirts and shoes and dresses, squirting potions and lotions under armpits and erogenous zones. When Bosco yelled that the limo had arrived they all gathered in a bunch and the door slammed shut, sudden silence. No wait, the door handle rattled again, they had forgotten me and were returning to check if I might be alright, if I needed anything, it was Megan she grabbed a pair of earrings from the dresser, blew a kiss and ran out the door again. It would be a long few hours waiting to hear how it went.

As the light dropped so did my eyelids. The Advil taking me into a deep dreamy sleep. It was dark when I awoke to the crank of a key the lock. Jimmy Jimmy and *Bosco* arm in arm singing the boys are back in town, gee-eyed. I lifted myself on my elbows to view the two of them lurching towards me.

"What a night," Jimmy Jimmy says , "what a night".

Unclogging my eyes with the ball of my hand I noticed specks of blood on Jimmy Jimmy's shirt.

"What happened to you ?" I asked.

"What a night", he repeated "what a night", shaking his head.

"What happened ?" I looked to Bosco for a reasonable explanation. He broke away from the embrace with Jimmy Jimmy and took a boxing stance.

"You should have seen it," he said.

"Seen what ? " I asked.

"Listen" he exclaimed, "the arena was packed, us on one side, them on the other". "We had the ringside seats as u know ?" he said looking at me for confirmation before resuming. "When Kelly came out there was a mighty roar, everyone up on their feet singing the Kelly the Boy from Kilane, it would have brought a tear to your eye," he said emotional with drink.

"Did he win ?" I asked impatiently.

"Hang on now" he said steadying himself.

"He was decked out in a pair of emerald green shorts Eddie had made up for him with King Kong Kelly Boy tastefully embroidered down the sides of them, a shamrock on the left leg, a harp on the right".

"Nice," I said feeling optimistic.

"Ya, nice" he agreed with a hiccup. "Well anyways he looked fit I tell you," he said staring at me, "but now" he stopped again, "the Puerto Rican fella was tasty too."

"Oh," I said surprised.

"Anyway" Bosco recapped, "the Puerto Rican in Gold shorts Kelly in the Green of Ireland".

"Got it" I confirmed.

"Any heroes or gyros in the fridge Jimmy Jimmy ?" Bosco asked "I'm fucking starving."

Jimmy Jimmy nearly fell into the fridge and Bosco took a speed wobble to the couch.

"The first round was cagey," he said "All jabs, all jabs" waving his hand "poking and prodding, showboating."

"Right" I acknowledged.

"Second round Kelly opened him up with a lovely left."

"Oh," I said excited.

"The crowd went wild" he stopped "but what happened then ?" he asked.

"I don't fucking don't know," I said.

"The bell went" he replied.

"Will ya eat a yoghurt," Jimmy Jimmy shouted across the room.

"No" Bosco replied. He refocused on me "Ding ding, third round" he paused "went to ………Kelly ."

"Very good" I sang, seeing victory in sight.

"But the Puerto Rican now" Mossy paused raising his hand again "but the Puerto Rican now, was tough stuff". He rubbed his hand across his mouth and considered something for a moment "Are you sure there are no chicken gyros in there, I bought some earlier."

"No" Jimy Jimmy replied.

Bosco focused on me again "Did I tell you the atmosphere was mighty ?."

"You did" I said urging him on.

"Anyway between the third and fourth Whitey and Eddie seeing blood got him really fired up so out he comes and rocked yer man with a beautiful right hook". "We all leapt up with people falling over chairs and chairs falling over people, pure delirium". I sat up in the bed, all pain having left me.

I almost dared not ask what next, begging Bosco to continue, he smacked his lips, his mouth drying rapidly from all the talk.

"Well ... " he said, his tone dropping.

"Well what ?" I despaired.

"Well what happened next you couldn't make it up", he said coldly. I felt the blood drain out of me, a sudden sense of foreboding. "While Eddie was sponging Kelly down, from the side of his eye he noticed one of the Puerto Rican fans making the *cat call* at Emmanuel".

"A cat call ?", I questioned.

"Ya, like a kind of hiss, like a Tom cat".

"Oh no" I said.

"She was ignoring him as best she could but he wouldn't let it go".

"Mercy" I replied.

"Kelly stood up to get a better look and Whitey not knowing what was going on tried to pull him back down onto the stool", "Kelly got up again", "Whitey pulled him down again but Kelly got up and shot out through the ropes".

"Disaster," I said.

"Near enough" Bosco agreed. "It was the Puerto Ricans on their feet now, shouting abuse at Kelly in Spanish, grabbing their balls and booing". I heaved a sigh and laid back down again on the bed. "We managed to get Kelly back in the ring but the ref had already made up his mind and awarded the fight to the Puerto Rican, raising his arm in victory". I wasn't sure if I wanted to hear any more but Bosco went on "The Belfast confetti started then, bottles, cans, shoes, hairbrushes, hamsters whatever they had to hand went flying into the ring".

"Where is he now ?" I uttered in a whisper.

"He was terrible disappointed, apologised to us all, especially Whitey for all the trouble" said Bosco sensing the need to defend Kelly's honour.

"Where is he now ? " I asked again.

"He gave Emanuel a hug and off he went on his own, gone on the rip I'd say, we won't see him for days".

"No harm," I said.

"What a night, what a night," Jimmy Jimmy says.

Bosco stands shakily, "Was some craic alright" and laughs and the two of them joined forces again and headed out to Sean Og's to meet Mossy, Megan and the Professor. I couldn't even find the strength for a good luck.

I followed the cracks in the ceiling wondering had it all been a dream, dissecting the story bit by bit when the phone rang.

"Hello Magee" I said unable to hide the weight of disappointment in my voice.

"Do you have the cold ?" Magee enquired sounding chirpy.

"I do" I confirmed "a bit of a dose alright" not wanting to go into the details of my nasal injuries.

"I suppose it's getting pretty cold over there ?" he questioned.

"Ya" I said, "cold and miserable", there was a pause.

"Did I get u at a bad time ?" he asked.

"Sorry" I apologised "feeling a bit sorry for myself is all".

"Not to worry," he said, "not like you to be down in the dumps, is everything alright ?". He was a decent skin and always saw me in a good light but I didn't want to get into any detail.

"You know what Magee ?" I said the thought of a new plan having suddenly come to me

"What's that ?" he asked.

"I've heard Australia is nice this time of year" I sounded him out. There was a silence on the other end.

"Sure why not," he said eventually "Isn't the world your Lobster".

Australia

Gay Byrne couldn't hold a candle to Uncle Frank, not according to the mother. He was far too witty and although not quite so polished in appearance was the more handsome of the two. To the extent women came to blows over him. He was supple as a salmon, fit as a flea and fleet as a deer. There was no doubt in her mind he could have worn the county colours had it not been for the vices of which there were many. He could sing like a blackbird, that was a fact, not quite Luke Kelly but not far off him, and it was said a session without Frank and the Sally Gardens wasn't a session at all. His greatest talent of the lot however was his ability to imbibe, a talent that earned him unbounded admiration among his peers. He could sink pint after short after pint without it knocking a stir out of him, in fact if anything he became stolid with the exception of the odd punchy remark, an occasionally infectious smile and a bolstered confidence for lilting. The strangest thing the mother often ruminated was that despite all the obvious talents and blessings he was never content. At the time he inherited the family farm, he sold it off, wanting to live in town. He bought up Harrison's and between himself and every hanger on going drank it dry. From the Phoenix bitter to the cherry liquor and Ruby ports left over from the erudite denizens that dispersed after its sale. Maybe the biggest surprise in this was he still managed to make a tidy profit such was his popularity. He wasn't long in it however when he caught wind from the returning immigrants of the high life in Australia and his head was turned.

"I remember the night as clear as day" the mother once reflected on the wake, "there were musicians from all over the country and you never seen the like of it for food and drink," "Melogeouse" she chirped with pride before a barb of angst pricked her conscience. "He had the finest young girl at the time" she uttered "Kate Kennedy", and not wanting to go into detail she paused before concluding with a sigh, "Ah sure now, all that glitters is not Gold".

Uncle Frank stood torpid against the coin tapped counter of the Mercantile. To his north, the sliding doors opened out inviting in the surging Sydney sun. Along with the light came the echoes of buoyant laughter drifting in from the intersection of George Street and Gloucester Walk. He stood in a loose white shirt, the sleeves rolled casually to the elbow. His hair like his shoes shimmered black with a boyish curl here and there freeing itself from the layer of lacquer. On his wrist a yellow gold watch glowed against the backdrop of his swarthy skin. He stretched a grin from mouth to crow's feet, extending the hello hand on my approach, until we stood, side by side, blood on blood, together torpid against coin tapped the counter of the Mercantile.

The Mother was delighted of course, to hear all the news. How Uncle Frank looked so well and was doing so good. "Uncle Frank says hello" I scribbled as a post script to the post card. On the front the magnificent facade of the opera house, which I had chosen carefully as a kind of representation of success and well being. I spared her blushes of course. The details of our night in the Mercantile, the fountains of golden larger, the countless Bundy's and coke. The jaunts back and forth to the bookie, with each and every crumpled betting slip ending up on the tiles of the floor. I was fairly lucid in the bottle shop paying for the six pack to take in the car. The Casino however was a blur, only a persistent recollection of Uncle Frank unleashing the gold clasp and whipping off the watch. The protestations of the dealer insisting he put it back on or vacate the premises. We left, ending the night careering into the communal rose bushes, the Val Doonican record skipping endlessly until old Mrs Breuer's feeble taps at the door eased Uncle Frank from his state of hibernation.

Three weeks on, experiencing a brief moment of clarity I landed myself a job in a call centre for a credit card company. Selling packages and add on's. Work that would turn a man to stone, but for now it served the purpose, funding the escapades of myself and Uncle Frank. Yes, there were more. On two occasions since I had to rescue Uncle Frank in his smalls from the landing. The second of which I was alerted to his whereabouts by the yelping of Mrs Breurer's toy dog, crumbs, which at the time she was leading out for his evening jot. I wasn't free from controversy myself although I might add, not entirely of my own making. It happened on Labour day.

Having the day off work I was in desperate need of a Tan, at least according to Uncle Frank who was referring to me as the Albino. I spread the towel on Bondai, flicked the flip flops into the sand and laid back. I was nibbling my way through Joyces, A Portrait of the Artist as a Young Man.

D. M. O'DOWD

I took it in hand but it wasn't long before my headlamps began to dim, the ink melting into the dry page. Stephen Dedalus languished in the sick Bay on a wet day in Clongowes, I was hale and hearty on the beach in Bondai, worlds apart. I was waiting for the magic of Joyce to possess me, until then happily distracted by any passing tong. I placed the book spread-eagle on my chest and within seconds was catching flies, baking under one malevolent orange ball of a sun.

A shiver of evening breeze woke me. Gritty grains of sand tinkling over my torso. Panic set in, looking down on my blood red feet, my huge bulbous ankles. I followed my luminous legs like streaky back rashers to my stomach, purple and raw as a nipple serving twins. Sally O'Brien could fry an egg on my shoulders (if she had an egg). The only place free from a scalding was, thanks to Joyce, a perfect rectangular patch of pale skin with a scrub of tangled hair. A surf dude and his girlfriend passed, arm in arm kicking swishes of sand as they went, tanned and toned with bleached hair stiff as Marram grass. I could see them giggle away under the shade of their baseball caps, furtively glancing as I went through the excruciating motions of dressing myself, twister style.

"No, no, no, you will not" I insisted to Uncle Frank as fell up the corridor half cut and half dressed, rooting in his pants pocket for the keys of the Ford. "Casualty" is all I remember him saying. I had to admit the Castlemane XXXX hadn't helped. We had taken in recent times to sitting out on the balcony, him in his chair, me in mine, both in our underpants, sing songing. He was teaching me all the old numbers, Fiddlers Green, Finnegan's Wake, Lanagan's Ball. It was true for him he had a lovely soft voice. Aside from the singing I awoke somewhere west of dawn suffering bouts of furnace-like heat. The heat dissipated, suddenly plummeting till I shivered like an igloo. Shortly after the heaving started, folded in two over the toilet till there was nothing left but yellow gloopy bile. After the heaving the blisters, bubbling on my shoulders, appearing one by one like little drumlins, on my belly a long flat one visibly expanding to the size of Patagonia. At that point, I gave in to Uncle Franks demands and we fell into the Ford forward bound for hospital.

Big mistake (the Castlemane XXXX) I was later informed by the nurse as she gently swabbed my shoulders while I sat shirtless slumped forward on the cot. "You're completely de-hydrated" she chided but I didn't mind, I was half out of it, rocking back and forth only half hearing the words animated in her flickering eyes. Over and back she went to the provisions tray, trailing delicate swirls of citrus perfume. "Oh dear," she said in her baby blue uniform pulling herself close to my contrite head, so close I could feel the static from her uniform touch the tip of my withered nose. I remained suspended just lolling in the sensuous odours of her mid-rift. Laura, she later informed was her name. Over the next three days she brought me back to health, pink and plump from unction's and laughter. As she mended me I studied every curve and angle of her face, from her soft round chin to the tip of her honey blond ponytail and dreamed of the day she bore my children.

D. M. O'DOWD

From the ashes of labour day came the phoenix of the Melbourne cup. Suited and booted two finer gentlemen you would struggle to meet on a day's walk. Watching *Makybe Diva* dash past the winning post opened a new chapter of prosperity for myself and Uncle Frank, at ten to one with a ton on we were quids in. The flight home was a no expense spared buffet of bubbles and peanuts. Labour Day turned to Australia day with Christmas Day falling between. It featured a momentous effort on the part of Uncle Frank and myself to pluck, stuff and cook the bird (the last of the Melbourne cup money). Mangled jocks from the radiators, gone, festered spoons from bean cans, ejected. The mother sent over a box bursting with Tayto and Barry's tea and soda bread and one of her special Christmas puddings. The redolent burst of aromas including roasted almonds, sweet fruits and cinnamon caught Uncle Frank off guard. He had to pinch the eyes and look away as the thoughts of a home he hadn't seen in years were unsuspectingly cast upon him. I called herself and the old fella for all the news back home. Mass was beautiful she said although she spotted Val Moran and he nearly came down after receiving communion, "he's very shook looking", she mentioned. It led to a discussion on the auld lad who was out to Michael Waters for the cure of the sprain, "there's power in the old cures" the mother let me know. "We left him a box of Celebrations and a pair of socks" the father chimed in. "Anyone else, sick, dead or injured ?" I enquired and sure enough Seamus Benson was found dead above on the tractor, he looked ten years younger in the coffin and you couldn't get into the church the funeral was that big. I handed over to Uncle Frank to say a few words, the mother was delighted, she didn't know where to start. The big day concluded in exhaustion, on the balcony, where else, just myself and Uncle Frank snoozing off to the Christmas chorus of croaking toads.

Back to Australia Day, as it proved to be another twist in the road. I was on a call at the time to one Miranda Miller. I nearly had her for the full package, travel insurance, hotel point transfers, car insurance, the works. She just needed to confirm with her husband of thirty years Terry. "Terry, Terry," she called up the stairs, I was imagining Terry sitting on the toilet wondering "what the hell now" or having a cat nap on the sofa, convincing himself that the rasps of his beloved's canter were nothing but the wind. While waiting for Terry to buckle his belt I stared at the screen wondering if Uncle Frank might care for rump steak and chips given we had mode it over the hump of another week. "Hello" Miranda rejoined the conversation just at the same moment as the email arrived in my inbox, bold font, marked as unread with a red exclamation mark denoting high importance. Sender, mossy.callaghan@hotmail.com. It read :

Hello

How's the body ? Myself and Bosco are heading down under, planning to go on Tour, Sydney -> Perth. Pack your bags boy.

p.s. have a look on gumtree for a camper

Later

Mossy

"Hello," Miranda says again and then she just hung up !.

Uncle Frank came along with me to have a look at the bus. A 1987 T25 VW 4 berth Camper, a real beauty. A lad from Borris Co Carlow (if you wouldn't smile) had it advertised. He answered the door, ruffle haired in his Bermudas but sadly lacking the muscles or tan to back up the look (but who was I to comment). He had just landed from a year long trip, himself and the babe and the buddy. The babe turned out to be from Nenagh, she ended every sentence with a *like*. " It was beautiful wasn't it Oisin, like I never thought I would like it so much, like". "It was ya" Oisin replied, his arm hooked over his head scratching his back. The Buddy also hailed from Borris. He was planning to head back home. Oz was good for a laugh but he missed the whitethorn hedges behind the house, the soft rain falling soundless on the cow, the clags on the bog, the goose grass on his jumper, settling for the quiet pint of an evening in O'Shea's. There was no way Oisin was going back, no way in hell, he mentioned, it was Singapore noodles for him any day over curly cabbage. Uncle Frank poked his head into a press, turned on the tap with a positive nod seeing it worked. "Does she have a spare ?" I enquired. Oisin the buddy and the babe all had a laugh at that. Did St Brendan have a life raft ?. "What'll you take for her ?" I quickly moved on from the ridicule of a responsible question.

We named her Saoirse (freedom) and parked her proudly on the kerb outside Uncle Frank's place. The boys would be arriving on Monday. We would be hitting the highway on Tuesday. It was Saturday so time for one last hurray. We hit the Mercantile (where else). The idiosyncrasies of which I had grown so fond of. The off kilter map of the old sod, the ornate lamp hanging from the moulded ceiling, the jagged ruby collars painted on the custard columns, one each side of the bar. The kink on the fan attached to the right of the two columns, throwing a hiccup half way through its rotation. I felt at home. I drew a finger down through the dew of my Schooner as Uncle Frank recounted the story of the Gold watch. The card game that went on all night and the big Aussie that offered him double or quits on an arm wrestle for the pot of cash Uncle Frank was gathering into his chest. A battle that went on for another solid hour until every drop of his sweat was drained, his arm starting to cramp up. The big Aussie was starting to suffer also by the sounds of things. His head dropped till only the wide rim of his hat was visible. By all accounts, judging by the anxious silence on the faces that sat round the table it was on a knife edge. It was win or bust for Uncle Frank, summing up one magnificent effort he shut his eyes firmly, slowly lowering the big Aussies lever until the knuckles cracked against the table. It was the thought of his own fathers (my grandfather's) strong hand as they shook for the last time before he set off for Dublin, which fuelled the surge that compelled him to victory. As it turned out the big Aussie couldn't match the wager. That's when the gold watch was proffered and accepted. That along with a bottle of Bundy and the rest is history.

We made our usual stop at the bottle shop to pick up a couple of six packs, then trundled on, Burger King drive through. On route, Uncle Frank requested a bar of a song to see how far I had come under his tutelage. I cleared the throat, switched off the radio and away with me. A One, a two, a three ….

Oh, Danny Boy, the pipes, the pipes are calling

From glen to glen, and down the mountain side,
"Lovely ...."
The summer's gone, and all the roses falling,
It's you, it's you must go and I must bide.
"Keep her lit .... ".
On the cusp of the chorus Uncle Frank reluctantly rolled the window down to the young Goth with the powder white make up and a hair net elevated in the kiosk above us. She had looked like it was the last place on earth she wanted to be. Uncle Frank joined in :
But come ye back when summer's in the meadow,
Or when the valley's hushed and white with snow,
It's I'll be here in sunshine or in shadow,
Oh, Danny Boy, oh Danny Boy, I love you so!
"Can I have your order please ?"
But when ye come, and all the flowers are dying,
If I am dead, as dead I well may be,
"Can I have your order please ?"
"Two burger and chips" ......
Ye'll come and find the place where I am lying,
And kneel and say an Ave there for me;
"Any drinks, please ?", the Marlin Manson fan asked.
And I shall hear, though soft you tread above me,
And all my grave will warmer, sweeter be,
"Two Bundy and coke...."
"Excuse me ?"
"Can you repeat please".
For you will bend and tell me that you love me,
And I shall sleep in peace until you come to me!
"Two what and coke ?"

STORIES OF A DIGITAL SPALPEEN

"Ah sure we're only joking, No drinks, your fine"
She handed over the warm paper bag, we paid and took off.

The last chorus took place with myself and Uncle Frank wrapped round one another standing straight in the rose bed.

Oh, Danny Boy, oh Danny Boy, I love you so!

Crumbs was out on the balcony, twisting, turning and yapping.

By the time the last note of *love you so* had fritted out, half to two thirds the lights in the apartment block were illuminated with curtains and shutters twitching.

The arrival of the boys in some ways was an anti-climax, they were jet lagged and completely shagged after spending the best part of a week playing pool, eating street food and encouraging lady boys in Bangkok on route to Sydney. I cleaned my room while they crashed on the couch, packing up what little stuff I had. Binning old bills and papers, counting out the few dollars I had. From the pocket of a pair of crumpled shorts a neatly folded paper fell to the floor. I opened, Laura it read, her number highlighted by an undulating underline terminated with a squiggly flower. I never called her. It wasn't like I hadn't wanted to. Too late now. I would think about her in my sleeping bag outdoors in the outback, staring up at the silver moon. Uncle Frank offered to help, more than once but there was little to be done. We withdrew to the balcony and slowly supped our way through the remainder of a crate of Castlemaine.

The morning of the departure was bright. The boys, Bosco and Mossy, after a good night in the cot had a renewed energy about them. We packed up the last of the gear. We had said our thanks and goodbyes to Uncle Frank. He stood to see us off, his white shirt the sleeves rolled to the elbows, his dark arms dipped deep into his black pants. Bosco turned the engine, it whirred then purred, he tipped the throttle twice to get a feel for her then pulled out gingerly. Mossy fiddled with the radio, settling on a station and turning it up full blast. I was in the back seat and lay my long arm along it, looking out the rear window at Uncle Frank. Without warning we spurted forward, the engine singing as we passed Mrs Breuer and crumbs, who stopped to stare us down. Half naked Mossy rolled down the window clawed at the air and let out a war cry above the banging music. The warm air gushed in and tossed my hair forward, Uncle Frank fading fast into the distance. Smaller and smaller he grew, unmoving, barely visible then gone like the last plucky cord in a reel. I turned round facing forward and called Mossy to pass me one of the cigarettes he was smoking while wondering if that might be the last we saw of Uncle Frank.

Two for Joy

Paddy was the local hackney, he didn't need a website, a social media presence or a two page spread to keep his business buoyant. If you needed a car you could find him in Cullen's Kitchen drinking tea. Paddy could predict the weather better than met Eireann, could drive to the hospital blindfolded, knew the schedule of every regular in every pub in the county, he even did the runs to the Joy although it was the one journey he preferred the least. Paddy had seen it all, never married, loved to laugh, always wore a suit and believed in the Faries. He let out one of his cracks of laughter leaving me to the airport the car wobbling on the loose chippings along the ditch. He was always watching for Magpies, "You're looking for his friend" he laughed, leaning over and peering at me, his face like a moon, his beard like lamb's wool full enough for a Magpie to set up shop in. It was true I was looking for the second one but I didn't let him know that of course. The Magpie perked his tail and stood plump and puckered, on a tilted fence post.

"Ah," says I, "I don't believe in your auld piseogs".

He let out another crack of laughter, this one louder than the last lighting up the mycelium of spider veins on his ruddy cheeks.

"You were indeed" he informs me.

"You'd better keep your eye on the road or we'll end up in the bloody ditch," I told him.

"O be Jaysus" said he, bolting upright realising I was right grabbing the wheel as if it was about to get away from him.

"Jesus Paddy" I suddenly realised the time, "you'd want to put the boot down or I'll miss me flight".

"Jesus" said he with a whistle, stooping his head, blinking at the small digital clock encrusted in the dash looking all serious. He put his foot on the accelerator and gave an almighty rev that propelled us only for a moment until we slowed again to a crawl, half on the hard shoulder, half on the main road.

I was still sick as a small hospital, the booze from the night before resulting in heightened bouts of anxiety. I fumbled for my inside pocket to touch my passport, relaxing only with the assurance it was there. The weather was cool, but I suffered hot flashes, sweating, especially, truth be told around the crotch area, forcing me from time to time to skid across the leather seat for relief. All the while Paddy assaulted me with questions, reliving his enduring relationship with booze through my experiences of the night before, his diabetes, gout and other conditions, a list as long as your arm having put an end to his participation.

"It's not the same when you can't take a drink" he professed, his left hand gesticulations enforcing the point.

"Do you get me ?"

"I do" I said. "I have you now but turn on your indicator or you'll miss the turn again" I remind him.

"O be Jaysus" said he with a whistle in his voice and swerved onto the hatching just after the large right angle arrow saying airport.

STORIES OF A DIGITAL SPALPEEN

He dropped me off in the disabled parking bay. He was about to tell me he was on eighteen tablets a day but I knew what was coming and cut him off at the pass.

"I better be off Paddy, there calling the flight".

"Oh you'd better" said he, looking all serious again, straightening his tie.

"Do you have everything now ?" he asked. Once upon a time I brought him home a Rolex from the night market in Malaysia, he always wore it, straightening his wrist he checked the time.

"Right !" he said, as we shook hands through the window, he threw me a louche smile and took off over egging her in first. I had meant to tell him to clean out the car of banana boxes and old newspapers I thought as the automatic doors swallowed me up. My path through the airport was well trodden, a swift right into the lower bar for the "hair of the dog", then out past the bust of Monsignor Horan, up the Monsignor Horan stairs, past the framed photo story of the Monsignor Horan airport and up to the Monsignor Horan airport development fee payment booth. Fifteen Euros emblazoned black on an orange background as if it was some kind of bargain. Will you do it for ten says I throwing in me last crumpled twenty. She counted out the five Euros in change, wilfully flicking the coins into her hand with polished French nails. French nails I mused, there's something about French nails. With a wry smile, she stabbed the money into my open palm. I looked into her eyes, they said, maybe I will maybe I won't. "Thanks, Clare," says I reading her name badge, gave her a smarmy wink and walked off. She rolled her eyes.

D. M. O'DOWD

A quick squiz through the duty free. One day I am going to buy that turf clock, I thought, or a turf Celtic cross or one or other of the inventive ways turf can be shaped into an ornate piece for the modern semi-detached. On this occasion, I settled on the Sunday World and three packs of Tayto, Cheese & Onion, Smokey Bacon and Salt & Vinegar. The three of which I was planning to eat after work Monday evening, one after the other, in that order while watching mindless evening TV, Come Dine With Me, Easterners and Blackadder, in that order. But tomorrow was another day, a swift exit to the bar with a pit stop in the gents. Some gap toothed kid sat on the mechanical tractor trying to buck it into life. I lobbed my hand on his head and told him to "ride her cowboy". He gave it an almighty back heel and it ground to a halt. Standing alone along the urinal, I exuded the relief of urination. Tilting my head backwards, piss slapping a steady stream against the hard white porcelain, I released a low sigh. A porter fart loomed in my gut and I was gently coaxing it along when the door swung open, three or four footsteps and then a shuffle, but no one came to join me along the urinal leaving me wondering was I still alone or if there was someone else sharing the same stale air. By that time the porter fart teetered on the brink, so I let it out. "Good arse" called the footsteps. Taken aback and half embarrassed I craned my neck backwards with a stupid looking grin, the stream of silver liquid still pouring out of me.

"Is it yourself Nathan" I say recognising him.
"How's she cutting ?" says he.
"Not so bad," says I.

"Are you heading off somewhere ? " I enquired all the while trying to manage looking comfortable holding my penis.

"No, just leaving Cara back".

"Oh,"

"What flight she on ?" I enquire, nostalgic flashes of his gorgeous sister in her school uniform, pouring into my salacious mind.

"Not sure", he said, "I think the three o'clock to Gatwick."

"Same one as myself" I let him know, delighted with meself. He said nothing after that except that he would leave me to it, that he only needed a tissue.

"Hold on there Nathan," I say, trying to re-ignite the conversation, "are you not stopping for a pint, let me buy you one at the bar ?"

"Ummm", says he, one foot holding the door open, tapping it over and back while considering. I could feel the power in my urine gradually waning, making it necessary to thrust my hips forward while waiting for his answer.

"Sure why not," he said, eventually, perking up.

"Sound so," says I, "I'll see you down there", "Oh and extend to Cara as well of course" says I trying to make it seem like an afterthought.

"I'll ask her," says he and disappeared out the door, just in time for me to collapse from my tipi toes and steer the remaining drops safely to the pungent trough with some relief.

Cara Hamilton, I mouthed a barely, audible whisper as I rolled my hands under the cold water of the hot tap, inspecting my complexion. Cara Hamilton, would it have been ten years since she used to pass my door ?, her school bag slung over her shoulder, her grey Aran socks bunched on her skinny legs. Cool in an understated way, hooking her long sandy hair behind her ear, glancing my way with her arctic blue eyes, the hint of a smile on her delicate mouth. In the weeks leading up to the graduation us townie boys would spend nights in my mother's prize sitting room of salubrious reds and dark mahoganies, engulfed in a haze of smoke as we played poker for pennies to the dim glow of the iridescent street light. Stoic ancestors, long gone, watched on from sepia-toned prints, framed and hung on the patterned walls. By the time I had mustered the courage to utter her name as a potential date, Egan, as if scripted, eagerly concurred that she was "a fine bit of gear" but that she was presently *en route* to the south of France to work on a horse farm for the summer. A fag dangled from his gob, the long ash tilting, a thread of smoke curling up like a serpent towards his fastened eye. He was dealing the cards mechanically around the table with little finesse. Stopping for a moment he looked towards me and cackled a laugh "Probably getting the garlic sausage as we speak" said he, as my enthusiasm for cards disintegrated like the snow on the telly that no one was watching. We'll see who has the last laugh I said to myself smoothing a handful of water through my hair.

"Hello there,", I gestured taking her slim velvet hand into mine, "So nice to see you again," I continued obviously sounding like a twat. She leaned against the bar, her right UGG boot casually placed on the brass foot rail.

STORIES OF A DIGITAL SPALPEEN

"Hello," she replied making an effort as she took my hand and leaned in to brush her cheek against my weekend of stubble. I drank in the spicy odour from her soft neck. She was older, of course, perhaps now a real beauty. I wanted to take her hip and hoist her into me, asking Nathan to take a walk. Instead, myself and Nathan launched into conversation while she resumed her sultry position against the bar, tapping on her iPhone, raising her head from time to time with vague interest. In truth, the conversation with Nathan flowed and before we knew it we had gulped two large ones and were on our third.

"Anything interesting ?" I broke off from Nathan in full flight outlining the difference between a two stroke and a four stroke engine.

"Just my boyfriend Conrad," says she.

"Oh Conrad is it" I say "Very good, very good", tempted to make a smart comment.

"An Englishman ?" I ask.

"From Kent" she answers, "and what is it that Conrad does ?" says I .

"Investment Banking, Stocks and Bonds, that sort of thing" says she succinctly.

"A good number so," I conclude.

"Pays the rent," she said "long hours though" as she paused to check the ding from her phone ."We are considering moving to Hong Kong" she resumed after digesting the text holding her phone apologetically.

I want to tell her that I have been to Hong Kong. Instead, I say "That's nice," and walk off to the toilet trying to look unimpressed. "Hong Kong," I mouth into the mirror as I wet the tips of my fingers to rub my eyes. "And Conrad, if you wouldn't smile," ... "and here's me thinking she was saving herself for me, pining for me, from the unmade bed of her Docklands apartment,". The bing-bong of the airport PA sounded with a muffled announcement of flight something or other boarding for somewhere or other, possibly Gatwick. "Shit," I mutter in the mirror quickly drying my hands. By the time I got back, Nathan was draining the last dregs from his pint.

"Where's Cara ? " I enquired.

"Gone," he murmured, mouth full, nodding towards her in the priority queue.

"Shit," I said, cursing myself, recalling my confusion at the plethora of options on the Ryanair website. Relegated to cattle class I strained to glimpse her, studying her phone, occasionally tossing back her sandy hair onto the bag slung over her shoulder. As the priority doors opened and she casually disappeared we were still being harassed by a melee of trollie dollies ruthlessly ripping boarding cards and badgering people to force rigid bags into tight iron cages. I itched to get out through the door past the family of whinging kids in front of me. I spent an eternity on the white Iron staircase, gently rocking to the sound of the jet engines while a heavy set Polish migrant at the head of the queue searched his pockets complaining that he had shown his boarding card ten or twelve times already. I couldn't see her at first, and then I did, flicking through the pages of the in-flight magazine, indifferent to the snapping of overhead lockers. I rounded an overweight woman contorting to remove her anorak, and then past her husband gasping from his sunken mouth as he struggled to find the energy to lift her vanity bag. The Polish migrant removing his jacket didn't have time to say "Hey comrade," before I had slipped by him and landed on the seat next to her. "Hey yourself," says I. I turned to her, fluttered my eyes and said "Naw, you weren't going to run off without saying good bye,", she smiled broadly. I struggled to remove my jacket in the confines of the seat. "Here let me help you" she said taking the collar. "It's a nice jacket," she commented. I told her I won it in a game of pool in Camden, she said I was always a good pool player. "I hadn't thought you noticed,", says I giving her a suggestive look. She laughed. By the time the drinks trolley came around, we were on the topic of school. I coaxed her into having a dry white from a plastic cup, myself an overpriced frothy beer. We discussed each of the teachers, their defining features and idiosyncrasies'. Kelly with his tag line "now we'll draw a little picture", Canden gaunt and leathered, Mc Loughlin fierce and unwavering. I asked her did she still have her school uniform and if she did would she mind wearing it to the school disco in Hammersmith one Saturday night. She laughed, flatly refused, poked me on the arm and called me a pervert. We caught the trolley on the way back and had another, I bought a lottery ticket. We scratched it together, square by square until all were revealed. "Useless," she said and ripped it in two.

In the baggage hall, I helped her suitcase from the carousel, leaving my hand a moment longer on the handle than needed, just to touch her soft warm hand. "That's it so," she said, an air of faint regret in her voice. I offered her a lift, told her my driver was waiting. Amid her ardent protestations, a bogman swept past, almost knocking her, jeans hanging off his arse his O'Neills bag read "Tara Gaels", In blue and yellow.

"We'll have ye next year," he says, referring my O'Neills bag.

"Round towers, pride of London" in green and white.

"Have your shite," I say, wrapping my arm around her protectively.

The sliding doors revealed my friend Mani, rocking on the balls of his feet, casually dressed in his polo and chinos sporting a broad smile. He raised his eyebrows, two large hairy arcs as he saw my travel companion. I dashed towards him, hand outstretched, his traditional gold bangle slipping back his dark arm as he reciprocated. "Hello Ashok" says I. "Ashok" he says to me bemused, his smile turning to a grimace. "One minute," I said to Cara, suggesting she wait there while I steered Mani sideways, maintaining a grab of his hand.

"You`re my driver, Ashok," I hissed.

"Fuck off," he blurted.

"For a mate", I pleaded.

"Fuck off," says he to me again "your only doing this cause I'm Indian, you're a fucking racist" he exclaimed.

"Fuck off," says I to him. "Now don't be such a drama queen,". Turning to Cara, I muster a fake smile "Meet Ashok," I said.

She was impressed by his new Mercedes, a sleek CLS, maroon with tan leather interior. We sat in the back our arms meeting on the armrest in the middle. "Where to Sir ?" says Mani sarcastically, oddly bobbing his head from side to side, his chiselled eyes devouring me in the rearview mirror. We still had the giggles from the plane which vexed him further. Passing Croydon the response to my suggestion of a pit stop in wasn't even considered as he unloaded our bags and sped off. In JD Weatherspoons we sat across a streaky round table, her iPhone was relegated to her handbag as we shared experiences of London life, occasionally dipping into a shared past, awash with memories. As dusk fell she took a call, I watched her silhouette passing over and back in the doorway, speaking heatedly as the lights on the slot machines jumped through their flashing loops. She returned and sat, a little saddened. I took her elbow with my hand, drew her in close to me and leaned across to kiss her, in the process unknowingly sliding her half empty glass of chardonnay across the table. She jerked backwards with a screech as it landed on her lap. "You tool," I said to meself. "Time I was making a move," says she with a shrug and a soft smile, patting her jeans with a tissue.

In my bedsit overlooking Chiswick roundabout I observed the orange tip of my cigarette move between the darkness of my mouth and the ashtray resting on my naked chest. It must have been four in the morning but the never ending traffic could be seen through the gap in the musty velvet curtains that drooped over the bay window. She awoke from a half dream and nuzzled her head to my neck, draped her arm across my belly and lifted her smooth leg onto my mid rift. She let out a low moan, "Conrad" she said. The next morning the clunk of the door behind me knocked the sleep from my eyes as I stood on the steps observing the day. I was late again for work but this time I didn't give a fiddlers. The unmistakable rattle of a Magpie sounded overhead from the branch of a Plane tree, he rattled again, bouncing on to the roof of the bus stop in front of me. What would Paddy say, I thought, where is his friend probably and just as he had said it in my mind a second appeared, together on the roof they jousted back and forth before taking wing in a flurry and out of sight. "Fuck Conrad," I said to myself as a blast of sunlight lit up my face the thought of Cara consuming me completely.

The Digital Spalpeen

With some travel the job description stated, my mind fixed on south India or some similar exotic location. It was one of those Friday afternoon, post interview conversations.

"So we like you", Brent says leading me out towards reception, "we just got a couple more candidates to interview but will let u know early to mid next week, how does that sound mate?".

"Sounds good" I confirmed pausing to look at him before we moved on, entering the realms of small talk and weekend plans.

"Cricket" Brent said "and a few beers if her indoors allows it," he said with a resigned chuckle. "Any kids ?" he inquired.

"No" I confirmed.

"Good for you mate ?" he said almost dreamily as if this was where the battle was lost.

The automatic doors swished open leading to the forecourt of fountains and Bentleys and exceedingly polite Security officers.

"Beats digging ditches," I thought to myself looking around, loosening the tie a couple of notches and exhaling deeply.

That evening I met Cara in the Coat & Badge. "Oh that sounds promising" she said, "I'm really proud of you darling", reaching across the table to cup my hands. I smiled, self satisfied. "Now we'll be able to afford the down payment on our own place" she continued excitedly.

"Steady on" I straightened up "I don't even have the job yet" I pleaded.

"No, no" she apologised, "Well....I'm just saying" and she paused again for a moment, withdrawing slowly her laconic eyes, "and then there's the baby", she said.

"Baby...baby ... baby " my mind like a bluebottle in a jam jar. "Rugby ... rugby ... rugby" and it all came back to me. The six nations, a grand slam, floods of Guinness all down the front of the jersey, streaky tears on my face, "I want to continue the bloodline" I implored her, clutching a war-torn menu from Mr Yung's.

I received the call midweek. "On behalf of our client we have an offer for you" she said in her polished accent.

"Not so bad" I said not wanting to sound like a man who was checking the phone a dozen times a day.

"Does that mean you would like to accept ? " she said a little more effete which got on my wick so I told her to ring me back in half an hour "I'm just about to go into an important meeting" I informed her.

"Very well" she responded.

I was straight on the phone to Cara. "Yipeee," she said unleashing the school girl I once knew. After that I called the agency back, informing them that I had considered the offer and, yes I would be willing to accept.

My first assignment would be in "France" according to Brent.

"Paris ?" I suggested trying to eek out the specifics, "a little outside" he confirmed.

STORIES OF A DIGITAL SPALPEEN

"You'll need to be onsite Tue to Thu, you can work from home or come in the office Friday, whatever is good for you mate" he said.

Cara was a little taken aback. Away three nights would have an impact on her schedules, both of them. She had two lists one for house hunting, areas, prices mortgage advisors etc, the second one a plan for making a baby, with a similar number of bullet points.

"You'll need to stop smoking," she said.

I nodded.

"And cut down on the booze."

"ok," I said.

"No hot showers, cycling bikes or wanking", I shrugged (wanking, as if).

"Want to get started now ?" she asked and took her top off. I shrugged again.

As it turned out the assignment was just outside Paris alright, Evreux in the asshole of Brittany. "E-v-r-e-u-x" I pronounced exasperated to the taxi drivers one after the other with the same mute shrug until I Googled the hotel address at a roaming cost of thousands, "Ah Evreux," an enlightened face finally, "Yes, that's right Evreux," I said. Two hours it took from Charles De Gaulle, at a clip. I checked in. One drink before bed I thought looking forward to finally crashing. The bar was quiet, just myself and one other guy, a tall dark handsome type leafing through a local paper chugging a beer. He looked up and crinkled an eyebrow "You just joined the project ?" he asked sounding like Sean Connery

"Aye," I said sounding like Dinny Berne.

"Is it the cheap suit ?" I asked.

"Ha ha ha" he gave a big meaty laugh and we instantly hit it off.

We weren't long into the pint me paying great attention to the in's and out's of the project when we were joined by another colleague, a Polish guy carrying a portmanteau old enough to have seen the pogroms, bedecked in a Forrest green suit. Robert the Scottish guy introduced him as Bartek.

"OK let us drink", Bartek said forcefully taking a bottle of Bison Vodka from his luggage. Robert gave another hearty rumble, I smiled nervously.

At 2 am the barmaid familiar with Robert left the key to lock up by himself. At 4 am I slurred submission and would take leave to my bed. "You are Irishman ?" Bartek slammed and filled my glass with another large libation. Robert let out another one of his big rumbles of laughter. At 7 am I was in the shower, beseeching God and his blessed mother Mary to help me through the day, my first day. At eight am I was down in the breakfast room nursing a lukewarm coffee. Robert wearing a pair of ray bans a bit quieter than the night before, Bartek chewed coarsely a slice of rye bread slathered with fish pate and slurped a black tea with lemon. I was introduced to other consultants who had arrived in the morning, Elise an older bejewelled Belgian lady who referred to herself as Momma, Luca an Italian eager to talk shop and Alok a motionless Indian who sat alone with a forlorn look, drifting home to Gujarat wondering how in the hell he ended up on a diet of root vegetables. At nine am we arrived at the office. I was introduced to the local team I was to work with, Dominque middle aged with the snarl, Michel, middle aged with a beard and finally Gilles middle aged with a penchant for burgundy, dressed head to toe in it. The project manager's name was Fabian, at ten am we had our first meeting, he appeared pallid skinned with a pinched nose, a pair of rat eyes softened a little by Joycean spectacles. He sat opposite me. At that moment approximately 10.01, I thought this couldn't be happening, could it ?, did I just gag ?. My mouth filling with a warm lumpy liquid. I was fixed on Fabian. I couldn't leave in the first minute of my first meeting. He was waffling on about the impact on the business, "not millions, billions", he said, "hence the importance of a smooth integration with the logistics providers". I needed to think fast, I bit the bullet winced and drank it back, flotsam Jetsam and all. *Oh shit,* it was coming back up again. "Ok ?" Fabian concluded his diatribe. "Em hm" I nodded forcing back the liquid for a second time not wanting to open my mouth, releasing the pungent gassy build up. He lifted his *Gitanes* from the desk and left for a smoke. At 10.20 I washed my mouth out in the toilets and wet my face, lamenting my bovine eyes. At 12.00 noon Michel took me to lunch, authentic crispy French fries and chicken legs with enough feathers to confirm it was farm reared. An espresso for digestion brought me back to life. At 2.00 pm I did some actual work. At 15.00 called Brent to check in but went straight to voicemail. At 5.00pm I was flagging badly. At 6.00 pm the Taxi arrived, like a chariot from the gods to take us back to the hotel. At 6.30 pm I was on the Gin and Tonic with Robert, hair of the dog. At 7.00 pm the program director Gerry floated in and took everyone to dinner, sea bass and potato dauphinoise, St Emellion by the bucket. At 7pm Cara rang, couldn't really talk with the background noise, by all accounts she had arranged house viewings and a meeting with the bank at the weekend. At 9pm I was back in the bar. At 12am Robert & Bartek agreed to call it a night, said tomorrow the nightclub was open so we needed to save ourselves for a big one before leaving for home on the Thursday. At 12.30am I fell onto the pillow, God is good I thought and was out like a light.

Brittany nightclubs were much the same as nightclubs anywhere, loud and hot. To save trips to the bar we procured a bottle of Bombay Sapphire and a bucket of ice replete with tongs and sliced lemon. Robert, he told me, was on the rebound from his second divorce and had managed intimacy to some degree with a local girl ten years his junior. They sat on a couch together giggling as she toyed with a button on his shirt, me and Bartek were positioned opposite. He was half deaf in his left ear so I had to roar in order for him to hear anything. He winced with delight on each mouthful of Gin "Ah that lavaely". Half way down the bottle Charlottes friend joined us, a petit blond with a massive chest. At some point Robert brought his shiny face to my ear, "She likes you mate" he said. I wasn't sure what to say, "let's get out of here" he said "back to Charlottes ?". I took a look at the blond, she had her back to me with her hands in her bum pockets, chatting casually, her rounded bosom jutting through the spandrels of her arms.

"I'll leave you to it," I said to Robert "I have a big one tomorrow".

STORIES OF A DIGITAL SPALPEEN

He sprung backwards and viewed me as if I were an imposter. "That gorgeous little piece of fluff fancies you mate," he said.

Twenty minutes later we were in Charlotte`s Renault, she was drunk as a monkey driving like Alain Prost down the back straight, Robert joined her in the front, puffing a cigarette, the blond squeezed in between myself and Bartek in the back, Bartek belting out the Polish nation anthem. We landed on the flower bed outside her house, the climax of the night. Inside Robert and Charlotte disappeared to the bedroom. The blond fixed us a drink, she had no Gin but anything would do, Bartek would have drunk out of a flower pot. It was possible she fancied me, she was showing me great attention with smiles and tactile advances, trouble was, every question she asked Bartek answered like a loud hailer. We weren't long there when there was a screech from the bedroom and the door swung open. Robert grabbed his jacket from the arm of the couch, "come on, we're off" he said.

"What happened ?" I asked standing up.

"Ach, she's gone mad" he said her outline appearing in the frame of the bedroom door dressed in a betty blue t-shirt.

"Git hout you Scottish prig" she said.

It would have been funny had it not been 5am. With an hour to walk home through the deserted streets, it left time for another round of scalding shower cold coffee. I called again on my good friends God and his blessed mother Mary to help me through another day.

D. M. O'DOWD

Heathrow was the usual chaos but I was glad to have gotten that far, I smoked a fag at the taxi rank and popped a mouthful of mints, it was raining. I was worn to the bone but an unshakable nervous wrench in my gut prevented me from dozing on the plane. Only the thought of Cara, a warm meal and our own duck down duvet kept me going. I fell in the door. She was just out of the bath and super excited to see me, exploding with a week's worth of questions and gossip. I barely had the gas to suck the strands of spaghetti she had prepared.

Pouring us both a glass of wine she asked "If I had been a good boy ?"

"I did my best" I croaked, feeling relief and guilt in equal measure. Relief that I had behaved with the blond all be it due to circumstance prevailing and the guilt of the thought of my unborn heir, spunk drunk on English Gin wasn't exactly the best start in life.

"Hang on she said" too excited to notice, hopping from her seat kissing my cheek returning with a bunch of property adverts. She laid them like tiles on the table, six of them, Putney, Clapham, Clapham Junction and Sutton in quick succession with a visit to the mortgage advisor pencilled in for late afternoon. I slurped the last strand of spaghetti, no sooner had it whistled into my mouth Cara had removed the plate, whipped it into the dishwasher, dimmed the lights and unhitched the bobbled belt on her bathrobe. "Baby making time" she announced.

Our mortgage advisor Kamal on first impression was only a boy, jerky and jocular in a slim fit suit, a flicker of lurking mischief. He rifled through the details with questions on salary, dividends and pensions. "Credit outstanding ?" he looked up, answering "none" before I could open my mouth. "Give me a moment" he continued, entering the details into the number cruncher. Cara left her hand on my knee for comfort. "Emm" he pondered reviewing the screen, a drum roll on the table. "What's your retirement age again ?" he asked.

"Sixty" I suggested.

"Don't you mean seventy ?" suggestively bunching his lips.

"Yes, of course," Cara replied "Seventy," getting the hint.

He returned his gaze to the terminal. "Looking better," he said, taking a printout and laying it on the desk, he used his ballpoint to encircle the figure with a whip. Was I seeing things ?, I wondered, £100,00 beyond what I ever thought possible. Cara chirped with joy. If he says so then it must be true I thought accepting the burden of responsibility that came with fatherhood. Cara was straight on the phone to her mother Carol while Kamal packaged up all the information. "We should meet for a drink once" he said as we shook hands confirming he would be in touch. I took Cara for a flat white in an ethical coffee shop to celebrate. "How am I going to pay all that money ?" I wondered reflecting on the meeting.

In the following weeks, the pressure cranked. The drinking increased. The humping, pumping and house hunting. Fabian haunted me, every move I made there he was his face like a funeral, exposing his yellow teeth in the smoking area. "Everything going smoozly ? "he would always commence attempting to unnerve me through a steadfast quizzical look in his rat's eyes. "Absolutely Fabian" I assured him wondering trying not to flinch. Robert had changed direction in the drinking, we were now on pints of continental larger and flaming Drambuies. Although we still went to the nightclub for the late drink his romance had fizzed out when Charlotte blanked him. He laughed it off. The blond was now working there in the coat room and would come to chat Robert, I tried to keep my distance, my hesitation only serving to increase her interest according to Robert at least, although I had noticed that each week she seemed to appear more and more sensual. Tight white hipsters with a gap just so sufficient to showcase her new tattoo.

"Ow are u ?" she asked plopping down on the couch beside me and suddenly on the cusp of a kiss, I could feel her sweet hot breath on my face. The response to the question ignored, all conversation ceased, we were eye to eye.

"I'll be right back" I said and hurried for the jacks to compose myself. I cracked and went back to the hotel, stumbled home leaving the blond on the couch. I crashed on the bed a ball of frustration, thought about a wank to take the edge off but remembered my unborn and settled for falling asleep fully clothed to the shopping channel.

"Where did you disappear to ?" was my good morning from Robert.

"I'll tell you later" I assured him, which placated him for now.

Fabian on the other hand was on me like a rash all day looking for updates on why we were tracking behind on testing and what was the recovery plan. I called Brent for guidance, voicemail again. By all accounts he was in Greece enjoying the Hilton with views of the Acropolises, impressing his newfound culture by drinking ouzo and eating sheep's eyes with the locals. My one meadow of comfort was lunch with Michel, we had slowly built a mutual admiration discussing matters of woodwork, the Lorien traditional music festival, bodhran beats in Donegal and how to cook the perfect Beef Bourgeoning.

I spilled the beans to Robert and Bartek, all the distresses of finding the perfect two bedroom in a modest postcode along with the performance pressures both in the boardroom and the bed. The conclusion was "She has you by the balls". Bartek agreed but more so from a nihilistic point of view of a post communist, he poetically put it that my day in the Sun was done. They weren't done there though, no, three unsolicited hours of it. From detailed accounts of the bachelor who delights in the excitement of a regular shag, to fertility diaries and thermometer checks before sex, "Viparita Karani, legs up along the wall, eh ?". Robert prompted. I pretended I knew nothing but he had me, Cara was now doing each time after we made love. We ended up at saggy tits, playboy subscriptions and education fees. No wonder I got the stomach ulcer.

It all came to a head on a Friday. Despite trying to eat healthy having had a salad and Kombucha, green bananas, and an Epsom salts bath I felt shitty. Cara managed to get a lunchtime appointment at a private clinic it being a matter of some urgency given I would be back in the air on Monday. Dr Odenwingey's smile was wide and welcoming accentuated with large lips.

"How can I help ?" she asked hands pitched on the desk Buddha-like.

She waited, I hesitated, wondering if I had imagined the groans in my stomach. She coaxed a little more information from me and confirmed that it was a simple case of excessive, too much hurry, too much curry and too much worry she informed me, too much booze, Marlboro and too little sleep she added. She wrote out a prescription with a long looping hand. "Make sure you follow the instructions," she said reminding me of the side effects, sliding the chit of paper along the table.

I had little time to admonish myself, louche lifestyle and all that, my phone buzzed with a voicemail from Kamal, a reminder of our drinks at 6.30pm in the North Star. If he didn't hear from me the assumption would be to see me there. There were two further missed calls from Fabian, a text from Robert asking *How's big Daddy ?* and a call and a text from Cara wondering *how it went?*. I questioned was she too good for me. The phone started buzzing again, Fabian with a late meeting invite entitled "Optimisations Review – Urgent," with options to accept or decline, *quelle horreur.*

I was surprised to see Kamal was in company, from a distance a shimmering beauty. Up close a confirmation.

"Meet my sister Fila" Kamal said, with pride. She offered a limp wrist hooped with gold bracelets, her face partly covered by a gloss of ebony hair.

"What's up Kamal ?" I asked.

"Oh nothing much" he joked, "just a few things to go through" he said, beginning to re-iterate details we had been through before. He took a call, excused himself and trotted off. Might as well have a drink.

"Sorry can I ask your name again ?"

"Fila" she answered in a low silky voice.

She didn't drink very often but said she would try a whiskey and ginger with me. She sank it and asked for another, my first drink of the day causing a loud spiralling rumble, that gave her a giggle. She had just arrived in London, studied economics, loved West Life, Wagamama and the freedom of living away from home in such a vibrant city. She had the face of a fawn with the magnetic eyes of a Leopard explaining further what she liked about London. We had another round. My stomach rumbled again, louder like a bear awakening after winter. "Are you ok ?" Fila noticed, a little concerned. I grimaced a smile while attempting to ride out the cramp in my stomach. I excused myself and made off penguin style for the jacks.

There was no lock on the toilet door, Bollix, I had to hunch forward and extend a hand to prevent intruders, anyone might think I was giving birth in there with all the moans and heavy breathing. I realised the likely causation that I had not followed the instruction mentioned by Dr Odenwingey, I had popped two pills in her waiting room although the instruction said one and at night before bed with abstinence from alcohol. "What about it" I had said. My phone rang, Fabian, fuck, at this time, on a Friday, aren't there harassment laws in France around this kind of thing ?. I shut off the phone. Holy Moses, there was no toilet roll. I spun the naked tube still on the toilet roll holder. I had been in there a good fifteen minutes without let up, beads of perspiration were forming on my brow from sustaining the uncomfortable door hold pose. I sat listening in silence to the urinal dripping wondering if that was the last of it, standing tentatively to check. I had to use my best pair of Calvin Kleins to do the toilet paper job, not exactly in line with the metrosexual branding, dumped in the bin. Going commando I washed my hands, my face glistened, I tucked in my shirt, puffed out the chest and made my way back to the bar.

No Kamel yet, where the fuck was he ?. I noticed that Fila was looking a little disoriented, she had finished her whiskey and mine along with it.

"Are you ok ?" I enquired, she looked at me with a big wobbly head, a dreamy smile and big glassy eyes.

"Your no Kian Egan but you're not bad", she said.

"Fuck" I thought "Taxi".

I took about twenty minutes to get her address out of her, 121, no 212 no 221, Dover Park Drive, no Dover House Road. I am going to kill Kamil, the little shit when I get hold of him. I helped her from the Taxi, the little red digits on the meter running like a stopwatch all the time took fiddling and fumbling with the keys to find the right one, hoping this was the right address. Bingo it opened.

"Will you be ok from here ?" I asked. She wobbled on her heels and fell into me, I held her up and she tried to kiss me, awkwardly. Honestly of all the years I spent scouring pubs and nightclubs from Manorhamilton to Mayfair unable to procure a ride for love nor money and now all this female attention.

"I think I love Kian Eagen" she said and started to cry.

STORIES OF A DIGITAL SPALPEEN

"And I'm sure he loves you too" I assured, seeing her in and closing the door.

Cara missed calls (3). She's going to crucify me. I leathered up the steps to our apartment, slipped and cracked my nut off the door. Jesus falls for the third time. The bang was loud enough to alert Cara. "What happened ? ", she cried automatically assuming the worst e.g. attacked by a gang of teenagers on asbos. She sat me down on chair and dabbed my forehead with cotton wool moist with T-Tree. Resting my chin on her navel I wrapped my arms around her waist and lapped up the attention. My hands wandered, feeling the outline of an incongruous object in her jeans pocket.

"What's this ? ", she didn't answer. I poked it out and examined, "a pregnancy test ?". She half smiled and nodded meekly. I took a moment acknowledging the single pink line meant negative, her eyes glistened.

"This time I was sure" she said. I held her as all the frustrations poured out, the petals of her heart closing, we stood like that for a long time, until my phone buzzed.

Brent, "I'd better take this one".

"Sorry mate" says Brent "been caught up these last few weeks, and again, sorry for such a late call, just arrived home from Athens".

"No problem Brent," I assured him.

"Listen" he continued "just wanted to call to give you some feedback from the project,"

"Oh, ok," I said fearing the worst.

"Ya, they are really pleased with your efforts and progress" he said.

"Glad to hear it", I replied with some relief.

"In at the deep end I know" Brent went on "but you are doing a good job mate" he says over the sounds of a crying child in the background. "Oh oh," says Brent, "that's my youngest one, vexed that Daddy, just in the door is on the phone so I'd better let you go mate."

"Yes sounds like you got your hands full there," I commented.

"That's life," he said, "but wouldn't change it for the world, would I mate ?" he asked to his son who's muffled response I couldn't quite make out. "You'll know all about it one day yourself" Brent says returning his attention to me and the phone. "It's hard to explain," he mused.

I looked towards Cara who was making a pot of tea, relaxed in a comfy cardigan.

"Time will tell Brent" I said and thanked him again for the call.

We sipped the honey and lemon tea watching TV. I draped my arm around her and switched off the phone. We didn't need to talk, all was understood. Thinking about Brent, "bitter sweet,", came to me, that was the oxy-moron he might have been searching for. Was it the lemon that made the honey taste so sweet or the honey that took the edge off the lemon, does it matter ?, could life be just as simple as a cup of tea ? Bitter sweet.

Meeting the Duvel

This was going to be a meeting to end all meetings for the project to end all projects. A global rollout over the course of the next twelve months, a standardization of process from finance to supply chain, promotions and operations. Due to the importance, the meeting was considered mandatory and would be held in the Brussels Office. The agenda and further details were as listed :

Agenda

- 08.45 – 09:00 - Morning Breakfast – A selection of coffee and petit gateaux
- 09:00 – 9.45 – Project Purpose & Introduction - Program Director - Jules Janssens
- 09:45 – 10:00 – Break & Refreshments
- 10:00 – 11:30 – A word from our Sponsors – Bernard Whitehead & Maureen Winterbottom
- 11.30 – 12:15 – Lunch
- 13:00 – 15:00 - Group Assignment
- 15:00 – 15:15 - Break & Refreshments
- 15:15 – 17:30 – Assignment Review & Q&A
- 17:30 – 19:00 - Dinner

Further Notes

a. Please arrive the night before to ensure you present prior to the noted start time

b. For an approved list of Hotels please contact Project Management Office

c. The Market have requested all attending to please present themselves in business formal attire.

The request for the attire had come from Jules, the Program Director who always looked impeccable and expected the same turn out from all participants. I needed to get this right and made sure that the suit was taken to the dry cleaners along with the silk tie. My ticket was booked on the Eurostar and all arriving attendees were directed to the same NH Hotel on Rue Royal Brussels. I would be staying the night before and the night of the event, the following day I would work from the office before taking the Eurostar back to London at 3pm. I kissed Cara on the doorstep, she was still in her sleep ware, uninterested, "see you Friday" she said and was back inside in a blink.

In the hotel bar on the evening, I arrived finishing my second beer the thought of one for the road crossed my mind but I paused, had a word with myself and agreed that I didn't want to fuck this one up. Not knowing what to do with myself in the room before 10 pm, I made a cup of tea enjoyed the complimentary ginger snap and watched an episode of Poirot in my socks.

In the morning I took care to shave every facial follicle and spent about twenty minutes attempting the Windsor knot, the last time I had done so was at Vincent and Nuala's wedding. A final inspection revealed the pink dry cleaners tag stapled to the collar which I removed and tossed in the bin. I enjoyed a modest breakfast and took a taxi to the office, a big roomy Merc. Jules was at the door to greet arrivals with the smile of an ambassador. He was beautifully decked out, as expected, in the palest of blue shirts, a Gray chalk stripe suit with an Oxford blue velvet dickey bow and a pair of Peyton shoes you could eat your dinner off. His hair of tight bunch of curls was carefully coiffured, his nails I noticed perfectly manicured as he offered it out complimenting me on turning out so well.

Jules handled the introduction smoothly, from the podium gave us an overview of the program, what the objectives were which included, consolidation of business process, standardization of business process, reduction of operation costs and associated IT infrastructure i.e. shrinkage of license costs. A lady from Bolton, Sue raised her hand with a question, "Would there be layoffs, as part of this consolidation ?". Jules handled it beautifully, he didn't say either yes or no, instead mentioned that in all large programs, there are certain sacrifices and certain gains to be won or lost in one area or another. Giles from Grenoble asked did the program have a name ?, to which Jules replied "Great question," and went on to explain that as part of the group assignment later in the day there would be a task to suggest a suitable name for the program. A prize would be awarded to the winning team. Sue raised her hand a second time, however, Jules, making an executive decision overlooked her (despite the hand flapping) and passed on to Dylan who enquired what would be the first business unit to adopt ?. Jules answered without hesitation, it would be "Barcelona," which sent a ripple of approval through the audience.

The speech from the Chief Financial Officer and the Program sponsors lacked the sparkle that Jules had kicked us off with. Too many facts and figures, too many slides and platitudes, Bernard says "One team one voice,", Maureen with "There is no I in team,". A heave of relief signalled the arrival of the caterers when in the background rolling in the trollies with lunch. Curls of smoked Salmon with cream cheese on Rye bread, blinis with caviar, ratatouille and rocket, an abundance of fruit salad, San Pellegrino both still and sparkling. It was all very civilized, white plates with maroon napkins, pinky fingers extended and conversations involving much reciprocal nodding. Jules floated, with his napkin tucked into the collar of his shirt as a layer of protection for the dickey bow. From one pod to the next in one moment listening intently with a wrinkle of concern the next beaming brightly with a light hearted witticism. He was one of the last to leave the area when we were called back for the Group assignment, where photocopies were handed out detailing a number of associated sub tasks. A business trivia section where groups were asked to estimate random facts and figures from number of employees in associated business units, longest serving employee, manufacturing locations etc, section two on third party service integrators and preferred partners, a third section on regulations such as Sarbanes Oxley and GDPR the fourth section more trivia with questions on the project sponsors and leadership team, what football team they support, can you guess who is a rolling stones fan etc, fifth and final section on a proposal for the project name.

My group consisted of Petra from Prague, Marcin from Warsaw and another girl that I had worked with in the past, Isabelle from Madrid. I had spotted her earlier but not had the opportunity to say hi, we greeted one another with an air kiss left and right, she gushed to tell me that she had just gotten engaged, presenting a rock to compliment the Rolex Daddy had bought her for her thirtieth birthday. We chatted for a while before setting down to the task with Petra assuming the writing duties, we all made a stab at the answers down to the final question coming stuck on the project name. Marcin suggested what we felt was a little too mundane, HAM - Harmonizing All Markets, Isabella came in with something a little more upbeat, BEBO – Better European Back Office, nice, we all agreed, what about, CUMT - Centrally Unified Market Technology I suggested. Petra wrote it down, she thought about it holding the end of the pencil against her top lip.

"Ya I like that,", she concluded "How might you pronounce that ?" she wondered,.

"Just CUMT" I replied.

"CUMT," she repeated.

"Yes."

"OK will we go with that one ?" she suggested to the group.

Isabella nodded in agreement and Macin said it was "Catchy, ya,".

Petra again assumed the position of group spokesperson. Taking a breath, stood with her notepad held to her chest as Jules turns to her.

"Right Group E what do you have for us ?"

Petra said that we considered many but finally agreed on "CUNT."

"I'm sorry" Jules replied from the podium cupping his ear, I put my hand to my face.

"CUNT" Petra repeated - Centrally Unified Market Technology.

"Oh I see," says Jules still wondering if had heard her right, "Thank you Petra, now moving on to the next and final group," he in the direction of their table.

Petra returned to her seat with a gasp of relief. Isabella looked at her holding up her crossed her fingers. Marcin patted her shoulder as if to say well done. We didn't win.

Jules wrapped up the event with a thank you and a reminder of the evening meal, with time to pop back to the hotel to drop our laptops and freshen up. There was a renewed energy in the room having made it through the day, the exercises and not embarrassed ourselves and of course the meal in a famous Belgian restaurant to look forward to with Moule Frites and Trappist Tripple to be consumed. Jules had also decided to stay in the hotel, even though he was a Bruxellois. Team building he called it. We had a quick beer in the bar before heading up to the room, a lovely Lambic recommended by Jules who gave myself and Herman form Hamburg the rundown on the history of the brewing process along with a story of King Karl, who visiting a pub outside of Brussels drank three litres of the stuff and proceeded to lech after the blond barmaid only managing to kiss her backside. The story got a great response, Jules was certainly beginning to loosen up and didn't even bother to drop his laptop to the room, just left it in the car he said. I changed into Jeans and a T Shirt came back down to ask the restaurant address from him, he would see us there shortly, still in conversation with Isabelle and a group of others, gauging consensus on how the workshop went while downing another Lambic along with the bowl of salted peanuts from the counter.

Some time later he entered the restaurant, it was subdued until then but Jules lit the place up. Oysters, Oysters, Oysters he called as he walked to the table catching the waiter before he made off.

"Yes sir how many will that be ?"enquired the waiter.

"Everyone" Jules simply advised with a blank look of surprise, "And Champagne, no wait Kir Royal," he added.

"Everyone I suppose ?", the waiter enquired dryly.

"Everyone" confirmed Jules.

Isabelle whispered to me that she was allergic to shellfish and would I eat hers ?. The Kir Royales were consumed and the waiter called out on forgetting a plate of Oysters for Sue from Bolton, Jules barked at him to bring the moule Frites before we die of hunger suggesting a pairing with a Golden Ale called Duvel. The waiter looked at him with contempt but held his water, Jules ordering him to bring a clean fork saying "This one is filthy,", although from where I was sitting there wasn't a mark on it. After coffee and a choice of Tiramisu and Panna cotta the group started to chip away one by one saying their good nights and thanking

Jules for an excellent meal and a wonderful day. On leaving Maureen in a hushed voice advised to "go easy" keeping it jocular but half serious, unfortunately falling on deaf ears and glassy eyes. A moment later I watched him stagger to the toilet coming back with what I hoped was a soap stain on the front of his pants. His interest gradually waning in acknowledging any farewells, sometimes not even bothering to look their way just raising a hand. He was downing the Duvel like there was no tomorrow moving over to sit on a free chair next to Isabelle and myself. Isabelle, having a woman's nose for danger, decided to present her engagement ring as an off limits warning. He examined the ring, lowered his lips placing a kiss on the back of her hand, Isabelle, not sure what to do, looked at me, inflated her eyes, I responded by raising my eyebrows. He proceeded to place a second one in the centre of her wrist, followed by a third half way up her arm.

"Oh" she shrieked in shock and whipped her arm out from under him. "Isn't he married ?" she hissed at me.

I was about to answer that I thought he was but was completely distracted when he suddenly sprang to his feet.

"Hold on" he cried to the waiter "l'addition," he spoke in French, the waiter quickly returning with a receipt as long as his leg before they got into a heated exchange with Jules insisting it was not possible that there were twelve bottles of wine drunk, twenty seven deadly Duval and eighteen Kir Royals consumed. Only when the manager arrived things calmed down and Jules agreed to settle the bill. He insisted that we head to the Wild Geese Pub, in my honour he reminded me, we must try the Irish coffee, the best in all of Belgium. I checked with Herman from Hamburg, who was also now well on and delighted to be invited by the Program director, Herman said sure he would go and I also half cuckoo agreed also, Isabelle and Sue were the only other two remaining, reluctantly they said they would go for one and only one. Jump in Jules says beeping open the silver Mercedes station wagon parked outside the door. There was a moment of shock from everyone that Jules was proposing to drive, but then again it was so convenient, we piled in. The two women in the back, next to the child seat, Herman from Hamburg in the front, I had to climb into the boot, on top of his laptop and a Fisher Price Laugh and learn that it started "Row row row your boat," as I leant on it. We sped through the streets of Brussels, screeching round corners, straight through lights, ignoring the flashing lights of an ambulance before coming to a hurried halt outside the Wild Geese Irish pub. Herman declared two more minutes of that and the Oysters were coming up.

We started on the Irish coffee, then left out the coffee and went on the straight Powers. Isabelle and Sue agreed secretly they would say goodnight and slipped out the door while Jules was on the dancefloor with the glass in his hand, being watched closely by the big bald bouncer in the black bomber jacket. Jules wondered where the beautiful Isabella had gone, noticing at the same time that he had misplaced his dickey bow looking back to the dancefloor so see where he may have lost it but quickly forgotten about as we were escorted to the bar for another drop of Irish. His eyes were gone at this stage, he started to say he knew it was me that came up with the CUMT acronym, turning very serious warning with a finger that such behaviour was a sackable offence before bursting out laughing and slapping me on the shoulder. "Come my friends," he announced to myself and Herman we had one last essential stop to make on our visit to lovely Brussels, so we bundled into the station wagon again and landed at Angels strip club. We watched as Lolita displayed her supine acrobatics on the brass pole, followed by Anastasia who drew it out before dropping the bra (as if by accident) to reveal a perfectly symmetrical pair of manufactured mammary's. Lola, the next act, particularly aroused Jules who couldn't sit still, it was impossible to stop him at that moment she descended from the stage, pouncing on her and taking her amorously into an air tight embrace, spilling all kinds of offers into her ear.

He was quickly spotted by the bouncer who grabbed him by the collar and walked him to the door. Jules looked truly dangerous as he was forced to settle the bill, including the Kir's we didn't even set our lips on. We left to a final warning from the bouncer that he was aware this was not the first time, "No fucking touching the girls,".

I couldn't face going into the office the next day, I just couldn't work up the courage. I logged in from the hotel room and noticed that Isabella was online.

"Morning Isabella, how is the head ?", I pinged into the chat.

It took a while until she replied with an emoji with a zig zag mouth, "Not as bad as yours I'm sure".

I let her know, "I am in the hotel."

"Me too," she replied, "No going to the office," she added "Not possible to face Jules, he is a maniac."

STORIES OF A DIGITAL SPALPEEN

I give her a thumbs up content that I was not the only one taking the cowardly option. I needed a shower which I was going to take but in five minutes, I was just going to rest my eyes, just for a moment, content in the knowledge that however bad I felt it couldn't possibly be as bad as Jules. I woke up with the track of the keyboard on my face to the sound of ping, ping, ping message after message after message. I looked at the clock on the bottom right hand corner of the laptop, it was eleven am, I was asleep for two hours, the ping was from Petra, wondering if I could share with her the presentation from yesterday.

"Are you there ?"

Followed by "Hello, it says you are online ?".

Then "Presentation ? ....."

I wondered in a daze what presentation but managed pull myself together, dig it out and send to her.

"Thank you so much" she replied with a smiley face.

I ordered a bowl of soup room service for lunch and by the time it was time to sign off I was close to getting back to myself. The Eurostar lounge was stocked with all kinds of beer, wine and Spirits along with mini pretzels and party mix. I spotted a row of Duvel in the fridge, I examined one, "Sure why not," was the decision.

It was Monday before we heard from Jules again, on a conference call, the first one post project workshop. He was back to his chirpy self, with an open question on "How everyone had enjoyed the workshop ?", to which there was a general murmur of acknowledgement, "I hope you found it useful.", he further added and paused for any specific feedback. It was on the tip of my tongue to say the Duvel was a revelation but instead I offered a platitude, "Great to meet the team and get to know everyone a little better" to which Jules confirmed it was indeed a special event and instructed everyone to pencil in the follow up which would take place in three months. Immediately the sensation of Oysters and Duvel gurgled up in the back of my throat.

The Invincibles

For six months after Cara left me I wasn't right in the head. I would have drank out of a sore toe to numb the pain. A year later I had become a social sot, every wake or wedding for five miles around, meself in the corner sure to be found, opening of an envelope or any excuse. All in the name of getting her out of my head, easier said than done, there was no one like her and I couldn't see myself with anyone else. I would call home and speak with the father or the mother and would yearn for them to mention her, just mention her name, was she home, had they seen her or even seen her mother Carol in Supervalu? did she ask for me? I couldn't bring the subject up myself, of course, it was an embarrassment, I was supposed to be the rake of the family but fuck it was a bitter pill to swallow because Cara left me for another fella.

It all started innocently enough, with a mention here and a mention there of Drew, her South African colleague. I went along with it till I saw a photo of him. "That's Drew she said pointing him out", the guy with swimmers shoulders in the starched white shirt. We joked about it, any small comment or criticism and I would throw in the Drew comment, but that was the thread and I began to realise that eventually the joke was on me. In typical fashion instead of fronting up, I avoided, started to go out more and came home late, things started to cool, in every area if you know what I mean, and the rest is history. She promised that we were only taking a break and that she needed some space and the next thing I know she was gone, the last view of her the back of her head as she wheeled out her wheelie bag, the door slowly brushed along the taupe carpet and then clunked closed. We talked but less and less until she didn't return my calls. That was the punch in the gut, the silence, followed by the slap in the face, seeing them together on Facebook arm in arm with matching smiles at an awards event in Covent Garden. I immediately unfriended her, pulled the duvet over my head and curled into the foetal position.

After that, I seemed to spend most of my life moping up and down Chiswick High Road, just plodding along, eating hummus sandwiches in Turnham Green, pint of mild in the Crown and Anchor, leafing through books in WH Smith, browsing the plastic containers in Robert Diaz, nibbling sesame sticks from Holland and Barrett. Time moved like treacle, changing my underwear was a chore, all colours were a shade of brown, every day it seemed to drizzle. I came out of the cinema wondering what the movie was about, rang Mossy and wondered who I had been speaking to, left my zip down constantly, brushed my hair and left the brush in. It was almost by chance I noticed her, in one of my usual bouts of comatose, waiting at the bus stop found myself staring into the window of Lombok. She was standing upright waiting for a customer to serve, her arms were folded and she checked her watch twice before noticing me noticing her. The Macintosh and the Tesco plastic bag may not have given the best first impression as upon eye contact she had turned away. I remained undeterred until the shimmer of the 391 appeared as a reflection in the window. I sat on the top deck and began to unpick the plan of how I was going to win her heart.

The plan was no plan, I found myself again stationary at the window peering in to see if she was there before I took the plunge to buy a large item of Indonesian furniture to gain access to her. This time she was on the move fixing cushions on a sofa with the long fingers of her elegant hands. I had gone to the trouble of shaving and wearing a shirt. The door jingled when I entered which drew attention to me from the four members of staff, they followed my approach as I tried to avoid eye contact with any of the other three keeping my head down making a bee line for her.

"Good Morning" she said very professionally with an accent.

"Good morning" I replied a little nervous.

Followed by her asking "How can I help you ?"

All very standard so far, but that's as far as the plan went, and for a moment I cursed the fact that she worked in a furniture shop, why not in a wine shop or even selling fishing Tackle. Since leaving, Cara had taken the dining room table and chairs, the Chinese chest and the Moroccan Dresser. The only effort I had made since then was the Ikea flat pack that remained unopened for the last nine months, most of my meals were eaten from cartons on the couch. I reverted back to the dumb stationary position.

"Um" I muttered, "I'm looking for a sideboard" and without hesitation she led me to a beautifully crafted Indonesian teak sideboard, her hand directing me to look it over, which I did slowly and carefully.

I couldn't ask the price, I didn't want to look cheap, she asked how I liked it and I said, beautiful referring to her who up close was even more sensuously stunning than at a distance through an inch of glass.

"It has been recently reduced from £5,999 to £5,500 she says without flinching."

"I'll take it" I said.

What the fuck was I going to do with it though, I thought as she walked me back towards the cashier but that was not the priority at the moment. The Priority was how was I going to ask her out, to work around to the subject on recommending anywhere to eat or drink, even though I knew in alphabetical order every restaurant, café and speak easy on the high road. She would surely recommend somewhere and then I would drop in, as if an afterthought if she would like to join me. Approaching the till, my heart began to pound, looping through the what if's and building myself up to the question. What if I didn't have enough money on my credit card, the sudden thought ran down me like fingernails along a blackboard. She stopped short, two feet from the sales desk and as if out of nowhere a senior sales assistant, a guy in a tailored black suit appeared behind the counter.

"My colleague will look after you," she says.

"Um," I say again, "Thank you," I add.

"Thank you," she replied with a half genuine smile and walked away.

"Payment by card or cash Sir," the voice from behind the counter wondered.

"Cash ... I mean Card .."

STORIES OF A DIGITAL SPALPEEN

The next time I looked up Christmas was coming, the sideboard had been sitting unused and unloved for three weeks. The Delivery guys had just managed to jut it in somehow between the sofa and the armchair. The spicy sales girl a distant memory but served as an interlude from the ongoing morose memories of Cara. The landlady Christina had done a great job on the Tinsel wraps and the flashing fairy lights in the Kings Arms, WHAM last Christmas was playing and it was filling up fast these evenings with the office parties. In the company of the usual suspects Mr Roy, a swaggering Jock with Sophisticated tastes, G-Man a Caribbean born Cockney and Mani my Punjabi mate we sat around a round table talking about Arsenal when I had to do a double take to confirm it was not a mirage. Was that her at the end of the bar ?, recognising also her colleague to whom I handed over £5,500 plus £120 delivery and installation charge, how could I forget that face ? Roy was waffling in the background, he was showcasing the tartan lining of his Burberry coat bought in Harrods, said Freddie Ljungberg wore the same one.

"Hey, are you with us ?", Mani asked, clicking his fingers in my line of vision.

I wasn't with him at all. She broke off from her conversation at the bar a smile lingering on her face and started to walk my way. I slowly rose to my feed half in shock, half in awe watching her motion through the crowd, half imagining that she specifically approaching me. I was on the cusp of murmuring hello, attempting to make eye contact as she passed with a puff of perfume and I was left like a lighthouse in a bog for the second time.

Things took a turn for the better however when the table beside us emptied and the sales assistant in the suit motioned to their group to pounce before some other gang gathered at the bar might move in. They quickly cleared the mess, taking glasses and empty plates to the bar and draping their coats over the backs of the chairs. Mani asked again if I was on planet Earth tonight as I leaned to the side eavesdropping on what might be going on. As the night wore on the numbers dwindled a little and G-Man struck up a conversation with the guy in the suit and I noted they were talking about me. He called across the table stating that he never knew I was an antique lover. The guy in the suit acknowledged with a nod of the head and I looked to her as she looked at me and I said "Hello again." She told me that it was the quickest sale that she had ever made in her three months in furniture sales. I mentioned that likewise, it was the fastest purchase that I had ever made, but the piece just spoke to me. Slowly the two tables merged until we were the only remaining table where the merriment prevailed until Christina rang the second bell. Outside she bunched the lapels of her coat around her neck and shivered, clonking her heels on the ground to warm up, her eyes glinted in the sub zero moonlight. I bit the bullet and asked if we could meet again. She hesitated.

"Why?"

I stumbled "Why not ?".

She laughed, warning me "Only as friends".

"Absolute," I said, "fat chance" I thought.

We met literally every night of the week after that to the point Mossy was wondering if I had emigrated until I called him back and let him know my situation. He was more than interested, nationality : Czech, hair colour : brunette, eyes : Hazel, age : gentlemen don't ask, tits : two.

"We're only friends" I said, sick at the sound of my own lame larynx.

"Ya right" he replied...."oh and by the way" he chirped "are you going to Nuala's thirtieth ?", I had completely forgotten about Nuala's birthday, "Cara will be there," he said and I went quiet. It's true I jumped like Pavlov's dog at the mere mention of her name.

"She will ?" I solicited "How do you know ?".

"How do you mean how do I know ?", "How does anyone know anything ?, fucking Facebook" he sounded genuinely bemused. "Don't tell me you're not still into her ?" he hooted. "Will you be bringing the new bird ?" he enquired "What's this her name again Iva ?".

I didn't answer.

The Friday night of Nuala's birthday Iva was nervous She hadn't met most of my friends, not to mention my ex and her pristine partner. I would be lying to say that part of me didn't want her there only to show how I had moved on, to massage my ego, even if that meant that it wasn't exactly fair or authentic to subject Iva to my petty grievances. We took a black cab and didn't speak much en route. I was too busy with the theatre in my head playing out the scene of introducing Iva. It would start with shaking Drew's hand confidently, and competently before launching a headbutt and him desperately clutching his nose, Cara staring at me in disgust before running to his attention. "Pull in here I instructed the Taxi driver", we were on the verge of West Hampstead. Iva wondered why we were stopping, I told her we both needed a drink descending the stairs of a cellar bar. I turned off the phone, placed Nuala's present on the seat, ordered two whiskey, put my hand on the hip of her dress and told her straight that I wanted to be more than friends. She knocked back the drink, winced and said it wasn't like she hadn't thought about it, but I was ...how does she put this without hurting my feelings, a little immature for her. I ordered two more shots, put my other hand on her other hip, we were both light headed from the heady mix of nervous emotions and twelve year old scotch. I pulled her closer, in as manly a way as I could, observing any resistance. Slowly as I could possibly restrain myself giving her time to still hit the eject button I moved my partly open mouth to hers, she blinked nervously, breathing more noticeably as our flesh finally met and we kissed. As it turned out we didn't make it to the party, in fact for the next nine months we didn't make it very far, the brakes were put on all plans because that was the night I impregnated Iva.

Yes, from a bun in the oven to a final gasping call "It's coming".

"Who might that be ?" I casually enquired stirring a fourth spoon of honey into her Nescafe. Iva had taken to drinking Nescafe recently along with biscuits by the bucket. "It's coming" she repeated in a wheezing drawn out moan from the couch. She was attempting to stand.

"Who's coming ?" I enquired again, confused.

"Who do you think ?", she hissed, turning to face me "Mother fucking Teresa ?".

I didn't know whether to laugh or to cry, "The baby is it ?" I asked, stirring a hole in the cup.

STORIES OF A DIGITAL SPALPEEN

"Yes YOUR baby" with spurted, exasperated, her eyes wide, wild and beautiful.

"Why didn't you tell me ?", I argued back and we stood in silence for a moment. It's not an easy thing trying to get to know someone and have a baby with them at the same time.

"Get my bag in the sideboard and call the taxi, pronto" she instructed as calm as she could manage. The sideboard had also gone through quite the transformation in the last nine months from laying idle to stuffed to the gills with nappies and wipes (unscented), play mats, onesies, burp cloths and nipple cream. I hesitated like I always do (don't ask me why), "now" she begged. "Oh Vienna" I said to myself "the baby is coming".

I won't bore you with the details of the blood and bawling, the feelings of ineptitude, not knowing where to stand, whether to laugh or to cry, ineffable joy, inexorable tears. That tsunami of emotion reaching a crescendo with a natal pop, followed by velvet veil of calm on the hospital cot with our bundle of bliss.

"Welcome to the world our baby boy" I tapped into my facebook timeline, "8lb 7oz", "Mother and baby doing fine", no, I reconsidered, too mundane, pecking at the delete button, "feeling ecstatic", I typed but also rejected as mush. I needed snappy, original, a fluffy barb that eluded me, the whole exhausting ordeal had blunted my wit. Iva was dozing off, the little man beside her wrapped in a blue blanket mouthing kisses to the new world. I wondered if I might slip out for a snifter, wasn't it in fact my obligation?, a pint would surely prompt the appropriate witticism needed to announce our new arrival to our social media network. The

D. M. O'DOWD

Albert, I knew was on Kingston hill I had clocked it earlier, much earlier, a lifetime ago, flashing into view between Iva's parturient heaves in the taxi, it spoke to me, it said "Solace found here". I lowered a leg to the floor, touching the tiles when the bed creaked and I froze at the feel of his liquid eyes fixed on the nape of my neck. It took him only a moment, a split second to realise the familiar feel of his placenta had gone west and a quiver rippled over his tiny face. A mewl pre-empted a patter of little croaks followed by a scream that tore the house down. Well anyway, that was the end of the pint.

Over the next week, we moved from one disaster to another, his waggling head failing to latch on and Iva being guided by the lovely midwife with purple spectacles perched high on her head. I learned that mastitis was not a condition solely for heifers and haemorrhoids itch to the point of mental madness. Sleep went out the window. I called the mother who matter of fact told me that back in the day nappies had to be hand washed. I was exhausted but managed one night to make it over to Mossy's place for some respite, we watched Dallas repeats, episode after episode and smoked a joint. I whinged about how work was so demanding at the moment, project after project, shareholders had ascertained the aura of the Greek gods on Mount Olympus demanding higher profits YOY, the fun had gone out of it somehow. I flicked through my photos showing him the baby. "Lovely" he said and returned to JR's giving Sue Ellen a devious look that was the precursor to the next bust up. I browsed through the photos and in the moment selected my favourite one where the baby had a sort of snarl and posted to facebook with the ambiguous caption, "a new rockstar in town". I made Mossy comment and share. In the back of my mind, I was hoping that Cara would see it. Two hours later, no reaction to the post but four more episodes of Dallas, five more cans of Grolsh and a large joint. Then I did the unquestionable, I fell asleep, zonked, stone dead.

Thirteen missed calls, all from Iva. I called back and she was silent on the other end.

"Well," I say.

"Well" she replies.

I dragged myself home, emptied the dish washer and made a pot of tea. Iva watched cash in the attic not taking her eyes of the TV while I mumbled "Sorry,". I had a minor hangover. I couldn't let it be known of course so offered to take the baby out for a walk. I took the sling and asked her to help me figure out how to put it on. I felt like a bit of a plank in the sling but the sunglasses would help and I knew she liked it, bonding and brownie points. We did the block a few times then stepped right into the beer garden of the Tap on the Line. A Baby in a sling being almost mandatory these days to drink a Beavertown Gamma Ray IPA. I lifted the soapy suds to my lip, his liquid eyes as always fixed on me.

"What are you looking at ?" but his eyes remained fixed "I promise, I'm taking up cycling next week", I hesitated, "you think I have the legs for it ?" which generated a gurgle that I took as his first recognition of Irish wit. "Well? What are we going to name you big man ?, Celt or a Bohemian ?". "Does it matter, one day you will end up a corporate Slave with a lifetime of debt to a German bank, drinking craft beer at eight quid a pop".

My phone pinged and I searched blindly across the bulge eventually pinching it from my pocket. A Facebook notification, to my astonishment it was from Cara. Excitement rushed through me seeing a thumbs up on the posting I had made which at this stage I had almost forgotten about. There was a comment to boot but I needed to unlock the phone to view it, it read a succinct sentiment of "So cute,". I swallowed, gulped even opening messenger, she was online, right now at this very minute, only a high velocity low latency broadband separating us. I wondered what to do.

"Hey stranger," I tapped and paused as another thought had overrun me, "what the hell was Iva watching cash in the attic for ?" and "She looked sad and pretty at the same time, she was right, I am immature, I need to grow up,", I slid the phone back in my pocket. The liquid eyes were still on me fixed faithfully. I looked at him meaningfully, and made a promise to him, a pact between us men, a secret never to be uttered, I even whispered it into his tiny ear, revealing what was going to be his name on his christening day, and remain so for all the days of his life. "Freddy" .. I said, "After Lunjberg, you know ?" ... after the Arsenal legend who scored goals and wore Burberry, "and you know what else ?, I assured him, you, me and Mummy, were going to be the Invincibles".

Amor Vita

This pandemic started so well but now I am in a mess. The initial Euphoria of not needing to travel for meetings, Zoom in the morning, Zoom at night. No overly concerned colleague looking over my shoulder in the office. No more small talk, no more shirts with rubbed up collars, pants with piles or socks with holes in the toes. In a family meeting with Iva we agreed that there was no point staying in London so did an exit stage left and went east to Bratislava. I set my office up in a corner of the bedroom and spend twelve hours a day there, jumping from Zoom to Outlook to Google to Youtube, then I get stuck on LinkedIn because I am trying to build up a following. To start I am going to write a feature – ten tips to become a tycoon - I only managed five :

1. Sleep naked (Steve Jobs)
2. Focus like a Cyclops (Jeff Bezos)
3. Wear a man bag (Richard Branson)
4. Drink Coconut water (Elon Musk)
5. Grow your nose hair (Bill Gates)

After some effort, I have completed it, but wonder if my ideas are even original or if I am simply regurgitating something I had absorbed through the menusha of it all. I get two comments, "What does 5 mean ?" (but I don't respond) and another from a random punter from Hyderabad "I am available for new opportunities, if anything direct message me". Suddenly the corner of the room was a very lonely place.

D. M. O'DOWD

Later in the evening, I focus on ratebeer.com, I am penning a review :

"Plush white head leaving textbook lace over hazy pale yellow body. Elderflower obvious, but not stifling other floral, vegetal and herbal notes. Obvious peppery tones as well as figs, nuts and other boreal vegetation. Interspersed Lemon drizzle, again elderflower, herbs with citrus-like characteristics"

I read it over and a voice inside my head snipes, pretentious git, "It's no wonder that Mossy and Bosco have disowned you". I validate the voice, ever since the leather pants I wouldn't blame them.

The huge retailer I am working for have launched a new website including omni channel experience, a seamless journey for the customer from bricks and mortar stores to digital platforms. Buy in-store and return online. We have a project manager who is a heady cocktail of mood swings. The test team are based in Bangalore, there must be about three hundred of them. They ping in different channels day and night along with the Project Manager and my manager Justin who likes to check if I am working with random pointless question carefully timed, morning, noon and evening. The Architects on the project, dress the best, speak the most and achieve the least. We spend thirteen months back and forth, we discuss, debate, disagree and finally somehow deliver. It is exhausting.

Iva asks me "What I am thinking about ?" and I say, "Oh this and that,"

STORIES OF A DIGITAL SPALPEEN

"This and that," she echoes "I would love to know what is going on in there," sighs and lays her sympathetic palm on my face.

The Town at home is gone to fuck, every time I talk to the brother another pub or shop has closed. It's not apparent at first more of a slow drift away from reality partly because I am cut off which makes way for the existential angst and life weights heavily but I am not sure why ?, the sick part is that I really have nothing to be worried about, wife, kids, career, friends, right up there on Maslow's Hierarchy of needs. I read Nietzsche, he says, "The thought of suicide is a great consolation: by means of it one gets through many a dark night". Kelly ended it all in the mental, he was on suicide watch but managed it anyway with the cord of the light. With Gallagher, no one knew he was suffering. He woke one morning poured the petrol on himself in the garage and lit a match, puff. His guitar plectrum still stuck to the grave, his picture fading a little but he still has that cheeky grin. Cormac Lavin went in over the hedge in the middle of the night, not another car on the road. He lay there peacefully for many hours, until night lifted and the arse of the car was seen elevated through the rushes. Emmet Mullen was mad, everyone loved him, he came freewheeling out of a pub in Sydney, tumbled to the road and was smacked by a taxi. It all ended for him there and then, seventeen thousand, two hundred and thirty six miles from home.

"You're Depressed," Iva says. I don't disagree, confirmed by the voice in my head. I thought I was bullet proof and I was for so many years but some nights I sit on the chair mewling like a lamb. "Why don't you get out a little more

?" she enquires asking if I want to go out with my Kiwi friend, the friendly guy with the underbite. Somehow I feel nervous absurdly imagining I am almost asking Kiwi Josh on a date. We meet for a few beers in Uisce Beatha in Old Town. My God, he can talk out of his mouth as much as I can in my head. We fall out of *Uisce* and end up in an eighties club where he is blaring into my ear about the growth of machine learning as the disco ball reflects shapes on his face, Nick Kershaw sings The Riddle. I was on the double JD's and Coke and enjoying a buzz. In an uncharacteristic fit I took to the dance floor, Josh followed. Talking heads, road to nowhere is on and I am moving my neck like a pigeon, Josh takes off his shoes and is dancing in his feet. I am growing more into it now from the Frug to the Twist to the Funky Chicken.

Two women, a mother-daughter combination bundle in beside us, some kind of family event based on the way they are dressed. Josh doesn't notice, he has his eyes closed, snaking his arms through the smoke, deep into the moment. From where I saw it, it was definitely an innocent mistake, laying his hand on the arse of the mother. The daughter took immediate offence and turns to me (why me ?), with a look of pure disgust and they shuffled away, heels against to the floor, unfortunately taking me with them. I didn't notice it happen, I guess Josh didn't either given his reaction when I was suddenly tugged forward.

"Hey man, where are you off to ?", he enquired. "Hey, I thought you were married ?" his voice trailed after me.

The truth was I didn't know where I was off to. I somehow managed to get hooked onto the of the drawstrings from the daughters blouse. In true eighties fashion these were drawstrings with gold plated hooks on the end and somehow in the art of the dance we became attached. At first, she didn't notice she had a passenger.

"Hey," I called, "excuse me" I beckoned.

The mother was the first to notice and furrowed her brow, "Pozor Petra !" she called in a baritone voice to the daughter, pointing back to me. The daughter whipped around, taking it as further confirmation of her being the family beauty.

"Hey" I called again "Wait," I pleaded, "It's not what you think" but she sped on up in the direction of the table where they had a bottle of white wine resting in an ice bucket.

From the shadow of the mirror ball to the side of the ice bucket he emerged, unfolding to a standing position. Hirsute and huge, I gulped. I tried to explain, he interrupted. "Look" I say again attempting to untangle to drawstring from the button of my shirt. My mind a fog of JD and fear and without thinking left my hand on her breast. She was quick to swat it away, the mother looking on in disdain, the brother threw off the coat and it dawned on me, pleading was pointless, my innocence a minor detail, you don't touch a sister's tit. The punch landed on the right eye it sent me crashing to the floor but worse was to come. Still attached the umbilical connection of the drawstring dragged the sister along with me and soon we were on the floor, her riding on top of me, hair spread out like yellow corn spaghetti all over my face. The smell of cosmetics consumed me and for a moment it threatened to be a pleasurable experience until she started screaming in my ear. Running to her rescue the mother called "moya, moya", pulling her upwards without much success. God save me this was worse than the brother, her elbows poking all over me, she managed to somehow crawl off. I sprung to my feet, free for a moment only, his huge paws descended twofold on my chest and for his next trick, he ripped the shirt clean off my back. I dashed for the door.

"Hey man, wait up" Josh called after me in a panic, he was shoeless, I was shirtless but we were free.

I sulked the next day like Bukowski off the Booze or the Popeye without spinach. I have this friend Iva suggested tentatively, "Would you be willing to try ?"

"Try what" I queried.

"Just go with it" she requested.

Her friend, turned out to be more an acquaintance rather than a friend. She arrived with her crystals, copper bowl and burning sage. It was an early Saturday morning but she was bright eyed, I still had the black eye and a dry mouth. She introduced herself as Suzanna and she spoke with Iva for ten minutes in the mother tongue while I stood mute until instructed to lie down on the couch. She lit the Chakra sage and let the threads of smoke drift through the air, purifying and neutralising (she informed me). Checking my chakras. Number one she said, very bad, two "emm,", three and the crystal on the dainty silver chain didn't as much as flicker, apparently it was supposed to rotate in circles to indicate the health of my aura. She moved the crystal up my body but still not a budge. She looked on in disbelief. Spiritually I was dead.

STORIES OF A DIGITAL SPALPEEN

Medically I was alive but travelled to Dr Pauls to see for how long. The receptionist instructed me to take a seat in a waiting room much like any other, a water cooler with a blue tap and a white tap but out of plastic cups, a little table stacked with Magazines all or most more than two years old. It was comforting to know that this was a global standard. The door swung open and Dr Paul towered above me, all two hundred and ten centimetres and sixty four years of him. "Come in young man" he beckoned in an American accent more American than a Frankfurter renamed Hot Dog. He took a little time leafing through the questionnaire before turning to me starting with the preliminaries, DOB, address, that sort of thing.

"We were going to do a general checkup and bloods,". I nodded in approval. "Let's talk about the lethargy", "Morning, evening or any time in particular ?". He asked.

"Anytime" I replied.

"All day" he scribbled on his notes. "And sleep ?" he asked, "can you sleep comfortably ?"

"Day and night," I told him.

"And dreams ?" he asked.

"Sometimes" I replied.

"Uncomfortable or any reoccurring themes ?"

I sat up, "no".

He paused and returned to the notepad, scribbled his analysis paused and looked at me.

"Vitamin D" he declared, "did you know that 67% of people are lacking vitamin D."

"Interesting" I replied.

"And QC10 he continued, 66% of sapiens are deficient in this mineral vital to vitality."

"Never heard of it" I acknowledged.

He ushered me to the couch to take off my shirt and lie down, which I did. He placed the cold stethoscope on my chest and listened intently.

"Heart failure accounts for fifty five percent of death in men between the ages of forty to fifty, that increased to 57% once the age sixty is attained". I didn't respond and let him continue positioning the cold orb while I breathed in and out as instructed. Helping me from the lying position he had the blood pressure strap around my arm as fast as bad news, twenty over forty, which he commented was good news if not a little on the low side which accounts for only 8% of the population. We moved on to the subject of stools, firm, tarry, runny, 45%, 35% and 25% percent respectively as Dr Paul took me through what the perfect poo should look like while he probed my anus with his finger checking the prostate (28% of male deaths). Popping his finger out, he snapped off the glove, tapped the syringe, slid in the needle and gurgled out three nice cups full. I left the office with a Vitamin D dose and a box of fifty allergy tablets which really wasn't going to fix a broken spirit.

Where might one go for solace ?, where else but Knock Co Mayo. I spoke to Kevin from customer service at theshrine.com, he mentioned Fr Benny who after speaking with put me down for the two week retreat. The bed and board would be modest a room in St Jarlath's, which was mostly used for visiting priests and nuns. Ryanair took me to Dublin, from there Heuston to Westport and Kevin would collect me. Iva was emotional when I was leaving, I didn't like the thought of her alone with the kids, after all we had been through, from feeding to winding to teething and tears we had done it all together. Now I was leaving her all alone, I felt like half a man but she was strong for the both of us.

Fr Benny was upright with a fine head of hair, he moved briskly through the corridors taking me to the room. It was a spartan single with a bedside locker and a bible.

"Grand" I said leaving my bag on the floor expecting Fr Benny to leave me to it.

"You like it then " Fr Benny asked again.

"Ya, grand, ya" I confirmed a second time looking around and waiting for Fr Benny to leave so I could flunk on the bed.

"You'll be wanting a drink then I'm sure," says Fr Benny "After your trip ?" he continued.

"Well ya, that would be nice" I hesitated thinking he was offering a cup of tea.

"Let's be going then ?"

"Going Father ?"

"Well I thought you might like to get out for a wee bit of fresh air, you know ?"

"Oh ok" I answered not sure if this was part of the retreat or not ?

"Do you have a jacket ?, it might be late when we get back" and before I knew it I was at a darts competition in Kilkennys lounge, Fr Benny and myself at the bar next to the sweet hiss of the Guinness tap.

Maybe this was part of the retreat, fucked if I know, but the majority of the conversation was on darts and if anyone could bate the Dubs. I don't remember much about making it home other than Fr Benny driving cautiously the red Corolla, 12 MO 191 and falling into the bed exhausted. The alarm went off, I tippy-toed on the tiles to find the shower meeting Fr Benny along the way, "hello young man" he said with a Tom Jones tan and a fitted Foxford wool knit jumper. I smelled like sleep. He spoke with me for five minutes letting me know a little about the retreat and what to expect before his mobile rang and he excused himself. I found the shower, it was freeze-your-balls off Baltic, I stood in it for several minutes my bones rattling but not a drop of hot. This was the first step in my repentance.

I didn't let Fr Benny know that I didn't much like meeting new people. So just my luck.

"The first thing we will do is give a quick introduction" announces Frances who was running the retreat.

I was one of about fifteen people attending, we mingled with tea on saucers after the introduction session which helped abate the nerves. I met Clare from Limerick who was having marital problems and Peter from London who was trying to get to grips with the loss of his mother. Why did I ever judge these people, I wondered. By the afternoon, Fr Benny stuck his head in, found me out in the crowd and gave me a wink. Was I reading into it too much or did the wink mean anything ?, it did and before I could say "Ah no thanks Father" I was in the Corolla heading down the N17 for Claremorris. We started off in P.J Byrnes and made our way to Wardes then Gilligans. Fr Benny introduced me as his nephew, told everyone I was a genius on the computers, by everyone I mean everyone, he shook more hands than the Pope or Bob Geldof. Thursday night we did Ballyhanius and on the Friday we had a hell of a night in Irish house, barCastle. As a bonus the retreat was going really well as I began to build friendships with the others. We listened to lectures, heard people's stories and something I hadn't done since I was a boy, we prayed.

Fr Benny assured me that there was a man to come and look at the shower, a Conlon from out Midfield way.

"Let me give him a buzz," he says, no answer.

"Don't worry" I assure him, "it is not important" but Fr Benny is thinking something different.

"Be ready at 5" he instructed.

Approx 5.05, back in the Corolla and heading for Midfield in Swinford. The pint was like new Milk in Horkan's. On the stool next to me, Fr Benny seemed agitated, the phone was in and out of his pocket as he checked for updates.

"Don't worry about the shower Father" I assured him "To be honest I am finding it invigorating" to which he smiled, said nothing, stood quickly and on his say so we were back in the Coralla heading for the Dalton Inn, Claremorris. He figured that Conlon was there at a dance there and before I knew it we were heading for the function room lured by the sound off the Yamaha F52 and a bouncing bass. There was the usual hand shaking as people lined up with news or petitions for prayers or advice.

"Are you a Longford woman," I could hear him say before introducing me to a recent widow Gladys.

With a hand on my back, he ushered me to, "Go ahead and take her for a spin". I gave her my best moving in and out, side to side, from a jive to waltz to foxtrot, with the concentration of a surgeon trying not to stand on her foot. Fr Benny cruised into the corner of my eye with a limousine of a lady whom he seemed all too familiar with. A rictus on his face, he raised the eyebrows as they passed. Could this woman be Conlon, after all, I had only heard the person in question referred to as Conlon. The band took a break and I bolted for the double doors and down to Wards.

"Your Fr Bennys nephew", says the barman.

"That's right" I nodded and before I knew it I was on the darts team.

No one seemed to know a Conlon. I tried to get away a few times, alas every time I did there was a new game or a fresh pint until it was one am in the morning and I jumped up and scrambled my jacket on thinking Fr Benny would be in a panic looking for me. He wasn't in the Dalton Inn when I went in, the function was long over the receptionist informed me, not in the front bar either or in the Blue Thunder for his favourite onion rings. Where else could he be? I made my way back to the car, it was dark and the windows were all fugged up. I leaned down and could hear the mumbled music of conversation. Through an opening carved by a droplet of rain, I could see Fr Bennys back to me, the head of his dance partner perched delicately on his shoulder, his hands where they probably shouldn't be. She jolted when she observed my naked eye observing Fr Benny who rolled down the window.

"Where did you get to ?" he asked, "I've been worried sick" raising the eyebrows again, "get in". He whistled like a blackbird the whole way home, the eau de parfum of his dance partner lingered large in the Corolla long after we had dropped her off at her mother's.

On my last night in St Jarlath's I lay on the bed, waiting for Fr Benny, he said my choice, wherever I wanted to go for the last laugh, so we agreed on Moran's in Westport. Opening the drawer of the locker I took out the bible and leafed through the pages. On the inside cover, there was an inscription - "Amor Fati – Love Your Fate, which is in fact your life". A quote from Nietzsche underscored with the name, Michael Mullen dated Feb, 2001. I wondered where Michael Mullen was now, I wondered if he ever met Conlon who threatened again to come on Thursday but - no show. It didn't matter I was believing the benefits of the morning ice water therapy and could last three minutes standing straight almost meditating. It was the perfect lead into the peace of morning prayer. I could hear Fr Benny coming down the hall, his whistle bouncing off the tiles his knock crackled of charisma. Tomorrow I would be back in Bratislava. I knew my family would be waiting anxiously, Iva getting everything ready, the kids wondering if Daddy brought them back anything from the stalls. He had the question out before I had the door open "are you ready son" he asks. I pulled the cover up to fix the ruffled bed.

"That depends Father" I say "what you have in store for me ?"

He laughs exposing two neat rows of teeth "Moran's" he says, "the journey home" he continued, "life" he concluded.

I took my jacket from the hanger slipped it on and mused for a moment on his response. I extended my hand on his shoulder, we were both now smiling – "Only time or fate will tell Father" I said "but until then let's Amor Vita in Moran's" and then he took me and hugged me as if he had known all along.

The Parting Glass

It was a waxing moon on the night he took his last breath. He was in his own bed, some comfort I suppose. I picture it, the moon motionless in a black sky, the clouds like tangled bar smoke slowly drifting past. The green lady stands and motions time to go Shane Mac Gowan. Mary Horan's poet, musician, story teller rises from his body. Victoria observes at the clock on the bedside dresser. It is five minutes to three am. She solicits a look of grief, she wants to be strong but can't stop the tears, one by one she slowly lowers his eyes kissing each one in turn. I am in my own bed too, not alone, Iva is there, she is my Victoria, along with two of our boys, one after the other they take turns in kicking off the duvet. I turn to the dresser and find the power button on the side of my phone. The light nearly blinds me, it is five minutes to four am, one hour ahead of Dublin. I walk to the living room and look out the window, the weather can't make up its mind if it is snowing or raining. Wet flakes drift slowly down and dissolve into the quiet street below. The Keeners have gathered by Shane's bed, Eireann, Eiru, Brodhla, Fodha, his mother is there now also, she takes him by the hand and leads him safely away.

Five days later and I still have an itch that I can't scratch. It was Friday night, Iva and I were on a date night which could go either way depending on how exhausted we both were. She had spent the last two weeks dealing with chicken pox, wobbly teeth and back and forth to the hospital where her mother was receiving treatment. I was on autopilot refreshing rip.ie every few hours for details of Shanes funeral which had just been announced, the mass would take place 3pm Friday the 8th in Nenagh. I looked across the table at Iva, "I would like to go to the funeral" I say, she had a glass of Merlot in her hand which she carefully placed on the table, looked up at me and asked confused, "Aren't you supposed to fly to Boston on Monday ?". She was spot on I was due to fly to Boston on Monday for a Quarterly Portfolio meeting for which I needed to prepare somewhere between one and two million slides.

"You`re mad," she said "but it`s up to you."

It was agreed then, all bar the formalities which involved the purchase of a plane ticket and a funeral coat.

The mother wondered if I knew him, I did I told her, I knew him in the bedsit on Chiswick roundabout and in the Camper van in Brisban as we headed west for Perth. I knew him in Singapore when I was working on an IBM middleware implementation for the investment bank. Or when I sat on Mannions pool and heard him sing about our Dirty old Town. I knew him when I was lonesome for home, drunk or in love. "Lovely so" she replied, "sure we'll see you on Thursday". Paddy the Hackney agreed he would pick me up in Dublin but not only that, he would take me to Nehagh, together on the Friday morning. In Vienna airport I grabbed two cans of Ottakringer and a tin of Mozart marzipan. The flight bumped along and I drank the Ottakringer sitting on the aisle seat next to a young couple with matching lilac hoodies sleeping on each other's shoulders, the guy in front of me was two times the size of the seat with hirsute knuckles, becoming agitated that he could not just find that sweet spot on the seat, the woman on the aisle across from me read a crime thriller, *three widows,* she wore glasses with beaded chains and ate a chocolate wafer, slowly turning pages. The lights of Dublin came into view and we landed with a thump. I clapped and the couple next to me woke and wondered what was happening. I wondered why doesn't anyone clap these days ?, the Irish used to love landing on the home sod, as the song I once wrote portrays:

> Josie do you remember years ago in this old town
>
> When the Christmas came and the roars from the plane
>
> as she touched down in Shannon town
>
> Davey got down and kissed the ground
>
> He declared he'd never go back,
>
> until he spent his last pound in a whiskey round and fell on the flat of his back

The mother had the fry ready, three Sausages, two Rashers, White Pudding, Black Pudding, Double Egg, Mushrooms, Fried Tomatoes soda bread and milky tea. It was just what was needed to soak up the Porter from Paddy's & Brackens in Kinnegad, with further libation provided in the house of the great troubadours Joe Dolans. After Mullingar the slump set in and It was nothing but cat`s eyes, that and wet rain on top of rain. Paddy insisted that we bring

D. M. O'DOWD

Sangwiches so we made a batch of ham and cheese in tin foil and with that along with the new coat for the cold, we were nearly out the door when the mother skited a glug of holy water on us and we stopped to bless ourselves. Petrol, Paper and coffee in Castlebaldwin, all front page spreads of Shane with slogans and excerpts of his songs, Legends Last *Trip to Tipp*, *Shane's Parting Glass*, *I Must Be on My Way*. A lot of babble on the radio also, about the cortege from Dublin to Nenagh, testimonies and snippets of nostalgia and on we went Carrick on Shannon, Athlone, a pit stop for coffee in Dromod, listened to Haunted with himself and Sinead O'Connor which brought a lump to my throat, Paddy had to pull in, "Gorgeous" he said through his nose, "What's that is her name again ?". Athlone and from there to Ferbane, Bypassing Birr and Banagher (which reminded me of the auld lad) and on to Borrisakane and finally we knew we were in Nenagh, the town was alive with people from all walks.

We positioned ourselves at the bar in Hibernian Inn next to two English gentlemen in elegant coats, silk scarves and gold rings. They had the look of record label A&R men. One was having the beef casserole and the other the turkey and ham, both wilfully consuming Guinness. Paddy had a Lucozade and took his tablets, I joined them with a couple of pints of Porter. The back bar was a rabble, a blond in a leather mini with a baby, a group of guys with dreadlocks, Fedoras and long coats and Mandolins. There was an older couple in the corner they were already half buzzed on Heineken, he seemed to be the God head of the whole crew, offering advice to all gathered round his table, his other half with pink lipstick laughed loud and often. A guy with a fresh face and a flat cap with a guitar on his back, walked in one door and out the other then back in the other door and out the first. We watched him and wondered was he alright in the head. On a normal day, we could have sat there for hours on end but this was no normal day and we made shapes.

The rain came in spits, the wind like a rusty knife. I turned the collar up on my coat and stood in silence. A guy with a placard stood across from me with the words *You are the pleasure of my dreams*, another in a tracksuit top held a Tri Colours high, it spun in the wind, punk girls in Pogues T-Shirts giggled to one another, an old gay couple stood arm in arm in velvet and tartan, one with a derby bowler, a group of local lads gathered in a ball at the side door of the church smoking and talking the country right. The first garda motorbike alerted the imminent arrival and the lump was back in my throat as the hearse came into view with a patter of claps, the coffin draped in the brightest of Tri colours, a monochrome photo of a moody Shane leaning against his own coffin. The hearse crept it's way up to the church door, we watched it all the way.

It was a kind of fairytale dreamworld, the Church, the mix of musicians, the booming eulogy of Gerry Adams, the heaving mass of bodies holding phones aloft, the towering windows shimmering a rainbow of light, the glamorous dark clad mourners the length of the Church, the splendour of the seating, the millions of heels that had trod on those tiles, Rebels to Rockstars, Bishops and Beauties. Paddy gave a hiss across to me, "whistttt", I looked in his direction and he motioned to come. I cleaved my way through the crowd noticing the guy with the guitar on his back causing chaos clocking into people left and right as he rummaged for a view. Paddy had his hand on a concealed door opening it as I arrived, it led to a spiralling staircase, his walk was bad but he managed to give a running commentary wondering if we were going up to the steeple or heaven or where to God. We clobbered on step after step finally entering the choir gallery opening a bird's eye view of the whole affair.

The greatest show on earth unfolded, Fairytale of New York sung brilliant by Glen Hansard and Lisa O'Neill, followed by honest Eulogies from Shanes sister Siobhan and wife Victoria. I listened mouth open, half stunned. When Siobhan said she was proud of him, some half sozzled punter broke the silence from the doorway, "the whole Ireland fucking proud of him". We watched as the Coffin slowly padded it's way from the chancel down the aisle coming to a standstill beneath us next to the exit door, in unison we inhaled, was this the end ? the dreaded leaving of Liverpool. Emotions raw and unhindered spilled over within the venerable walls with cries of "good luck Shane" and "thanks for the memories", it was as if Tipp had lifted the Liam Mc Carthy. I fixed on Johnny Depp, and watched him react with a proud pat on the side of the coffin as if to say, I'm the rusty tin can and you're the old hurley ball. For a long time after the church emptied, I couldn't find the will to leave, sitting in one of the front rows surveying the scene as the local laity were busy with the ramp down. Paddy was limping around them trying to beg, borrow or steal a mass leaflet which were for invite only guests but like Joseph of Nazareth got a closed door with whoever he tapped up. "Ignoramus" Paddy huffs walking ahead of me and straight out the door.

STORIES OF A DIGITAL SPALPEEN

Down in Philly's The Pogues never sounded so good, the Porter never tasted so sweet. We managed to find a pair of stools in the back bar where the DJ not much bigger or younger than Miggeldy Higens sat in the corner with a waistcoat and a ponytail and belted out the tunes. There were two behind the bar taking orders left and right. On that night in that back bar, every class of lunatic seemed to have converged, from corduroys with cowboy boots, slits past the knee, Turbans and Berets and the Fedoras were back in town. A Chinese guy with a drum was staggering round the place, giving the odd slap on the drum. I settled into my first pint which the barmaid served me in a plastic glass. I told her I didn't want a plastic glass and she shrugged and moved on to the next order. A guy over six foot in his sixties in a perfect navy suit with a red tie was jumping up and down doing the lasso move to Streams of Whiskey. A girl along with him with a Sligo flag wrapped round her like a skirt bouncing with him. In terms of Berets, there were two, A Punjabi a denim shirt who was equally if not exceeding the levels of intoxication of the Chinese guy and a girl from Cork who wore hers with a turtleneck and John Lennon spectacles, she was in town with her mother who proudly informed Paddy they were Roy Keane's neighbour from Mayfield (boy). The Turban was a Tipperary man, who in terms of height, in his sandals exceeded the guy in the navy suit, with the dreads falling to his waist. I ordered another at the bar and told her to make sure it was a proper glass. She shrugged.

The Irish Rover kicked off and the roof was nearly taken off the place, the guy beside us with a big bunch of keys on his belt and a beard straight from the Irish Rover stood on the rung of the stool punching the air and sang every word. A French girl, a tourist, sitting at one of the barrels converted to a table wondered was this a normal Friday night ?. Paddy said, "You`re right, it is a bit quiet tonight, isn't it ?". She wasn't sure what to make of it. Just at that time, the guy with the guitar on his back came in through the exit door pushing into a local who along with the friend was in a good hearted quarrel with the barmaid, he said they ordered bottles, not pints. She shrugged. "Here will you drink this" the local said to the guy with the guitar on his back, handing him the pint of Heineken. He took it then and the second one he offered to the French tourist sitting at the barrel. She accepted it as local custom. Paddy wondered if the guitar guy was he going to give us a tune an answer to which he put down the pint opened his wallet and handed Paddy his business card, *Terrific Tunes* and went off again for a walk.

I ordered another round and another and Paddy got the next one in, the barmaid didn't bother to charge him. She was too busy arguing with a customer if she had given her the right measure for a Baileys or not. It was about the time of night when things started to fall, the Punjabee fell a few times once on top of the Chinese guy with the drum and a couple of times on top of Roy's neighbour although they may have been engineered. She had another admirer also, a grunge guy with a jumper all frayed at the cuffs with long greasy hair. He was trying to work up the courage to dance with her as she made moves on the floor but at this stage, he had overshot the mark and was falling round the place. The next man to go was a guy with a bleached head and a home job tattoo under the left eye, he lilted sideways across a table and toppled until assisted by the hand of a girl with thick eyebrows and lip filler. She was the kind of girl that needed a guy that needed to be saved. He was the kind of guy who had the potential to munch his way through the beach boys back catalogue. The Mac he was wearing opened to reveal that somewhere along the way he had lost half his shirt, she looked down at his naked belly and lay her hand on it. I didn't see them after that.

I was beginning to slow up, slip up and slur myself and took hold of Paddys arm who was talking to a guy in a black suit a bob cut and a pair of eyes like pinwheels. A bar owner from Dublin he introduced himself to me as, "not touched a drop in two years" he said then ordered us two pints and was about to tell me his life story until suddenly he spotted the DJ and made a beeline for him. He was replaced by a pair of mischievous schoolgirls that were suggesting to Paddy to buy them a Rockshore, he said, "I will ya". The bar owner from Dublin was too much for the DJ, leaning into him, talking profusely to the top of his head, Paddy had to go to assist, slipping in a request to play something a bit more on the mellow side. The barmaid asked me if I wanted a pint before they closed up. Just as she handed it me the Heineken sign fell from off the front of the tap, she threw it into the sink and disappeared. It was the last thing to fall as shortly after that, the DJ ground to a halt and the lights went up, the only man standing was the guy with the Guitar.

Down at the chipper, I went for the Curry Chips, Paddy for the Sausage and chips. Three young lads wet and weary asked if we would bring them to Puckane, Paddy said, "We will ya,". A band was starting up outside Philly's, we rolled down the window and listened to them play *A pair of brow eyes*, sung so simply. A passing group of girls in long boots and puffer jackets joined in. We ate the chips and hummed on from the car. Just as they finished who turns up but the guy with the guitar on his back, was this the moment he made a name for himself? No. We had one final job to do, drop off a couple of battered sausages to Roy's neighbours who were sitting in the camper van waiting for Johnny Deep to arrive back in town. After that it was all cat`s eyes again, nice and connie, all the way West.

The mother had the fry ready, three Sausages, two Rashers, White Pudding, Black Pudding, Double Egg, Mushrooms, Fried Tomatoes soda bread and milky tea. Paddy said that we would need Sangwitches for the journey, that we would stop at Lough Owel on the way up for a kip. I fumbled my way through Dublin airport and managed to buy a six pack of Tayto and bag of Emeralds and a bottle of Versace Yellow Diamond from the Ryanair catalogue. I downed two lovely pints in the Gate Clock at departures. Three houses later I huffed & puffed down the street super excited to see my lads, they jumped up and down at the doorway with pictures of hearts and Preying Mantises a Spinosaurus and a letter from the tooth fairy.

Monday morning back in Vienna airport, on an Austrian Airline ready for take off to Boston, a little nervous, not having really prepared as best I could for the week of meetings. The laptop was stored like a guilt trip in the overhead locker. A shave and a shower cleared that feeling of being hit by the Spider tray. I had a new energy also, one of elation, that I had actually done it, backed myself and the urge to go to pay my respects. To share that parting glass and made it back and now on to Boston. Despite the gallons of Porter, the odd snakey fag, the driving all hours, the sleeping in the coat I had an emancipated energy of the true me. I opened my phone and flicked through the pictures, arm in arm with the Punjabi Pogue in Phillys, Roy's neighbour's family photo, the Beach Boy in the half shirt, the Messianic Manager from Dublin handing Paddy the Mass leaflet. The show put on by the artist community in Ireland, by his closest family, his wife and sister, to learn some of the intimate details of his life brought us closer, made us prouder. And what about Shane himself, did he demand a state occasion, was the national outpouring a rub to his ego ?. Not likely, the opposite probably, he was humble and true, no pretences, no compromises, a complex man who loved simplicity, that is that way I saw it at least and maybe why they mobbed to pay homage, the daydreamers, believers, the meek and the mad. The captain turned on the speaker and made an announcement that we were waiting for clearance and should be on our way shortly. An air steward in a red uniform was passing down the aisle checking seat belts and armrests. I returned the phone to the inside pocket of my coat, raised the collar, sat back and closed my eyes. What happened after that, well, I suppose it was at that point I smelled the Curry sauce off the collar.

About the Author

Originally from Ireland with a background in IT, currently living in Bratislava Slovakia.

Milton Keynes UK
Ingram Content Group UK Ltd.
UKHW010149270624
444787UK00001B/18